Other books in Quest of the Vampire Trilogy:

VAMPIRE'S REQUEST   VOL II
REQUIEM FOR THE VAMPIRE   VOL III

These books can be ordered direct from the publisher
www.authorhouse.co.uk

QUEST OF THE VAMPIRE

VOL I

Paula Meek

authorHOUSE®

AuthorHouse™ UK Ltd.
500 Avebury Boulevard
Central Milton Keynes, MK9 2BE
www.authorhouse.co.uk
Phone: 08001974150

First published by AuthorHouse 7/16/2009

ISBN: 978-1-4389-8875-7 (sc)

This book is printed on acid-free paper.

I dedicate this book to you, my readers. I wrote this for you.

If you're a vampire fan – sit back and enjoy.
Or if you just love a good romantic
adventure – fasten your seatbelt.
If you're a vampire; do what you like -
'cause I know that you will…

One

CALLUM PULLED INTO THE KERB, balanced his throbbing motorbike between his legs and scanned the high street. He was looking for a hostel; somewhere to rest his weary bones. He needed to find one. The heat of the early September day was stifling beneath his black leather cladding although it was still only mid-morning. The journey from the north of England had felt endless. On top of this, his emotions were running so high; stress was the only thing driving him.

The town was situated amongst a vast forest, south west of England; a great place to remain inconspicuous for anyone wanting to hide. This luscious forest was so dense with a million hiding places you wouldn't be seen for weeks. Yet Callum couldn't ponder this now. He had another dilemma. His limbs were tiring. It took all his strength to grip the handlebars. With clammy, prickling skin threatening to melt beneath his leather exterior, and sleep beckoning, he had to find some safe haven soon.

He could see no hostels. He would have to search further since he'd never been here before. He was a tourist; hadn't even heard of this town called Sanctuary. But that had been before his world had turned upside-down. Before his mission, that now meant more to him than life or death. Now his task was becoming so huge, so vital, the more he thought about it the more it drove him crazy.

Callum made to pull off when someone caught his attention amongst the shoppers. Although he had more urgent needs, he became paralysed. He watched the bustling people, hoping to catch another glimpse of this woman while suspecting he might be hallucinating.

Sophie strolled along, enjoying the sun against her skin; arms laden with sandwiches from the nearby cafe. She had overslept and had missed breakfast. After pleading with Mr Lucas, her supervisor at the Town Library, he had allowed her to fetch brunch for herself and the other library assistant, Roz.

Sophie was lost in a daydream, the sounds of the world passing her by; shoppers chatting, music playing through open car windows. She was vacantly dodging the pedestrians when she sensed eyes on her and she focussed past the bodies through a gap. She spied the lone rider. The man in leather was sitting astride a black and chrome motorbike. He was wearing a crash helmet and the tinted visor was down, yet she felt his gaze.

She drew closer, becoming self-conscious; intimidated by this dark motionless stranger. The weight of his stare constricted her movements, and a bag slipped through her arms to her feet.

Transfixed, Callum watched the young woman resting on her haunches to retrieve the bag. He digested the way her bare arm was extending. Her skin was so white, so distracting, so dazzling: purer than the white of her long gypsy dress. She smiled at a passing lady, her long, spring-like curls dancing in a dark veil about her face.

She resumed her stroll. The gentlest breeze blew about her dress, fanning her hair against classic features. Unblemished skin upon perfect bone structure, and eyes as blue as any sky he could remember. Again those eyes turned to him and he felt exposed, abandoned of disguise. Was she aware of the effect she had inflicted? He doubted it. He was too exhausted to clamber off his machine to go tell her.

This delicate, delicious creature turned to the library steps, lightly skipped up them and disappeared through the double doors. She had left her impression as if he had been smacked in the stomach by a demolition ball. He didn't need any distractions from his mission because the job would prove difficult enough. He tried to dispel all images of the enchantress, but they remained haunting with a radiance that refused to fade.

Callum had to get a grip. Stay focused. He pulled off and merged with the traffic. Banking the bike, he turned left into a side road, centre of town; and there, further along was a sign reading, '*Vacancies*'.

After viewing the room and paying the landlady one week's rent, Callum went to the en suite bathroom, and bent to the washbasin to swill his face. The cool water couldn't refresh him from his journey. Fatigue was capturing his body, rendering him useless. Using reserved energy, he dried his face and took his round, gold-framed glasses from the shelf and put them on.

He studied his reflection in the small mirror above. His twenty-five-year-old appearance looked good. He focused on his light-blue eyes, then on his pale complexion. His long blond hair was tangle-free from his journey since he had worn it tucked well inside his jacket. Tiredness stole his focus.

Sleep was imminent. He drew away from the basin and staggered into the adjoining room. He slumped down onto the bed and pulled off his leather boots, hurling them to the floor beneath an old wooden chair.

He lay back. The light of day was blocked out by heavily lined curtains and the door was locked. Now he could sleep. He tried to plot a scheme; deciding upon waking later, he would explore the town by foot then take a ride out to search the forests. He stared at the darkness above, trying to imagine what perils would stand in his way before his mission would be complete.

Through that darkness, the lady returned, approaching him in full Technicolor. Illuminated by an inner tranquillity, those blue eyes again burned him to the core. Her soft femininity reached out and snarled his attention. He discarded his helmet, ran to her and helped retrieve her lost package. They rose together. With that sweet smile being paid him, he held her and lowered his mouth to hers; his fingers searching her slender arms, that distracting flesh, all the way up to those dazzling shoulders. Onwards they travelled, over the curves, the bone, the soft and fragile skin towards her white and perfect neck...

Darkness began blotting out the colour. Blacker than black, it engulfed the figures, drowning them. He couldn't control it. He had no means left to prevent the inevitable. The figures died as he fell into a deep and dreamless sleep.

⊱✦⊰

Night was falling. The sun was lost beyond the horizon of trees. In the forests, nocturnal creatures woke and scurried to collect food. Deer stood foraging. Foxes and badgers poked noses out of holes and sniffed the air before advancing forth.

Jon swung his car into the small lane that meandered through the forest, south-side of Sanctuary. His three friends sitting with him were anticipating a night in the pub.

"Stick a CD in," Liam said, leaning forward from the rear seat. "I'm in the mood to party."

"Oh great," Jon said sarcastically, ignoring the request.

"I'll do it then," Liam demanded, glaring at the back of Jon's dark, spiky head. Bending between the front seats, he reached towards the glove compartment.

Jon took his eyes from the fast-approaching bend and glanced at Liam wedged there, with his short red curls seeming more red with the flush of annoyance on his cheeks. It was too much a temptation. He glanced across at Greg, who was smoking in the front passenger seat. Then, with full force, he slammed his foot to the brake.

With the screech of burning rubber, Liam hurled forwards. Grasping the dashboard, and locking his arms to brace himself, he stared at the expanse of glass, which threatened to rip his face to shreds. "What are you messing at?" he hissed. The car halted then rocked back. He slumped into his seat. "What did you do that for?" Liam asked, slapping the side of Jon's head.

"I don't want to listen to music?"

"You just wanted me to hit the tarmac."

"I thought it would give you something to think about other than being an annoying arsehole." Jon smirked.

"Not funny."

Daniel, sitting beside him, had been flung against the back of Jon's seat; he was laughing.

"It was hilarious," Jon said. Pulling off, he instinctively glanced at the rear-view mirror, but could see neither a mop of red hair nor Daniel's collar-length fair hair with his usual 'hacked-at' fringe. All he could see was the lane and trees behind becoming a blur due to the increasing speed. Their reflections were gone, maliciously stolen in the sixties - along with their souls.

"I've got to get some fags," Greg said, throwing his cigarette butt out the widow.

"Me too," Jon said. He gave way at the junction then turned the car onto the road leading to town.

"There's a fag machine in the pub," Liam reminded them. "Use that."

"No chance," Greg said over his shoulder. "Technology sucks, mate. The last time I used it the poxy thing swallowed my money and wouldn't cough up the fags."

"We'll go to the shop," Jon announced. "Then I'll drop you lot off at the pub before I go and see Sophie."

Liam was agitated. "I can't see what's so difficult about using the machine, it's simple. You'd have to be a complete moron not to figure it out."

Greg said, "You do it then. Being as though you're so smart; you use it."

"I don't smoke." Liam shrugged.

"Fine," Greg said. "Then we're going to the shop. And just so you know; I'm not a moron. I'm a vampire."

Liam's mouth fell open. Speechless, he stared at Greg as did Daniel, and although Jon was driving he too stared dumbstruck at Greg who paid a winning grin and confidently relaxed back in his seat.

"Excuse my ears all to hell," Daniel blurted, wanting to laugh with shock. "He said the 'v' word. He said the goddamn 'v' word!"

"Shut up," Jon snapped. "Just shut up." He swung his attention back at the road. They were travelling on the wrong side and heading for a bend. The opposite embankment loomed. They were going to hit it. Headlights lit the car as an approaching vehicle appeared. Jon snatched a hard left on the steering wheel and swerved away as the car blasted its horn, passing with an inch to spare.

"Maniac! Slow down!" Jon yelled out the window.

"Yeah," Liam hollered, excited by his adrenaline rush and wanting to try it again.

Rattled, Jon glanced across at Greg. He had said the 'v' word.

Although they were vampires, the four couldn't use the term. It stuck in their throats. The word spooked them. It reminded them of their sinister capabilities and of the general consensus that vampires were evil; made of evil: creations of the devil and none of them wanted to believe that.

They knew their creator. They all shared the same tainted blood back in 1969. They had each met the same bitch from hell. Destiny had turned her pretty face their way, picking on the vulnerable. Each one was in their mid-twenties. Only after the deed was done did she smile with those long white fangs gleaming their warning. By then it was too late.

Much as each vampire would like to forget his true undying self, each night as the moon grew high the hunger for blood would return, the true active vampire would materialise - and his conscience would fade. Besides this, they only had to look at each other to realise their immortality because it was in their appearance.

It was in their eyes.

Their eyes were a constant reminder of their soulless bodies that appeared normal to mere mortals with souls intact. But to each other, their eyes appeared dull and empty. Dead. Their pupils were matt black, with no twinkle from a light source reflecting. No surroundings mirroring. Nothing. The life force was snuffed out. Their soulless eyes depicted their soulless bodies, and only a vampire could see the emptiness of another and instantly recognize him as undead.

Civilisation could notice nothing irregular because their souls were ignorant to the warning. To the mortal, a vampire's eyes were seemingly normal and twinkled as though alive.

Jon turned the car into the high street. Approaching the main part of town, he slowed to the speed limit.

"Will you look at that?" Liam gloated out the window at a leggy teenage girl in shorts.

"Yeah," said Daniel. "Tidy."

Jon checked her out in the rear-view mirror. "Will you guys pack it in? The girl's about fifteen."

"She's older than that, at least eighteen," Liam stated.

Greg said, "It's hard to tell these days."

"Jail-bate: even if she is fifteen, she isn't a virgin," Liam said, taking a deep breath of air.

Jon said, "Are you trying to wind me up?"

"Stating a fact. Stick your face out and cop a load of that."

"How am I supposed to trust you to behave yourself when you talk such bollocks?"

"What did I say?" Liam smirked.

"You know, dim shit. Do you want me to come with you and wet-nurse you?"

"No," all three stated simultaneously.

Jon parked outside the off-licence, wrenched up the handbrake and turned to his friends. "Are you girls going to be alright there for a minute?"

He took the keys from the ignition and got out of the car with Greg. "Take these," he said, handing the keys to Greg. "I've had enough of those two for one night."

"They're only yanking your chain. Ignore them," Greg said.

"Keep to the speed limit, and don't let Liam drive. He's being a right dick lately."

"You're going to catch up with us later?"

"I'll come to the pub. We'll go to the feeding grounds together. Just try and avoid trouble in the meantime."

Greg nodded. His dark curls falling into his dull and lifeless green eyes.

Effortlessly, Jon pulled open the heavy glass door and entered the shop. Leaning against the far wall, he casually pushed his hands under his loose tee shirt into the front pockets of his jeans, and waited for Greg to purchase two packets of cigarettes. His friend approached the counter. Greg was as tall as him with the same solid frame; he was also wearing jeans, tee shirt and trainers.

As if he enjoyed anguish, Jon checked the circular mirror in the corner above the shop assistant's head. He felt the usual chill. He knew he was there. He was solid; of flesh and bone. He could feel pain and emotions. If he were cut, he'd bleed, albeit for two minutes before his skin would knit together and heal. Yet in the mirror, the shop was void of him, empty of his friend; the assistant handing two packets of cigarettes to thin air, the packets floated there, wavering then dropping as Greg lowered his hand.

Outside, Greg handed Jon his cigarettes. The car rocked violently, moans, cussing and laughter emanating from the rear seat.

"Bloody great kids," Jon said at the two vampires play-fighting in the car. "You'd think they'd have grown up by now."

"Forever young." Greg shrugged, getting in the car.

As it pulled off, Liam and Daniel waved maniacally out the rear window. Jon flipped them his middle finger.

Discarding crumpled cellophane to the pavement, Jon leaned against the shop wall and lit a cigarette. The night was darkening. The high street lights glowing orange in a straight line to the distance either side of him. The occasional car drove by. Further along a gathering of youths stood huddled by a bus shelter, up to no good and scanning for onlookers.

Jon was drawn to approaching footsteps. A guy of about his age, height and build was walking towards him. The biker, wearing jeans and a leather jacket with long blond hair and glasses, noticed him, hesitated then stopped.

"Good evening to you," the biker said. "I wonder; perhaps you could help me?"

"What can I do you for?" Jon was instantly amused by his quiet and snobby manner.

"I have just arrived in town, and I wonder if you could enlighten me as to the nightlife in these parts?"

"Yeah, sure; it's dead, mate. It's a frigging Wednesday."

Callum regarded him more weakly. "That's it? This is the only street alive with activity?"

"There's the Bat Inn Hand pub, north-side, if you're looking for a decent beer. It's a small town, what can I say?"

"Thank you. You have been most gracious."

"Don't mention it," Jon grinned, blowing out smoke. "I'd stick to the main roads. Keep out the forests at night. It's not a good place to get lost. It gets black out there."

The biker nodded a 'goodbye' and carried on his way. The guy was completely up himself, Jon thought. If he carried on talking like that in these parts, he was going to draw attention. If he wasn't streetwise yet, he was going to be. Either that or be dead. "Bloody tourists," Jon mumbled. He and his friends had moved to the area a decade ago, so Jon felt he was native. He dropped his cigarette butt and began walking in the opposite direction to his girlfriend's flat.

He passed the bus shelter. There wasn't a virgin among them. Liam was right; had made a valid point. Anyone seeking pure-sweet innocence pumping through vulnerable veins would have to stoop to a lot lesser age. He visualised virgin veins; so tender, so easily pierced; blood spurting, coating his tongue and blowing his mind, his senses.

His groan gurgled as he fought addiction. Here he was surviving on animal blood in the forests while wanting to chow down on a virgin. To rid all tempting images, Jon concentrated on his girlfriend, Sophie. The woman he adored, the one person he'd do anything for, would be at her flat waiting for him.

He quickened his strides.

Two

IN THE DIMLY LIT KITCHEN of her top-floor flat, Sophie poured another herbal tea. She looked out the window at the dark sky, then down at the quiet side road, aware of her faint reflection begging her approval.

Jon would be here soon, but he would use the conventional way; the door. The ghostly figure was wearing a long white dress. Sophie gazed back at the apparition allowing the indulgence. Half a reflection was better than none. She felt the usual hint of sorrow for her lover. She pulled down the blind, dismissing the sympathy she had for anyone without a reflection.

She sipped her tea. Sounds of rock music from the adjoining living room were growing steadily louder. Her flatmate and fellow library assistant, Roz, had raised the volume.

The air filled with energy. The bass was kicking, visibly vibrating the walls. The husky male vocalist was wailing. The electric guitar, played distortedly, held the thrashing melody in ruthless torrents.

Sophie groaned. The neighbours would go mad. She walked along the hall. The main door was ahead, with the bathroom on the left, central to the two bedrooms. The noise-polluted living room was on her right. She stood in the doorway and watched her taller, leggy friend.

Roz was dressed to kill, as always; her short tight dress highlighting her every curve. She was bent over brushing her long, golden mane, her curves remaining firm, uninfluenced by gravity.

The music was getting inside Sophie's head, the noise agitating. Roz began swinging her head and wailing as unintelligibly as the vocalist.

"There's a baby downstairs." Sophie lowered the volume.

Roz regarded her. Roz was twenty-three, Sophie twenty-five; yet Sophie was pricy, always wearing flowing dresses that reached to her ankles and always mothering her. Yet Roz couldn't help but like her.

Although the two friends were as different as night and day, they seldom argued. Perhaps, like night and day, they complimented each other? There was no competition. Both were different, and both, ultimately, accepted the other.

Roz said, "It's Nirvana. You can't listen to it quietly. It was meant to be played loud."

"Grab your ipod then. Be my guest. Blast your mind senseless. But I like my hearing the way it is."

"You're boring," Roz said affectionately.

"I like real music."

"You don't understand; it's pure passion."

"It's pure noise. I can't even understand the lyrics."

"It's better than the la-de-da, classical crap you listen to."

"That's passion," Sophie corrected.

"Whatever…" Roz took her glass of red wine from the coffee table and offered it to the gods for a toast. "Here's to passion. And long may it reign."

"You're incorrigible," Sophie said, dismayed with her friend's easy attitude to life, to men.

Roz took a huge gulp and sighed with satisfaction. "You better believe it."

"I'm taking a bath. Jon will be here soon."

"Well that's just great. Perfect. Give me five minutes and I'll be out of here."

"You don't have to go out each time he visits. Jon's alright. You just haven't given each other a chance."

"He's weird, Soph. He's a frigging screwball. But will you listen to me? No." Roz flicked her long straight hair over her shoulder. "I keep telling you there's something odd about him. He gives me the creeps. Love must be blind, deaf and dumb if you can't tell that."

"He's not weird; he's just a bit different."

"You're too kind," Roz said sternly. "You love him. I loath him; I've had enough experience with men to know what I'm talking about. I'm telling you, I'd rather spend the night with Freddie Kruger. I'd have more of a laugh."

"We can't put it down to you being picky."

"That's a fact." Roz took no offence.

Defeated, Sophie went and prepared a luxurious bath filled with pink bubbles from her vanity case. As she sank into the frothy depths, she remembered the day she moved to Sanctuary. It was two years ago. She had taken the lease on the flat, and started work at the library where she met Roz. Two months later, after becoming firm friends, Sophie had suggested Roz move out of her bed-sit and into the flat, for company as well as to share expenses. Sophie didn't feel Roz was indebted to her, but she wished her friend and her lover would get along better. The two people she cared for in the entire world were constantly bickering; both equally headstrong. Stubborn and hardened, neither would back down, and in the middle was Sophie, hurt because of her protective love for her vampire and for the friend she considered a sister.

Roz leaned over to the mirror on her lap, applying make-up. She had to get ready for her date with Sam. She had met him on Saturday night at the Crypt, the local nightclub. He had been shy, nervous; and although she hadn't made tremendous advances that night, tonight she would bring out the man in him.

She traced blood-red lipstick to her lips and smacked them together, listing what she might just do with the nineteen-year-old to initiate him in the wonders of life. He wouldn't know what hit him. She made it her mission to bring any man she wanted to his knees. She knew what men wanted, what made them tick. As she pouted her 'come and get it' expression, she considered herself an expert.

She applied black mascara to her long lashes. Banging on the door caused her to blink. "Shit." Her eye make-up smudged.

She grabbed a handful of tissues on the way to the door. Still the visitor hammered.

"Alright; I'm coming," she called, hiding her annoyance in case it should be Sam. It might be the cretin. Her heart plummeted. "Who is it?"

"Me."

The cretin.

She slid the chain off, opened the door and took a determined step back, keeping her face lowered and hoping he would sweep past with his usual arrogant swagger. Instead Jon leaned in to observe her.

Her face was pretty even though her black encircled eyes were ghastly. Her lips were full, generous, and possibly inviting, having been painted his favourite colour. Her tongue was sharp. "It's an improvement."

"Screw you," she hissed, making her way to the bathroom door.

"Well, now you come to mention it," he joked. Her voluptuous hourglass figure was shrink-wrapped in red shimmering material, so that her firm buttocks glinted with each stride. Eternally long, bare legs carried her.

Roz knocked on the bathroom door. "Sophie, His Eminence is here." Jon's approach resulted in a chill as he invaded her personal space deliberately. He went to the living room and flopped onto the sofa. "Loser," she uttered.

Jon took Roz's half bottle of wine and drank the red liquid thirstily. He knew it was Roz's since Sophie seldom consumed alcohol and loathed red wine. He knew it was hers because he had smelt it on her. Sensing her disgust, he took several more gulps.

Roz went to him. "That's mine."

"Here, have it," Jon offered. "It's a bit too sour for my palate."

"Keep it. - I'd sooner die than drink out something your gob's been around."

Hurt flashed across Jon's smug expression. "Not delighted by me? I take it you're still not partial to me?"

"You're having a bubble?" Roz said, hands on hips. "Anyway, it doesn't matter how I feel, you hateful shit. But, since you asked, Sophie's wasting her time on you. She deserves better. She could be with a real man - a man with a job for instance; a man who has self-respect, who brushes his hair sometimes instead of never. But she makes do with scum. I mean - have you looked at yourself lately? Your life's a mess. You couldn't give a damn about anything. You're selfish and egoistic, swaggering about like you own the place. Taking what you want. Drinking what isn't yours; and your friends are just as bad. Shall I continue?"

His dark-brown eyes narrowed in contempt. Swiftly, almost unnaturally, Jon was on his feet, face against hers. She instinctively leaned back.

"You're not so perfect, little Miss Slapper," he hissed so Sophie couldn't hear. "I don't know who died and made you Sophie's keeper, but I'll tell you this: you bad-mouth me, and brainwash her, and I'll break your bitter sweet neck, got it? Over in a second. The pleasure's all mine."

Roz had overdone it this time. She saw anger flash in the twinkle of his dark eyes and the madness behind it. Although he had just proved to be insecure in his love for Sophie, Roz had no intention to remark. He would break her neck. She had heard the usual threats, but this time she had seen the promise.

She grabbed her cosmetics bag and went to her bedroom. She didn't need the hand-held mirror there. Sophie allowed wall mirrors in this side of the flat: the two bedrooms and the bathroom. She wouldn't allow them the other side, believing it would bring bad karma surrounding Feng Shui. Although Roz didn't believe in this Chi business of yin yang energies, she allowed Sophie her New Age notions.

Jon lit a cigarette and slumped back in the sofa, blowing blue-grey smoke. "Bitch," he mumbled, her icy words tormenting. He didn't need a job, goddamn it.

He needed to calm down. His heartbeat had quickened. Adrenaline was wreaking havoc on his sensitive body. If it wasn't for Sophie, he could easily kill Roz. But then, Sophie was the cause of his anger. No other subject would have aggravated him so badly. His love was blinding, physically stifling. And he couldn't get enough. Sophie was his world: his first thought as he opened his eyes from death's sleep, his last thought as he closed them at dawn. Without her, he would perish. Yet, although she was mortal and would one day die, he could never hurt her. He couldn't envisage exchanging blood and taking her soul to discard it to oblivion. The thought of making her undead to dwell with him forever sickened him. His love was mightier than universal restrictions. He loved her soul; the essence of her purity. He would allow her to grow old and die, so her soul could take its place in heaven alongside the angels. But whilst she was alive, she was his.

More timid knocking sounded and Roz hastened from her bedroom in case Jon beat her to the door.

"Hi, Sam," she smiled at the tall, lean, spotty-faced lad in his sports cap, seemingly just this side of puberty.

"It's Sean, actually," he said timidly.

"Oh, right. Well, come in." Dashing to her room, she called, "Wait there, I'm almost ready."

Standing beside the telephone table and green leather chair, Sean scanned the layout of the flat, and then politely entered the living room to make himself known to the man on the sofa. "Alright?" he jigged.

Jon took a steady breath and savoured the intense aroma. He decided to indulge the youth after overhearing the conversation. "You must be Sam?"

"No – Sean."

"You're Roz's date? Sit down. A friend of hers is a friend of mine."

"You live here?" Sean asked, sitting in the armchair.

"Just visiting." Jon blew smoke in his direction. "Are you ready for what she's got? She's a man-eater."

"Oh?" The lad's eyes darted about, as if checking all exits.

"I've been told she's like the Praying Mantis. She gets her savage claws into you and won't let go until the lady's devoured you. She'll chew you up and spit you out - and that's if she likes you," Jon beamed. He swallowed his words hard, picturing blood red lips supping Sean's virgin flesh. He envied Roz her task, then realised she was a missionary, a true saint amongst sinners; eradicating the temptation of virgins across the land as she went about doing what she was renowned for doing best.

Roz appeared in the doorway. "Ready," she announced, hiding her dismay at finding the two guys chatting.

"Good luck, Sam," Jon said.

"It's Sean," he quietly reminded deaf ears and followed Roz out the flat.

Jon was at the window in a heartbeat, curtain flung sideways. Shoving up the sash pane, head thrown out to the night, he breathed deeply the cool fresh air that would cleanse his system from the intoxicating drug screaming to him by name. He downed the remaining red wine to help shift the scent; heard Roz's voice drifting up from the road below and caught her gravely, dirty laugh a she flirted her wares. He slammed the window shut. She had rattled his cage enough for one night; he'd take his chances with the scent of virgin blood still in the room.

Bored with waiting for Sophie, Jon took her period novel from the coffee table and began scanning the back cover. Having never been able to get lost in fiction, he admired anyone who could find an escape from the real world. But then, his world was different than most.

Jon's mood grew lighter as Sophie approached from behind, wrapped in a blue towel with pale limbs glistening. "It's cold in here."

"I've had the window open. Fresh air. Good for the system. Clears the mind."

Her aroma was so sweet it stifled all others. So sweet, he could smell it a mile away. Her long dark curls, cascading about her face and shoulders were wet and smelling of wild-flower shampoo. He thought he would explode in rapture as two loving hands on his muscular shoulders moved downwards to his chest as she leant over him.

"Have you missed me?" she whispered against his ear, releasing tingles.

"With every breath." He turned, held her face, planting soft kisses on her lips. He shifted round, wanting more of her mouth, and deepened the kiss. He felt her body tense as she abruptly broke free.

"You've been drinking."

"A little bit."

"You've been drinking red wine." She became distraught. "And later you're going to drive."

"I had a few sips," Jon said, desperately. "I'll be fine."

"I know you will. But the other road users wouldn't fare so well if you were to have an accident."

Jon was on his feet and rounding the sofa to her. "I'll drive carefully, go real slow. - I don't want to hurt anybody. You know that."

"Promise me?" she pleaded. "Sometimes I lie awake at night worrying."

"I swear. I love you, Soph. You're the best thing that's ever happened to me. I'd do anything for you. I won't hurt a living soul as long as I have your love."

Sophie searched his handsome face, his mournful eyes imploring her to have faith. She submitted. "Fine. I'm over-reacting if it was just a sip or two. Come with me. Reassure me. I need you to love my body." She led him to her bedroom.

Jon recalled the first time he had seen her. She had been new in town. He and his vampire pack had been in the Bat Inn Hand when he saw her across the crowded room, gazing back; and he hadn't believed his luck. Soon they were engrossed in a deep conversation. Over the following weeks he saw more of her. His feelings developed into a mad possessive love. Now he could hardly remember his existence before her - nor did he want to.

Jon's expression was ardent as she helped him undress. The bed was inviting with feminine frills and fringed with delicate lace. Now naked, Jon drew her to him, and falling into her blue, sparkling eyes full of kindness, he whispered, "I love you."

"I know." Sophie smiled. His kiss was deep, triggering her passion. Yet, as always, as she tried to manipulate the hunger, to get lost for once in lust, to lose themselves in each other, he remained restrained. His kiss was always so good. His lips were firm. But he was too considerate, always controlled. Her insides burned. She longed for him to discard caution, rip the towel from her and take her down to the bed or floor as if she were a seductress needing to be served. Her thoughts manifested into dampness.

Jon removed her towel, and lowered his angel to the bed. He lay beside her, planting soft kisses on her lips and face. He moved onto her bare shoulder, licking, kissing her skin. Her white, supple neck allured his attention. He groaned. Her skin was soft. He could smell the sweet scent from her bath, but was more aware of the red rivers flowing beneath. He kissed along her shoulder to the nape of her neck, drew her flesh into his mouth, and began encircling her skin with his tongue. He pressured her flesh between his lips. Her blood pulsated past. Could he sink his teeth in, take a sip or lap it up? Enjoy such mind-blowing sweetness, and dismiss the terror of hurting her? Disastrously, he banished such images from his disgusted mind since his desires along with his rock-solid penis were rapidly deflating. Releasing her flesh abruptly, he moved his lips back onto hers to somehow begin again. Since his thoughts had nearly lost the whole situation, he realised the only good thing to have come out of his nibbling at her neck was that she felt safe. She was completely safe.

Sophie placed his free hand on her breast, inviting him to explore. His touch was softly caressing, kneading her. How she longed for that kneading hand to go lower: to go between her legs. For his strong fingers to force their way inside, delve deep and prod rhythmically to her end. She squirmed; hips heightening from the bed as his fingers ran their course; over her flat tummy, lower, before pausing.

Jon noticed her delirium, the eagerness in her eyes, and knew what she wanted. But he couldn't use fingers on an angel. Not his angel. He teased her delicate lips with four dampening fingertips. As she delighted, gasped and moved her hips, threatening to swallow them, he retracted his hand and moved onto her, entering her compassionately with his reinstated erection. He took his time, moved with self-control, his aim concise; to gratify the woman he worshiped.

Sophie realised his feelings were unreal. This mad, never-fading love engulfed him, reigned over him and prevented him from doing what comes naturally. She realised, with Jon, it could only be all or nothing. Although she appreciated it, she wished he would keep the respect but lose the inhibitions, find the passion that would drive him. Thrust harder, be forceful, send her body to a new dimension, and drive her brain to insanity so she would grasp the bedposts in some crazed state and scream out to the world.

Delighted, Jon knew he had done it again. Muffled gasps escaped her, and her body convulsed. Her hands were clasping his back. Again he had pleasured his Sophie. He could leave her now and feel satisfied with a job well done. But she egged him on; gyrating her hips, indicating he reach his own satisfaction. And he did, collapsing. They lay entwined.

Jon lay back, resting his arm on his forehead, grinning stupidly.

Sophie loved his grin and, although his hair was dishevelled, it was also endearing. She imagined him as a small lad. He would have played all day in the sun and wind. Then, seeking his mother with his unkempt hair and cheeky grin, she would have forgiven his torn trousers and grubby face. Although Jon was a grown man oozing confidence and masculinity, Sophie could sometimes glimpse that small boy peering out: forever cheeky, but always forgiven.

"Do you want to go out tomorrow night?" he asked, propping onto his elbow.

"Roz and I will meet you in the pub on one condition; no arguing with her. I know you have your differences but you hurt me when you bicker."

"She gets under my skin. She's such a bare-faced tart. And she thinks I'm the one with no regard. If only she knew."

"She's my friend and if you hurt her, you hurt me."

"Roz - hurt? I doubt it. She's tough; gives as good as she gets."

"She's not as tough as she makes out. Go easy on her, for me?"

"Okay," Jon said, allowing her anything, so long as she cared. He glanced at the far side of the room, at the dressing table, the long mirror and saw her beautiful white body reflecting. A real English rose.

Then he peered to where any person would to see himself in all his glory. - Patterned wallpaper. Pretty flower print. - Frustration burned. If he could just look fast enough, somehow trick the looking glass, would he catch a glimpse of his features before the mirror callously stole them? The mirror was always too fast. He relied on his faded memory: gorgeous, tall, dark and handsome? No scars remaining from his mortal existence? There had been no accidents or bottles in faces. Did he have a big nose or measly thin lips? Was there hair in unsightly places?

Jon excused himself, dressed, and went to the living room. He snapped on the stereo. It whizzed and scanned the selection of tracks, then played some funky music. Jon lit a cigarette, becoming aware of the more understandable lyrics from a different band. The man sang about the sin and pleasure of sex, drugs, and rock 'n' roll. How very sixties, but he didn't need this patronising twerp telling him about eternal misery of the flesh. Unsightly hair: - no chance. He hadn't needed a razor because his face produced no hair. He felt his lips. They seemed alright. His nose didn't seem so big; the slight cleft in his chin was not some yawning chasm. Paranoia, that's what it was; planted by a vindictive bitch.

Above the music, Jon detected two distant sounds: an infant crying and a woman humming. He concentrated on his hearing. Raising its sensitivity as easily as the volume on the stereo, the infant's cries grew louder. Honing in on it, the vampire detected the small baby to be in the flat downstairs. He heard the mother's soothing lullaby and the distinct creaking of a rocking chair. The baby quietened. He heard a drawer gently close in Sophie's room. He lowered his hearing and went to the window where his mind drifted out to the darkness.

Now clothed, Sophie sat at her dressing table, brushing the dried tangles from her curls. Jon would have to leave soon. His need of fresh warm blood would start to burn dangerously. She held no fear for her safety.

Jon had explained everything soon after his love for her had grown. He had disclosed the deeper part of the vampire within. And she had understood, never doubting his words to be the truth, and she had accepted him. For, although her vampire was a killer, she could see his struggle: his conscience endeavouring to be clear; and his battle for his three vampire friends to behave likewise.

She knew their capabilities. A vampire was an empty shell, having exchanged his soul for inhuman qualities with the exchange of blood from another. Besides all other attributes the vampire possessed, the most important, and most called upon were the qualities of his senses. They were more than animal-like. They could concentrate on each of the five senses, heighten each one, and hear the faintest sound, or smell the purity of blood and detect its source with precision. However, a vampire could heighten only two senses simultaneously; more than two would upset their bodily balance and progress them swiftly towards the transgression of the blood-hungry vampire with extending fangs.

Jon had explained in some depth that a pack of vampires together had a tendency to manipulate each other's changes. If one were to raise three senses and begin the irreversible transition to active vampire, the others would be affected, also regressing as ruthlessly.

Still Sophie felt safe. Even in the company of the four together, she knew they couldn't harm her. Jon's love for her was incredible. He put her needs first and she trusted him. She felt protective and would endeavour to please him in return. Although her love was not as strong, she had met no one yet who could tempt her away.

She was staring at her reflection. The memory returned of the mysterious lone rider in black. The crash helmet and tinted visor were still hiding his gaze. She was curious of the stranger's features. She was ashamed of this betrayal. But the visor wasn't masking the weight of the stranger's stare...

Sophie went to Jon's outstretched arms. He said, "I'll have to leave soon. I've got to meet the others. Go dine."

"I know it's not easy for you, Jon. I know your conscience fades as you grow hungrier, but please, if you can, remember to stun your prey first, ease their suffering?"

Jon tried to hide his desperation. Anything witnessing the flight of a hungry vampire, fangs ready, would be stunned. He sank into the eyes of his vegetarian lover and said, "I promise - if I remember." Jon pulled away and turned his back. Roz was right; he wasn't good enough. He was cruel and sinister so must be evil, killing countless creatures of the forest each bloodied night with no control over his hunger or deeds. Yet his angel wouldn't harm anything. She wouldn't eat meat, couldn't bring herself to handle it in any way because killing was barbaric. He was barbaric.

"I've upset you." Sophie massaged his shoulders. "I never meant to offend."

"I'm having a bad night. Sometimes it all crashes down, around." Jon turned to her. "You're so gentle and kind; always searching for the good in everyone, always caring for everyone else." He toyed with a few of her curls. "You don't drink, don't smoke, and don't eat meat. You don't even swear, damn it." He dropped his hand. "So what are you doing with me?"

"It doesn't matter that we're different, so long as we're together. You're not as bad as you once were. You've amended your ways since we've been together."

"This thing inside me - what I am - can never be beaten. I can never be good enough. Not for you. Not when it counts. What gets me the most is that I try. Shit, Sophie, every night, every minute I really do try."

She held a finger against his lips to quieten his mild hysteria then kissed him. "That's all that matters."

Her kiss was reassuring; clarifying she loved him as her magic touch drove out all pain. Was he worthy of her? He gazed into the soul-filled eyes of his guardian angel and realised if he were to love his goddess more his heart would break open.

"Perhaps, it's as Greg says: opposites attract?" he croaked.

They cuddled for some time; Sophie feeling content, Jon feeling adoration lightening his mood and making him giddy as he breathed in her scent. He had heard rumours of vampires being capable of intense love, and he knew it was so - because this was it.

He kissed her, concentrating on how her lips felt, wanting to carry their memory for the remaining night. All he wanted was to be able to spend one complete night and day with the woman he loved. He opened his eyes, the room appeared brighter.

The light of the two lamps faded to natural daylight flooding his vision. The scent of wild flowers from her hair and skin intensified. He could taste them, picture luscious green meadows with the sun beating down. He could almost remember what the sun felt like against his skin.

The clock ticked louder. The heat of her arms and body seeped in, warming him more. "I've got to go. It's time." He managed a weak smile. Without kissing her again, he fought to let go. He lit a cigarette, appreciating the stronger, acidic taste. His body-clock was screaming speed was of the essence.

Jon left having sapped her energy, and Sophie needed to sleep. She had overslept this morning so she had to be punctual tomorrow. Although the library was just around the corner, and only a five minute walk, she hated rushing, hated the inevitable lecture at her age.

In the kitchen, she made a concoction of her herbal tea mixed with chamomile to assist sleep. As she sipped her drink, she rolled up the blind and stared out at the blackness. Where was the stranger, the lone rider? What was he doing right now? Why should this intruder invade her mind so freely? She tried banishing him by turning her back on the night. Glad to be a daylight person, she finished her tea.

Three

ALFRED LUCAS POKED HIS HEAD around the door of his back office and scanned the library. One minute then Sophie and Roz would be late. Yet another day in Paradise.

He didn't need the dilemma of running this show on his own. Stress was taking its toll, and the weight on his shoulders was burden enough. Deciding to make a start, he strode to the front reception desk, passing freestanding columns of books and tables and chairs.

The building was a monument to the past as it dated back several centuries. Sandwiched between other buildings, the library had no windows to let in natural light, which suited Mr Lucas, since brightness caused his head to ache. He liked the older building and felt at home in his domain.

Outside, four stone columns supported the tall porch, and five shallow steps led up to it; lending the building significance. In days gone by it was the Town Hall until all business moved to the new upmarket complex of the district council. Mr Lucas felt his library was as important as any other task he was overseeing in Sanctuary.

At Sophie's reception desk, he lifted the cover from her computer monitor, as she pulled open one of the heavy, glass-panelled doors and entered.

Sophie's eyes adjusted from brilliant sunshine to the room's fluorescent light, and noticed Mr Lucas waiting to pounce; a lanky, middle-aged man with slicked-back dark hair and gaunt face.

Behind thick glasses, his tiny eyes narrowed. "You're late."

"Yes, I am - barely," she agreed, nearing her desk like a child to a teacher. "I am truly sorry."

"And Roz; how sorry is she?"

Roz had overslept and she'd had left her getting ready. After a debate, Sophie had reluctantly promised to lie. Sophie hated lying. "She's got one of her migraines. She says she'll be along as soon as the tablets start working."

"Don't you mean a hangover?" Mr Lucas's eyes narrowed further, disappearing amongst creases.

"If Roz says she has a migraine then I believe her," Sophie said, wrestling with her conscience.

"So you say." Mr Lucas dramatically threw his hands to the air. "But this is a business, and literature has an importance. You suffer too many late nights at the hands of your lover, and it's just not good enough." He slammed his hands onto her desk and leaned closer. "I'm in charge of this vessel. And without my crew the ship will sink. Do you understand?"

"Yes, Mr Lucas. It won't happen again."

"We shall see." He straightened. "Send Roz to me when she eventually drags herself in."

He stalked the length of the room to his office. Sophie was concerned he was at breaking point. The poor man had never been so sharp with her before. Never before had he mentioned her love life. He was acting strange; out of sorts. These last few weeks he had spent mostly in his office with the door closed, warranting more awareness that all was not well. Yet there was nothing she could say as the man was unaimiable.

Typing lightly at her computer, she failed to hear the approaching rumble from outside. The throbbing drew nearer. She casually looked through the glass-panelled doors at a motorbike pulling up.

Not *a* motorbike; *the* motorbike. Its rider, familiarly clad in black leather, was swinging his leg across the seat to dismount. Her heart surged. He was coming up the steps. He was coming in. She wanted to appear busy but became all of a fluster as the stranger entered the library.

He stood hesitating, while appearing like an astronaut who had landed in uncharted territory. His crash helmet was on and the visor was down. It seemed he was surveying the room. He pulled off his gloves, and began unfastening the strap under his chin.

Please be ugly? Let him be hideous. He removed his helmet and pulled his long blond hair free from his jacket. No such luck. The guy was handsome. No, more than that; pretty. His light-blue eyes were gleaming, his complexion pale. He was wearing glasses, which deemed him intellectual.

"Good morning," Callum said softly.

"Can I help you, sir?"

"Sir," he repeated distantly. "I am new to Sanctuary. I wonder; would the library have literature on local history? Perhaps maps of the surrounding forests?"

Sophie smiled kindly, rising to her feet. "Come this way."

Callum followed her to a sidewall strewn with books, all the while admiring her grace. Her long navy skirt and white blouse were official yet feminine. Her hair was tied loosely in a piece of white ribbon. She was beautiful; demure as he had remembered from yesterday, and seemingly more wondrous by nature. He was engrossed in digesting her when she stopped.

"You'll find all you need here." She gestured at the line of books.

"Thank you. You have been most helpful."

"Shout if you require any further help," Sophie called, returning to her desk.

"Isn't shouting against regulations?"

Sophie giggled. "I was being metaphorical."

Callum found a relevant volume and sat at a table to read. Strategically, through the freestanding shelves, he could see her at her desk. The book was of interest, but couldn't hold his attention. Something she radiated demanded his focus. If he missed a moment, even due to blinking, he would miss an eternity's worth.

He had seen her entering her obvious place of work yesterday, and if he had been bolder, or less tired, he could have followed her in. But he was here now: imagining standing behind her, massaging those shoulders, pulling her blouse to one side. She moved her head, allowing him to kiss that flesh... her delicate white shoulders; that supple sweet neck... whilst his hands reached down over each breast, and lower, over her flat tummy, and lower, down over each leg to her knees. Then, slowly dragging her skirt up, he searched the warm flesh of her thighs. She relaxed her legs, inviting him between them. He heard a main door open to the noise of the street, and came back to be seated squarely in reality. The temptress frowned.

"Where have you been?" Sophie asked Roz. "Mr Lucas is on the warpath. He wants to see you, and he's not very happy."

"Did you tell him I had a migraine?"

"Yes, I lied for you. And I didn't much enjoy it. He's in a right mood. Now go to him and on bended knees, apologise."

"Get stuffed," Roz snorted. "I'm not grovelling to him."

"Then he could have you dismissed. Is that what you want; a trip to the Job Centre?"

Roz shrugged, making to head for her supervisor's office when she noticed the biker at the distant table, reading. She turned back to Sophie. "Who the hell's that?"

"Quiet; he'll hear you."

"Now that's horny." Roz gawped freely at the stranger. She glanced out at the motorbike. "Yeah," she confirmed, and then turned to Sophie. "There's only two things as erotic as a gorgeous body on a meaty bike with such power between his legs - and that's a guy with passion running through him as he plays guitar with capable, masterful hands and agile fingers." Roz caught her breath as her imagination ran amok.

"That's two. What's the other?" Sophie asked, trying not to sound interested.

"A bloke with loads of money; is a must."

"Well, I really wouldn't know," Sophie mumbled dismissively. "Now go and see Mr Lucas before he lynches you from the rafters."

"Come!" Mr Lucas bellowed from his desk. Roz entered the small office, which felt more like a closet, and shut the door. He studied her attire. Her blouse was as tight as her skirt, yet although her skirt was a little too short she was otherwise presentable.

"I'm sorry I'm late, but I woke with this migraine that wouldn't go away. You know how it is."

Mr Lucas leaned back in his chair, placing his hands on the table. "Are you being obstinate, child?"

"No." She smiled. "I'm apologising."

"You are giving a feeble excuse, presuming I may well have been born yesterday. And I don't need it." He stood up. "Not today, not anymore. I don't need your insolence. It's by the grace of Sophie that you remain in employment here. She's been carrying your work load."

"You're sacking me?"

"I'm afraid that's for the powers that be to decide. Listen…" he said, rounding his desk. "The only attribute you seem to possess is that of a tidy appearance. Your attitude and punctuality leave a lot to be desired. If you don't smarten your act, I'll have no other option than to report you to the hierarchy."

"God," Roz said, spontaneously chuckling. "Keep your hair on. It's a library not the bloody Home Office."

"Again, you show no respect; and very little more to the general public. Your attitude appals me. Your education was obviously wasted on you, child. Little wonder your parents have washed their hands of you."

"What?" Roz was astonished, since she had left home three years previously of her own freewill.

"You heard," Mr Lucas said. Her expression was hostile. "But then it's not my place to remark on such things. It's for you to find your own course through life. No matter how much we might wish, we cannot put wise heads on young shoulders."

"Damn right," Roz agreed. "But, I need this job, Mr Lucas. - I did have a migraine, honest. Give me another chance. I will try harder."

Mr Lucas sighed submissively, regretting his irritation. "Go back to work."

"You're not going to report me?"

"No," he said quietly, disappearing back into the library. Taking few strides to cover much ground, Mr Lucas marched, noticing the biker. The young man glanced back. Mr Lucas noted this man's presence. Stress levels rising. He reached Sophie. "I'm going out for a few hours. Hold the fort whilst I'm gone." He handed her a bunch of keys.

"Are you alright, Mr Lucas? You seem a little edgy?"

"I'm fine," he said stiffly, pushing his glasses more securely on his nose, glancing again at the newcomer. "I trust you to keep Roz in check, if that's at all possible."

Sophie studied his sallow, haggard face and sunken eyes. "Are you sure you're okay? You look a little off-colour?"

"I've got a lot on. Guard them with your life." He ordered the safety of the keys and marched out the library.

"What's got into him?" Roz asked.

"I don't know." Sophie mused. "I think he must have personal problems."

Roz laughed at the notion. "Lucas the locust has personal problems? - I don't think."

"Why?" Sophie asked, annoyed at her friend's lack of compassion.

"Because he hasn't got a personal life; he's not married. He doesn't go anywhere or do anything. He's a complete anorak."

"How can you be sure?" Remembering the stranger, Sophie glanced through several strands of hair that had escaped her knot and were veiling her face. He was reading. His blond hair catching the fluorescent light was mesmerising. Sophie swallowed hard and whispered, "Just because he doesn't mention his private life doesn't mean he hasn't got one."

"Where's he going to go for a social life? He's a dork, a nerd."

"Roz, you're being cruel."

"I'm just stating a fact."

"My grandmother had a quote: If you haven't anything nice to say, say nothing."

"And as you always say: Honesty is the best policy."

"Not when it hurts others."

"You win. Anyway, I'm starving. Do you want your usual salad sandwich?"

"That would be nice. Thanks." Sophie handed Roz some money.

"I'm going to have a lavish bacon roll dripping with fat and oozing red sauce." Instinctively, Sophie screwed up her nose in revulsion. Roz said, "I'll be back in a minute - or ten - or twenty." She strolled to the doors, swinging her bag, feeling content that 'the locust' was no longer there keeping a beady eye on things. He always had his eye on things. He missed nothing. Not a trick; as though he had a sixth sense.

Heaving open the door, Roz noticed the biker was approaching the reception desk. He paid her a look of indifference and turned his back to face Sophie. His summer blond hair was free-falling and shining with health, contrasting against the blackness of his jacket, his rear was neatly wrapped in leather trousers. Catching Sophie's attention before she left, she mouthed, "Nice ass."

Sophie stifled a giggle as the stranger regarded her curiously.

"May I take it out?"

What did he mean by that?

Callum placed the book on the desk.

Was he referring to the book? Sophie's mind scrambled. She picked it up then placed it down, his gaze intimidating her. "Have you moved to the area permanently?"

"Why do you ask?"

She blushed. Was her curiosity that evident? "Because if you're just passing through, I'll need to open a 'temporary borrowers' file."

"I'm a tourist." Callum watched her type. Her pretty features being highlighted by the glare of the screen, his attention swung again to her hands. Her fingers, thankfully free of all rings, tapped rhythmically. He studied them more closely. They were long and delicate; so fragile. Like the lady herself, so vulnerable yet yielding. He wanted to reach out and touch her paint-free manicured nails: touch her fingers and feel their agility; the soft white skin on the back of her hand; the slender wrists, and trace his fingers up her long bare arms to her neck, to her lips.

"Can I have your name?" Sophie asked, fingers hovering while catching the stranger staring unguardedly at her lips. He seemed neither surprised nor embarrassed. In fact, he seemed to have to prise his eyes away.

"Callum," he said smoothly. "Callum O'Donnell."

"You have no accent. Are you Irish?"

"I'm well-travelled." He smiled weakly. "I was born in the Emerald Isle. My parents were Irish." Callum explained, memory drifting. "They died a long time ago. I was very young."

"Oh, that's tragic. I'm so sorry."

To change tact, Callum asked, "You'll want my address and some form of identification?" He patted his jacket then felt his trouser pockets. Annoyance flashed through his cool expression, and his light-blue eyes hardened. "It seems I may have left my driver's licence back at my room."

"It doesn't matter," Sophie said, dreamily. "You seem honest enough. I trust you."

"You do?"

His eyes sparkled with vibrancy. Only after her unexpected delight caused her sudden discomfort did she reluctantly break their gaze. She turned to her monitor. "Your temporary address is?"

"I'm staying at The Lodge, Forest Road. I'm in room seven."

Typing, Sophie said, "I know it. My friend used to live in room four." She reached for the book, but swiftly Callum was there, holding it. He was inviting her to take it. As she did their eyes met.

Through paper the void had been bridged. Heavy anticipation flooded the air, asphyxiating her as he stole her breath. Their hands were not touching yet energy flowed between them through the binding. Each knew the other was feeling it. Strong desires were being stirred; chemistry electric. Callum was astounded by the ferocity of his emotions and was knocked sideways to realise that the young woman felt it also, but he remained externally cool. When all he wanted was to convey his admiration, he remained silent, scared that if he was to open his mouth and speak his desires, words would spill in a haphazard frenzy and he'd sound foolish. How could he say she had awoken his dormancy without terrifying her, scaring her off, or - worse - without her laughing?

Sophie caught her breath, broke eye contact, and retracted her hand. She opened the front cover hastily, more aware of his gaze, and scanned the bar code with her infrared detector, printing the date stamp to the page with a flick of her wrist. Taking no risks, she placed the book on the desk for him to take.

Although he had overheard it, Callum said, "Can I ask you your name?"

- No, I have a boyfriend. Burst the bubble. - His gaze was fixed on her lips so that she could almost feel his kiss reach out and brush them. "It's Sophie."

"Sophie," he repeated. "Sophie is Greek for wisdom."

"I don't know about that."

"You are too modest," Callum said thoughtfully. "But it is an attribute." He pulled down the front zip of his jacket and slid the book inside. White cotton lay beneath, hinting at a firm physique.

Embarrassed by her sudden yearning to slide inside his jacket and snuggle up, Sophie nodded towards the doors. The sun was blazing, the day scorching. "You're going to bake out there." She failed to notice Callum flinch.

"I wear leather for protection," he remarked guardedly as he fastened his zip and took his crash helmet from her desk. "Maybe I will see you again. Until then, be safe."

He put on his helmet and secured it. - I've got a boyfriend. I love him - her brain demanded - tell him! She bit down hard on her lip and said nothing.

Muffled, Callum said, "Goodbye, Sophie." Casting to memory her pure-white teeth, sunken against the pressured red of her lip, he pulled on his gloves. He'd see her again.

Sophie watched him leave. He straddled his machine, heaved it upright and started it. It erupted to life. He pulled away, leaving her with the deep feelings his penetrating gaze had demanded. The haunting kiss she had seen in his eyes, threw her again into such despair and bewilderment, she was still staring into space when Roz returned.

Four

"ONE OF US IS GOING to have to learn to drive," Roz complained, that evening, stopping yet again to rub her aching ankles. "My feet are killing me."

"Then you should wear flatter shoes," Sophie stated a little too coarsely.

"I don't see why we've got to trudge to this pub all the time. The ones in the town centre are just as good."

Sophie knew the Bat Inn Hand was the only pub in the district with no mirrors along the rear wall of the bar, which suited the vampires. She could hardly tell Roz this, instead she said, "It has the nicest atmosphere."

"Is everything alright, Soph? You seem a little tetchy. In fact, you have been for most of the day."

"No, I haven't. Now, can we go?" Regardless, Sophie began walking, leaving Roz to catch up.

With the evening breeze cooling her flushed face, Sophie tried again not to think of Callum. He was staying not too far from her, breathing the same air, experiencing the same weather. Perhaps she should confide in Roz? Tell her of Callum and her turmoil, but Roz wouldn't understand. She couldn't know the complexity of her relationship with

Jon, and would only encourage a newly found passion away from the man she despised.

"So, how did your date go?" Sophie asked, turning out of the short cut through the residential estate and into the road, leading to the pub.

"Sean. - Thought you'd never ask." Roz shrugged. "It was okay. But he's not my millionaire come to whisk me away."

"I can't believe all you think about is money. There's more to life, you know? There's love?"

"Love is for romantics fools. No offence," Roz said breathlessly. "It means nothing to me. My parents had a hard time showing me any, and so did everyone else. I've never been in love," she offered casually. "I've been in lust. Infatuated a few times, and once, possibly, obsessed - but never in love. Which suits me fine; I don't want it. But I will marry. I ain't destined to work in that frigging library for the rest of my life, no way. I'm going to find a man that'll take care of me, let me party all night and flatly refuse to let me do another day's work. - He's out there, somewhere. Even if I've got to go through the whole damned lot to find him, he's out there."

⁂

The Bat Inn Hand was situated in the northern, more rural part of Sanctuary. Close to fields that bordered on the forests, the pub stood next to the local cricket ground.

It was now dark. The green car pulled into the rear car park. Four vampires got out.

Jon slammed his door. Sophie would be here in a room packed full of drunkards leering, testosterone flowing.

"Come on," he urged, striding off. "We've wasted half the bloody night as it is."

"Ooohhh," Liam sang sarcastically, waiting with Daniel for Greg to finish lighting his cigarette.

They followed Jon, coolly swaggering along the street. The low droning voices and the music from the jukebox grew louder. Jon yanked open the solid-wood door to the rowdy voices and smoke-filled air. Nobody in the area gave two hoots to the government policy on smoking.

Sophie was standing in the busy room to one side of two lads who were chatting to Roz. Over her glass of orange juice she spied Jon. She was hoping to see long, blond hair and pale-blue eyes. She felt the steady onslaught of guilt, and had to focus hard on the vampire heading toward her.

Jon sauntered through the crowd, wondering how he could have feared her chatting to the other guys here. Loyally as ever she was waiting for him alone. Her radiance was beaming an illustrious aura that he never had to scan the room. He knew where she was; he could sense her.

Then he saw Roz. Her face was glowing with flirtation. Her short, skimpy dress was so tight her curves left little to the imagination. Both of the guys were drooling, seemingly eager; attention on her breasts, none on her words, they smirked at each other. To Jon it seemed Roz didn't care. He wouldn't be surprised if the bimbo didn't get down with them both and copulate there on the floor in front of everyone.

Jon was also quick to notice desire on Liam's face, and realised his intentions. Liam made to divert course in the direction of Roz. Jon demanded, "Bar."

Liam decided a drink to be his main priority anyway, and went with Greg and Daniel to line up the pints.

Jon reached Sophie. "Sorry I'm late, but the girls had to get ready." She was amused because the three other vampires were anything but effeminate. "How's your day been?" Jon asked, wrapping his arms around her and loosing himself in her sparkling blue eyes.

"Fine, except Roz and I overslept. Then Mr Lucas left in a hurry and didn't return for several hours. He's acting a bit strange. But other than that everything was normal. - And you?" - Normal; she lied.

"Oh, I had an awesome day. I did the usual while the sun's out. Went for a picnic, and then for a swim which barbecued my skin."

"Jon?" Alarmed, Sophie checked the developing crowd.

"Sorry," he lamented, his own words now causing him to cringe, yet the fear of the burning sun was in his imagination, for he hadn't seen the fire ball in the sky since the sixties. "I slept, sweetest Sophie - as always."

"Keep your voice down."

"I do the nightshift," Jon paid his boyish wink. Then gently, he did what he needed to do since waking. He kissed her.

"Fuck it!" Daniel exclaimed, carrying two pints of lager. Half the contents of one splashed out of the glass and splattered on the floor.

"That had better not be mine," Jon said.

"It is, mate." Daniel handed him the half pint. "You'd still have a whole one if the numpty behind hadn't nudged me."

The lad turned to Daniel, grunted something and turned away.

Ignoring the lad, Jon groaned, "Shit, Daniel. I was looking forward to downing that."

"Ain't it just a bitch? - Want a game of pool?" Daniel asked, aware the table was occupied.

"Later," Jon said, noticing the two lads attempting to finish their game as the balls rolled back and forth, bouncing from the cushions and eluding all holes.

"They'll be there all night at that rate. Let's finish the game for them?"

"You can't!" Sophie exclaimed. "Don't cause trouble. They're only young. They're just learning how to play the game. Let them finish what they've started."

Daniel liked Sophie; she was such a New Age type of hippie.

Roz scanned the crowd for any male face not from her past. She had a short attention span and got bored easily. She saw one: a fit guy, whispering to another and slipping a cellophane wrap into the other's pocket. He was attractive with a confident air. He was wearing designer labels: possibly her millionaire?

Swaying her hips, she thrust breasts at him. "Hello, honey. I'm Roz."

"Alex." He stuffed money into his back pocket, looking her up and down. "What do you need?"

"A fast mover - I like it."

"I meant, what's your poison, darling?"

"Vodka and coke."

Taken aback, he studied her naivety - then her breasts. "Okay, whatever."

They wound through the crowd towards the side of the bar nearest the door. Roz wondered what sort of car he drove. Her attention diverted to a guy vaguely familiar, yet couldn't place him. She was sure she hadn't slept with him. She was positive she hadn't spoken to him either.

The guy had long, blond hair and wore glasses. He was carrying a bottle of beer and crash-helmet towards a small, round table for two near a window where he sat down alone. Then she remembered him from the library earlier, disappointed that she had met Alex first. Never mind, there was always tomorrow.

Daniel was loading balls onto the pool table. Jon held Sophie in an embrace. Every moment was precious. Every waking second, he wanted to be with her, loving her. The only consolation he could find was that summer was drifting into autumn and these nights would grow increasingly longer.

Her lips tasted good. Her long, summer-dress, hiding all that lay beneath, teased his memory, his imagination as, tracing his fingers lightly over the thin straps at her shoulders, the vampire felt her warm smooth skin. Moving his fingers lightly up to her neck, he pressed her flesh with encircling fingers, and deepened the kiss.

He felt something like 'firm flesh' run from his forehead, over his nose, stopping, blocking his mouth from his lover's. It was Daniel's invading hand.

"When you're ready, man?" Daniel grinned mischievously.

"Fuck off," Jon cursed, wanting to grab Daniel by the throat and punch his dull lights out. He snatched the pool cue Daniel was holding, went to the table, and leaned down to the cue ball.

He took vampire aim, fuelled with annoyance, and fired. The white ball thundered towards the triangle of balls and smashed into the spheres, scattering them in all directions.

Choosing red that had mostly disappeared down the holes, Jon proceeded to down the rest. His aim was precise. His keen eye detecting distance and angles; the physicality, all the balls rolled to their destinations, slamming against the back of the holes before disappearing downwards. No contest. He noticed Daniel's irritation out the corner of his eye. Leaning down to take the next ball, he noticed long, bare legs, walking suggestively by. - *Those* long legs: *her* long legs - Roz's.

His eyes travelled their length, so taut and slender from her ankles to her hem: her thin waist, enhancing the size of those breasts: her yellow hair, threatening to touch that pert rear: those sweet smiling lips of delicious blood red.

He missed.

He missed the ball? Shit. The white ball bounced off the cushion, hitting nothing.

"Ha, ha," Daniel sung, excitedly approaching the table with his pool cue. "Move out the way and let the master show you how it's done."

Indifferently, Jon stepped aside, allowing Daniel to finish the game, as Roz talked to Sophie.

"I've met this gorgeous guy, Alex," she said.

Jon studied her next victim, beside her. - A right prat. - He heightened his sense of hearing, blanking all background noise to catch each word.

"We're leaving now," Roz said. "We're going to visit a few more pubs; he's got some business to take care of, and then I'm going back to his."

"Fine," Sophie said. Nothing she could do or say would make Roz change her ways.

"If I'm not back before morning, I'll see you at work," Roz said, instantly unnerved as Jon neared and took his drink from the table.

"Be careful. Don't do anything stupid," Sophie said.

"Worry not; the party's only just begun." Roz glanced at Jon. "Found myself someone really generous and nice." She had invited the usual ridicule, and waited for his response. He said nothing. He just stared at her blankly and she was unsure what the cretin was thinking. For his benefit she gloated, "Don't wait up." As Roz and Alex left, she didn't turn to see Jon still staring blankly after her.

If Sophie had looked past the bodies towards the window, she would have seen a guy watching Jon curiously and her with unwavering interest. Perhaps she would have noticed his discomfort as Jon began affectionately kissing her? Then she would have understood his motive as he diverted his attention out of window. Perhaps if she had asked, he would have explained, then, why he insisted on gazing so distantly into the night, at that now darker than dark sky.

Seeing Jon preoccupied with his New Age girlfriend, Daniel had pestered Greg into playing pool. Liam was beside the pool table, the balls rolling along green carpeting. The game bored him. He looked at Sophie, necking his mate. She was a babe. In his opinion she was a real-life hippie-chic. With her cascading curls and flowing cotton dress, all she needed was a flower in her hair and some beads, and she'd be made. She had an attitude of peace and love to the world that made him want to retch. He supposed Jon was attracted to her because he was from the sixties - that era of free love with beads and hair, and kindness of soul; tuning in and opting out, not to mention all the sex on tap.

Liam asked Greg, "Shall we go to the Crypt tomorrow night?"

Greg shrugged. Cigarette drooping from his mouth, he took aim and fired. The balls cracked together. "Ask Jon."

"Are we going to the Crypt tomorrow, or what?" Liam hollered across the table at Jon, interrupting his canoodling.

"Yeah," Jon snapped back. He softly asked Sophie, "You want to go, don't you?"

"It's Friday tomorrow, so I'll only have to work Saturday morning. I think I can cope with that," she replied against the warmth of Jon's lips which muffled her answer and caused Liam to concentrate on his hearing to catch it.

Liam sighed noisily, hinting he felt on the verge of brain-dead, but the others were too engrossed in their own activities to notice or care. The lovers resumed kissing. He watched their mouths moving and sensed their tension and rising desire. If he were Jon, he wouldn't bother with all the mush; he'd take her outside and give her a damn good seeing to.

Liam scanned the room, ignoring the unwritten rule: no lovers should be taken within their own territory in case of accidental death. But here and now, females in all shapes and sizes were scattered about the room, distracting Liam from the rules. To him, they were all beautiful. Their summer clothes were skimpy and lightweight. Some were transparent.

Raising his sense of smell, he savoured their aromas.

Of all blood, human blood was the sweetest. So tantalising, so tempting. But, as most vampires had, at some point discovered, virgin blood was the ultimate fix. Once tasted, it could never be forgotten: the purity, the quality. The feel of it coating the tongue would deliciously blow the mind and senses like an orgasmic rush, the best drug on earth.

"I need to get laid," he groaned, shoving away from the wall he was leaning against.

Excited, Daniel watched with amusement as Liam emphatically made his way to a petite girl in her early twenties. She was standing alone, fixed on the television in the corner above the bar. Although the sound was muted, she seemed riveted by the soap. Daniel checked Jon was preoccupied then watched Liam entrap the girl. He whispered something in her ear. The girl shook her head, shunning him for the television.

Okay, so she doesn't give blowjobs to strangers. Liam glanced at her vulnerable neck, exposed by the short length of her hair. In obscurity, although she had ignored him, subconsciously she was begging for it.

Watching Liam stroke the side of her face, Daniel shifted his weight from one foot to the other in infantile delirium, as again, his friend dared to make lurid suggestions.

Jon was busy with Sophie. No vampire noticed the man in his mid-thirties, weaving out of the crowded bar area towards his girlfriend.

The man was carrying two drinks, biceps bulging, threatening to tear the short sleeves of his tee shirt. He noticed his girlfriend and the red-haired loser chatting her up. He dropped his drinks onto the nearest table, and flexed his steroid induced muscles: time for a workout.

"Game over," Greg announced, dropping his cue onto the table as a man grabbed the cue, swirled around and headed directly for Liam. The cue was swinging up and down to his outstretched hand, slicing the smoke-filled air to the beat of each stride. "Oh, fuck," Greg muttered, frozen by the vision of the wooden stake as it twanged in the man's palm.

"Yeah," Daniel winced.

Both vampires were mortified. The cue was long, sturdy and sleek, and gleaming with reflected light along its length that was turned to perfection, narrowing to a finer point. A cleaner incision.

The man reached Liam. "What the fuck do you think you're doing?"

"Chatting up your girlfriend; what does it look like?"

"Yeah, that's what I thought." He turned to his girlfriend. "Move out the way." The girl moved. To Liam, he hissed, "You must be on a fucking death wish."

"No, mate. Been there, done that." Liam smirked, not breaking eye contact and ignoring the wood swinging menacingly. "I knew she was yours. Seeing she had no taste, I thought I'd be in there."

"Oh, a fucking wise guy," the man leered. "You like pain, do ya?"

Liam shrugged. Knowing the man would sooner wrap the cue around his head than lunge it through his vulnerable heart, he said, "Try me."

Obviously wanting to feel some of the pain he would deal, the man dropped the cue, clenched a hard fist and swung it hard into Liam's jaw.

By now all the vampires in the room were watching and feeling less jittery as the cue bounced with a twang to the floor.

Liam straightened up, lip throbbing with pain. He glared at the man. His temper rising, his heart pumping adrenaline; igniting his every sense, he snarled, "Is that it?"

"You want more, do ya? I'll give ya some more." The man readied his fist again.

"Come on then, chicken shit. What are you waiting for?" Liam jibed, spitting blood, which distracted him. He frowned, wiping his lip, and stared at his hand now smeared red. He ran his tongue over the swelling wound and tasted nectar; blood seeping. He glanced at the others.

"Ah. You want your friends to come help ya, is that it?" the man said. "Little boy split his lip?"

"Fuck you," Liam spat pink saliva, grabbing the man by his collar and head-butting him on the nose so swiftly, the man didn't know what hit him.

The man was groaning, face in his hands to nurse his nose. Liam sucked hard on his open wound, knowing in two minutes he would heal, his skin would knit together. But, with anger reigning and the sweet taste of blood, the inevitable began happening. Helplessly, he looked to Jon for support.

Jon could feel it too, as could Greg and Daniel. The sounds from the jukebox and droning conversations were growing louder. Their eyes were filling rapidly with daylight vision. The smoke-filled air began burning their nostrils. Liam was transgressing into the active vampire. The combination of his fury and the taste of blood were now too great a mix to subdue his raging hunger. His transgression was overpowering. His five senses were thrown into chaos and out of control. All five senses were heightening; he had begun manipulating the other vampires.

"Come on, we've got to get out of here," Liam heard Jon speak, but was distracted. The man was removing his hands. Mesmerised, Liam saw what he had been anticipating: more human blood oozing out of both nostrils: trickling, worming red tramlines. More blood shimmering in cupped hands. He wanted it all.

"Liam, move!" Jon grabbed Liam by the arm as still Liam gawped.

"You broke my fucking nose! You wanker! - You ain't going nowhere. I'll have the fucking lot of ya. All of ya, outside; come on!" the man bellowed.

"Bring it on!" Liam raged, daring him to take his chances. He wanted the bloke outside. He wanted the bloke's insides while urging his fangs to hurry and extend.

The man lunged at Liam again, but with one forceful strike, Jon shoved him backwards. "We're leaving. And you're staying here."

"No I fucking ain't."

"Yes you fucking are." Jon tried not to acknowledge the sweet distracting liquid.

"Let's be on your way now lads," a male voice said. The landlord of the pub was standing before them. A tall man with authority in his eyes behind yellow tinted glasses acknowledged the man, dripping blood, then turned to the four vampires. "Go on lads, you'd better leave now."

Liam disguised his mouth with his hand to hide the healing process. Jon pushed Liam in the direction of the door. The four vampires made their way through the crowd of spectators.

Jon turned to Sophie. "Sorry."

"It's not your fault. Go and take care of them, and I'll see you in the club tomorrow."

Jon tried controlling his developing senses but all attempts were futile. His entire body was awake. He was aware of the slightest noise, the smell of iron and some form of steroid, the people surrounding: and more aware of the distance to the door. He had to get to that door. He had to get away from the bodies pumping blood. Time was against him. His body clock was against him. He had to get away from the town and get the others to the safety of the feeding grounds that were the forests.

Following the others, he sauntered as casually as he could through the crowded bodies while feeling their heat, hearing their breathing. Sensing the oxygen being delivered to the vital organs via the stream of life: those delicate veins, such delicious arteries, - that blood so divine. Soon, his conscience would fade, all rational thinking would leave, and he would have no self-control. His primal instincts would reign: leaving him without thoughts for consequences or empathy for the inevitable pain dealt.

Reaching the door, Jon barged through it, ran at his three friends huddled on the pavement, and grabbed Liam by his collar. "What the fuck are you playing at, you crazy shit?" Jon was too livid to notice his healed lip. He shoved Liam hard in the chest, causing him to take a step backwards, then, glaring at the others, he snapped, "Get to the car park."

Sitting by the window, Callum had watched the entire spectacle with fascination. He had seen the troublemaker's lip swiftly heal and all the spilt blood disappear. Although Sophie was in the room, and he wanted so much to go to her, he closed his eyes, lowered his face, and rested his forehead in his hands.

Samuel Lawson pushed his glasses more securely on his nose and bent to retrieve the wooden cue.

Sophie hovered. "I'm so sorry for the incident."

He studied the stake, turning it thoughtfully between his figures. "It could have been worse," he said distantly. "These things happen. – I've been around long enough to know that."

"You're not going to ban them?"

"No. If I were to ban everyone who caused a fracas, my pub would be empty." He glanced at the timid girlfriend then turned to the man. "As for you: wash up in the gents, wait ten minutes, then leave. You can return another night when you've had time to reflect on your behaviour. - Am I being fair?"

"Fair? The bastard broke my fucking nose," the man hissed. "You should've got the pigs in, had them arrested, not let 'um walk free."

"Maybe, but you threw the first punch. Anyway, you're bleeding on my carpet, and the sight of blood makes me queasy, so go and wash, and let the matter drop."

There was nothing keeping Sophie here. She made her way to the door, to grab an early night. Through the crowd she saw Callum. His face was in his hands, massaging his forehead as though he had a headache. She caught her breath. As though sensing her gaze, he looked directly at her. He seemed troubled. But then his light blue eyes glinted behind his glasses, his handsome features broke into a charming smile, and his agony seemed to subside.

Callum noticed her dilemma. The lady of his dreams was indecisive. He thought she would leave. He knew it best that she should. She had a boyfriend. Callum had witnessed the intensity of his love.

She made her decision, weaving her way towards him. All thoughts of her boyfriend disappeared. All problems concerning his mission dissolved back to the haze. All inner-turmoil diminished. If he only had this moment with the ethereal Sophie – so be it. She stood before him, her serenity paralysing him.

In her angel voice, she gently spoke, "How are you enjoying your stay?"

"It is pleasurable, thank you. The forests are most breathtaking. Sanctuary is quaint, though the townsfolk are less endearing, you omitted, of course." He gestured to the chair opposite. "Would you care to join me?"

Sophie shrugged and uttered, "Yes."

Callum pushed her chair out from below the table with his foot, and before she could sit down, he was standing. She faltered, astonished by the biker's etiquette, and only after she had sat down, did he follow suit.

"Have I amused you?" he asked.

"I'm not used to such gracious manners. There aren't many men who would rise for a lady to be seated."

"Then I'll take your amusement as complimentary." He glanced out of the window and surveyed the scene.

Sophie caught the glint of a clear stone stud in his ear, and wondered of his upbringing.

"Your boyfriend will not return for you?"

"No. They have cause to go there own way."

"And now you're here in my company, which is his loss. I sense your discomfort; you feel you're betraying him?"

"Excuse me?"

"I don't mean to be intrusive; your affairs are your own. It's just - I feel drawn to you." His fingers knitted together to save grabbing her hands. "I long to know you, Sophie. Yet if your lover is between us I may never know the real you. Since I first fell upon your beauty, my desire is to learn your heart, your mind; you intimately."

"You're not backward at coming forward are you?" Sophie gasped.

Callum leaned closer, intensity dancing in his crystal-blue eyes. "I confess, I'm not usually so out-spoken, but with you I find it's a necessity. My feelings are controlling my tongue that I am embarrassed. So much time is wasted in the world. So many missed opportunities thrown to the gutter. You took something of me, I'm not sure what."

Sophie giggled. His expression was so serious, his manner so earnest. Never before had she considered bikers could be such ardent romancers.

"I've got to go." Sophie rose to her feet. "I could stay here all night. Your words are hypnotic, but..."

"Then stay," Callum urged. "Please?"

"I can't. I'm sorry."

"Then I'll come with you." Noticing she was about to protest, he added, "You leave me no choice. You are too fair a creature to be travelling alone by night. God knows what dangers could befall you. I'll see you safely to your door; only then shall I feel content."

It was him she feared. That kiss promised in the library. Not any creature of the night, some sinister vampire lurking in the shadows. It was her emotions she feared – her own raw desires.

"You fear me?" Callum felt his stomach twist. "You shall come to no harm. You can trust me."

"I just don't think it would be wise."

"Then, you're afraid I may tempt you with kisses and try to seduce you?"

"No," she said alarmed then uttered, "Yes."

"I promise; I shall do nothing you don't wish of me. Ever been on the back of a bike?" Callum grabbed his crash helmet. Noticing she was faltering due to his bottle of beer, he added, "I'm intoxicated, but not with alcohol."

Samuel Lawson watched the pair leave. He pushed his glasses more securely on his nose, and snorted a scoff.

As they walked to the car park, Sophie tried to sum up the stranger. She could have thought his words were corny, yet somehow they suited him. It wasn't a display, a facade. This was him, his way, his manner. Much as she wished to deny it, she liked it. She found comfort in his eloquence, a certain reassurance.

Callum celebrated her innocence, again glimpsing vulnerability beneath her calm exterior. He was pleased he had found the nerve to speak his feelings. The fact she had a boyfriend had given him the jolt he needed to be impulsive. But it was more than a jolt, more like a swift kick up the rear. Inwardly, Callum was still reeling from his emotions; alive and to the fore. He was still reeling from all his discoveries of the night.

Jon's car was still parked. This meant they had flown; taken to the air, risked being seen in their urgency. As Sophie neared the bike, the glistening metal stole all thoughts of Jon.

"Beautiful, isn't she?" Callum said, stroking the black petrol tank. "I call her Black Bess, after Dick Turpin's horse."

"The infamous highwayman of the eighteenth century; I like it. Mr Turpin's horse was reputed to be a fine creature. And this..." she placed her hand on the seat. "This seems to be a fine motorbike, though perhaps a little too powerful."

"Dick Turpin's horse was mighty enough to keep him on the run for so long." Callum said, enjoying the otherwise bizarre conversation.

"But, sir, you are not Dick Turpin in fear of being hanged; you are Callum O'Donnell proposing to take me home."

Callum laughed, and realised he had not felt so happy in a long time. "I'm not Dick Turpin; but on my fine steed I shall, most cautiously, take you. First I ask one thing of my honourable fine lady."

"And that is?"

"Where is home?"

"All Saints Road, near the library."

"I'll find it. Fancy them naming a road after you."

"I wish. Actually, there's a church at the far end." Sophie giggled. But his cool gaze stole that giggle, her breath then her smile; and both stood in silent wonder at the other. He was now far less intimidating. The silence was no longer uncomfortable.

Callum was first to break the still. Handing her his crash helmet, he choked, "To protect that pretty head." He took a step closer to help her fasten it. She let him. She kept her eyes lowered and refusing to be drawn. With conviction, he softly told her, "I will take you slowly, so that you'll hold no fear for your safety, or any doubt in my integrity."

"Oh," Sophie was perplexed; should he be promising his slow, deliberate taking of her sexually?

She sat behind as he started the machine: his Black Bess. She tried holding the rear handrail, but didn't feel safe. She wanted her hands in front, holding something sturdier. As they pulled off, she grasped his firm waist.

Callum was aware of her touch, and tried to concentrate on his steering. He was aware of her legs wrapped about his, her inner thighs warming his legs, her hands pressing his sides.

As he pulled into the high street, he noticed the change in his pillion through the handling of his machine. Her grip had loosened of hands and legs. He sensed her trust; her submission.

They rode with the roar of the engine in their ears, with each other in their minds. Sophie lifted her visor, breathed in the cool air, and lowered her face so his hair gently tickled her nose and cheeks.

She wanted to tell him to keep going, past her road, and on, and on, to the forests and beyond. Callum was masterful; controlling such power as though it was an extension of his body, leaning this way and that with self-assurance. Roz had been right, Sophie realised in wild abandonment. This was truly erotic.

Approaching the library, Callum dropped the bike down through the gears and banked left into All Saints Road.

They pulled up alongside the pavement opposite her flat and Sophie dismounted. In the orange haze of the streetlight, she lifted her helmet: curls fell, bouncing to surround her beaming features. "That was amazing," she blurted breathlessly.

Her cheeks were flushed pink. Her eyes were glistening from the cool breeze. So healthy, so alive and so vibrant; Callum felt he was falling, lost forever. "I'm glad you enjoyed it."

"How fast does she go?"

"Fast enough," he said proudly.

Her excitement faded to seriousness. She handed him the helmet. "Ride safely."

"You have concern for me?"

"You've been a friend. You've seen me to my door." She took a small step closer. "For that, I thank you, sir." She saw his kiss again. She remembered the kiss she had seen in his eyes that had haunted her for much of the day. It was back in full view. She could kiss him, and truly know what his lips would feel like. Then surely this kiss would no longer haunt her every moment? She would be reinstated. Her mind would quit pestering. Her stomach would quit somersaulting. He had also promised not to kiss her. His word was his honour.

Sophie needed to know. Her lips softly brushed his; instantly it awakened the need in each other. She kissed him again. The denial made it more desperate to obtain. She kissed him once more until he could no longer deny himself the pleasure; he wanted her. He returned her demand, and pushed deeper, urgently. He wanted her every breath; he held her throat to feel her pulse quicken. He released the kiss to gaze at her. His hand moved from her throat, slowly down towards her breasts and stopped short to rest against her thundering heart. He knew her desires in this moment. He grabbed her to him to deliver such rapture she would return to his arms and beg for more.

Hungrily, they entwined, kissing until they were holding each other's heads to control and manipulate each other; neither wanting this moment to end; that the taste of each other would be only a memory.

Butterflies flitted in Sophie's stomach and churned her insides like never before. Thousands of them flitting to emotions, and moistening her gusset.

Callum gasped against her mouth, scrunching her curls desperately. He uttered, "Sophie."

Jon entered her mind and in stomped guilt. But still, she wanted this kiss, for him to again breathe her name, touch her heart; feel anything he wanted. She drew him closer, manipulating him to deepen the kiss again. The passion overwhelmed them, until, to his distress, she broke away, visibly shaken. Callum longed to wrap his arms around her and hold her close, never lose her. But her expression was too distraught, too damning. Her eyes glistened with tears.

"I'm sorry," she blurted. "I shouldn't have done that, Callum. I can't do this. More depends on me than you can ever know. Forgive me?"

Before he could respond, she had fled to the safety of her gate, then behind the slamming of her door. He wanted to follow, beg mutual forgiveness and wipe away her tears.

He rode away, knowing he had caused pain and realising he would do best to concentrate on the mission, his only true purpose for being here. Yet, all his yearnings could conjure was the taste of her kiss and the urgency of their desires.

Five

FOUR VAMPIRES FLEW TOWARDS THE wide-open fields in their wake. Silvery moonlight coated the farmland, casting shadows from hedgerows along the fields, intensifying the borders in shrouds of sombre black. Amidst this land, a lone house stood lifeless. The occupants were asleep, absent of the sixth sense their livestock possessed.

Side by side four vampires glided an inch above the grass.

Chickens in their coops began flapping and clucking. Detached feathers floated in dusts of chaos as the chickens clambered over each other to get to anywhere that was safe. The predators were flying swiftly in their direction, on course for blood. They only calmed after the dreaded chill from four soulless freaks past soundlessly over.

Horses in their stables stamped their hooves and ground them across concrete, dragging up straw. Nostrils flaring, they tossed their heads in unease. Eyes bulging in the rear sides of their sockets, they sensed danger looming briefly overhead, before it past them by.

In fields, sheep and cattle grouped together. Shivering, they rocked in quiet discontent and fouled the grass. They sensed the onslaught. Gliding in their direction was death. They stood silent and waited...

Obliviously the mortals slept. Silhouetted by the moon, four mysterious figures gathered muster as they did a flyby, skimming the roof on their way to nearby forests.

The vampires flew low. Their consciences were fading as rapidly now as their fangs were extending. A few minutes later, and they wouldn't have cared whether they were to feed on forest creatures or the counted farm animals. But they still had a small sense of rational thinking, dictating they get to the forests. As they neared the start of these trees, they vaguely realised they had made it to safety.

The northern forests were unfamiliar to them. They normally used the southern forest closest to their den for blood. Tonight they had to leave the pub in a hurry; their transgressions taking a ruthless grip of their bodies, they had taken to immediate flight away from human inhabitants.

Under the cover of trees, near the edge of the forests, a brook trickled; it's fresh water silver and glinting on course for a huge expanse of pond, nestled in the woodland. Ducks were nesting on the embankments when something startled them. They sat in attendance to their senses. Fear washed over them, demanding they leave this place. Danger was heading straight for them. Evil was on course for destruction; and death knew their numbers. Stretching their wings in a flapping warning, they took to the air.

Reaching the trees, the vampires swooped over them, gliding low to the green canopy. Their consciences and logic had now escaped. Their only instinct was destination bloodbath.

Their five senses were heightened to their capacity, and the vampires could see through the night as though it was midday. They could hear water trickling below, and could smell fear drifting on the air.

The sounds of thunderous flapping rose from the trees as the ducks quacked taking to flight up over the pond.

"Dinner is served," Liam lisped.

The ducks flew in confusion over the vast pond. Unsure which way to turn, most of them flew away from the predators; the stragglers faltered then went after the more dominant ones. But doom was faster.

Honing in on their chosen prey, the vampires sped faster in a frenzy, weaving, darting; circling the pond. With one fateful swipe, each vampire grabbed a duck from the air. Clenching the beaked heads, they turned the ducks over to expose their chests and raised the feathered delicacy to their ready, drooling mouths.

The vampires pulled at the feathers with sharpened fangs, ripping feathers from flesh. The feathers floated delicately downwards to the water. The ducks remained struggling. Vampire fangs pierced through the hard flesh. It succumbed, popping to the force. In mid-flight, the vampires sucked harder, drinking the sweet blood. They drank hungrily, draining the ducks until they flopped lifeless and limp with bent necks and still beaks.

Focussing on their next feed, the vampires flew on. Discarding the emptied ducks, they snatched the second duck, and sent more feathers scattering.

Liam slowed up. Jon took the lead and grabbed the next feathered victim. Liam held no true thoughts. His conscience was gone. His primitive instincts were driving him now. He felt annoyance and frustration and, as he watched Jon, his agitation unexplainably grew.

Jon changed course for a picnic area, dropping with feline grace to his feet. Greg and Daniel landed either side of him.

"Where's Liam?" Jon demanded.

"Don't know." Greg scanned the skies.

"For fuck sake," Jon cursed, unsure why he cared.

From above, Liam hollered, "Duck!"

A duck carcass was hurtling towards Jon's face. Jon ducked. The carcass skimmed his head and landed to the ground behind. Liam landed in front, wearing a menacing smile of bloodstained teeth.

"Wanker," Jon hissed.

"Yeah, you got it," Liam said, glaring aggressively into Jon's dark, dead eyes. He wanted a fight. He was heading the right way to having one. Yet still he couldn't logically comprehend why through the fog? Although he couldn't think clearly to call upon his vacant memory, Liam sensed Jon had done something to annoy. His body was tense. His muscles were filled with pent up energy. Without being able to reason, he knew he wanted nothing more than to smash Jon's face in.

Jon sensed this; unsure and unconcerned why Liam should be spoiling for a fight. - But if the aggravating prick wanted a fight, he could have one.

Daniel said, "What next? I'm starving."

Liam took to the skies. Instinct was driving him onwards, but amnesia wouldn't budge and his brain refused to work. All he could see was the murky red colour swamping his eyes. All he could feel was the burning need to rid the frustration. And still he failed to understand why. Deep within his psyche, something was driving him to return to the forest edge; back in the direction they had travelled; back to the farmland.

In their field, cattle sensed the approaching doom. They sensed determination. The doom was real and coming fast and furiously straight for them from some invisible place. They could hear nothing: no flapping of wings, no swishing of material, not a growl or a squawk. But they knew the wingless predator had death within it. The predator had death in mind like a slaughterer holding a stun gun.

They sighted death. Gliding over the distant trees, it swooped down inches above the grass and continued heading for them like a missile. Unstoppable, it honed in on them. They huddled together, urinating. As the dark figure descended upon them more vigorously, pathetically they began to trot.

Liam singled out the largest cow of the herd. Not caring where the rest were heading, he concentrated on her. Light brown and heavily muscled, well cared for, well fed. Perfect. He could smell the blood from his teasing subconscious and knew how this particular blood would taste - good enough. He licked his lips, admiring his sharpened fangs, and sped onwards as the fattened cow tired. It broke from a clumsy trot to a walk. Then, surrendering to her fate, the cow stood trembling, and waited. Her hefty body was rocking to each laboured breath. Her only employable eye, rolled to focus on the killer storming in from the side.

Doing likewise, the other cattle stood stupidly between them, unaware that the vampire had already made his choice.

Like a ball hitting skittles, the vampire flew in, knocking into those in his path and sending them sprawling heavily onto their sides. There before him stood the prize; the kingpin. Waiting, watching, mocking him with indifference, she refused to budge even though he was hurtling towards her at speed. Liam knew the stubborn female was going to have it. He was a vampire and should be shown some respect.

The vampire landed alongside the cow. He lowered his face to her, stared her hard in one eye and, although he hadn't a clue why he should ask, he lisped, "Do you give blowjobs?"

The cow remained motionless, as though if she didn't move, she couldn't be seen.

"I bet you give good head?" Liam smiled hatefully, reaching out to the obstinate female and stroking the side of her face. Hunger was in his eyes, the devil on his shoulders.

"Come on, stupid cow, stop fucking ignoring me. You know damn well I want you. I'm going to sink my teeth in and suck you dry. You know you'll enjoy it."

Deliriously, his hand moved, his fingers pressing hard against the short brown hyde. Vacantly, he withdrew it, folded his fingers and slowly made a fist. Knuckles whitening, he twisted his hand, surveying the fist from each perspective. He caught eye contact with the cow.

Not feeling the need to kill her outright, not yet, Liam refrained from swinging his fist back too far. With a force mighty enough, he jabbed his punch hard into the side of her face. The cow fell.

Landing sideways, her eyes rolled in delirium. The vampire leapt onto her stomach. The full force of his body restrained her main torso. But he didn't lower his mouth, as promised; instead he used the vampire strength of his fingers. Pinching her flesh together to take a firm grasp, he yanked hard. The flesh gave way a little. A small tear appeared. The cow remained protesting. Using both his hands, the vampire curled his fingers under the gaping flesh to greet the warm, sticky blood that had found its course to the surface. With a better hold on it, he yanked even harder. The hyde tore. The cow snorted, moving her head to look behind as her pathetic matchstick legs tried to find solid ground.

Liam marvelled at his handiwork. With one final tear, he had made a hole large enough to lose his head in. Her intestines broke free so that miles of the stuff seemed to unravel and spill past his knees down to the grass. The putrid stench was bliss. Lowering his head to the hole, Liam began lapping up the blood.

The three vampires saw the sight from above. Some cows were standing; others were fighting to get up. Gliding soundlessly in, each saw the main cow; the main course; her intestines glinting, and the blood drenched grass. The vibrant colour was beckoning, the addiction overwhelming.

Greg landed straight to bended knee alongside Liam. He tore a larger hole in the cow and dove his face straight in. Daniel sank to his knees and joined them. Jon was about to do likewise when he saw the cow move; a shallow breath as her chest exhaled, a slight nudge of the protesting head. The cow was still conscious?

Without conscience, none of them could care. They could feel no empathy for the pain it was suffering, yet deep within Jon's subconscious something pestered. He couldn't logically wonder what, except his instinct was to stun the prey first. This wasn't to appease his conscience since it had long gone: this was for someone else's sake. Someone he cared more for than himself or the beast lay dying: although without true thought, he couldn't picture whom.

He walked directly to the cow's head and kicked it hard. The head jolted. Vertebrae popped and snapped. Her neck broken, the cow breathed her last.

Unburdened of his nagging instincts, Jon marched back to his companions and dropped to his knees to take what was left.

Gorged full, Liam sat back as his three friends finish the main course. The carcass was lying in red grass. Its head lay at an obscure angle. Her eyes were open and were dull and lifeless as his. Her tongue, hanging sideways from her mouth dripped strings of saliva. On the sunken body, straggly hyde lay oversized on prominent bones.

Eventually, Jon stood up and wiped his face in his tee shirt. He held no compassion for the animal, but deep within, again, something told him not to leave it there for the farmer to discover. He glared at Liam. "Get rid of it."

"You get rid of it," Liam retorted.

Greg stood up. Staring at the carnage as though seeing it for the first time, he nudged Daniel and said, "We'll get rid of it."

The two vampires grabbed the carcass and held it effortlessly between them, then began the flight back to denser parts of the northern forests to drop the evidence for the foxes and flies.

Unsure why he wanted to wipe the smirk from Liam's face, Jon lit a cigarette, turned his back and stared vacantly towards Sanctuary.

※

Amidst the forest, southern side was the vampire den; a forgotten, disused coalmine. The entrance was square and hollowed out in the side of the hill, and well hidden by surrounding shrubbery. Across the pitted track, shrubs and trees concealed it from most vantage points.

These trees stood in all their splendour. Tall and proud, they reached towards the skies, dug in their roots and defied gravity by refusing to lean or bow over. Proud to be standing near siblings and saplings, the carpet of a hundred thousand trees and a million leaves coated this peaceful world in a sea of green. The only break from green was on the distant horizon to the right, the shimmering orange and white glow of Sanctuary.

Jon drove carefully up the dirt track and, reaching the mine entrance, swung the green car into his parking space opposite, amongst bushes. He yanked up the handbrake, switched off the engine and stared momentarily at the trees. His hunger salved, his senses had lowered almost back to normal, his teeth had retracted back in their gums, and his true logic and memory had returned. Because each vampire manipulated the other, he knew the others were up to speed.

Now he remembered why Liam was such a prick. He was the reason why Jon had left Sophie so prematurely. He, with lustful whims and empty-headed stupidity, had been the cause for their overwhelming advancement to the active vampire that could easily have wiped out the entire pub in a frenzied bloodbath of selfish greed.

Jon spat, "You took out a cow; - a fucking cow." Still he stared ahead, knowing if he saw Liam gloating in any form, he would swing for him. Both were equal in strength, and the interior of a car was no place to brawl. With mighty swipes and kicks, the windows could break, the doors would be kicked from their hinges; and the car needed to appear legal. Although Jon wanted to re-arrange Liam's face, he got out the car and crossed the track to the mine tunnel. Keeping his sight heightened to see his way, he flew its long, meandering course down into the earth.

The large, circular cavern lay before him. In front was the living area with three armchairs, a sofa and a coffee table. Curtains, pallets and old doors sectioned off the sleeping area, which held four beds, surrounded by more curtained screening like a hospital ward, since the curtains reached neither the floor nor the high roof. But this provided each vampire with privacy.

Jon made his way past the furniture to the far wall to a small, underground spring. The water collected in a rock pool before continuing its course through a small pothole to disappear downhill. He swilled his face free from blood, pulled off his blood-matted tee shirt and threw it into a box that substituted a bin. He went to a box of stolen, new clothes, and pulled on a fresh tee shirt.

His friends' echoing voices droned through the tunnel, and Jon again tried calming his anger. He lit a cigarette, grabbed a can of lager from one of the many crates stacked high along the sidewall, and sat down on the sofa.

The conversation muted as the three vampires past him and went to the spring to freshen up. Jon was still seething because of Liam. He couldn't help it. The arrogance in his saunter was riling him more, that Jon almost detested looking at the back of Liam's head: the red flaming curls hiding the smugness, the deep satisfaction. He had killed a cow. An entire cow had disappeared from the face of the planet leaving red grass. Like flipping the middle finger at the farmer, they had left his grass saturated in blood.

"You took down a cow," Jon repeated.

Liam sighed. - Like he cared. He pulled the pull-ring on a can of lager. "Get a life; it's no real catastrophe," Liam said, slouching back in the armchair opposite.

"You - killed - a - cow," Jon spat out slowly, as though Liam was deaf. "What's the fucking matter with you? You want everyone knowing we exist?"

Liam chuckled. "Get real; they're not going to think some Dracula flew in and did it. And if they did, they'd be sectioned under the mental health act. No, mate, they'd put it down to a fox or something."

"A fox? Bollocks - a fox. Did you see the mess you made? Did you see the size of the canyon we left in its guts?" Jon snapped, rolling his cigarette between his finger and thumb irritably.

"So?" Liam shrugged; his green soulless eyes not missing one move of his friend.

"So, you fucked-up-prick? So - what if we'd left it there? What if the farmer found it, and came searching with his farmer buddies on a witch-hunt for us?"

Greg sat down in a chair. "Jon's got a point, Liam. You know the rules; no humans, no pets and no livestock."

"Well, I didn't see you turn your nose up at it," Liam stated, refusing to be scorned.

"It tasted nice, didn't it?" Daniel asked, standing amongst his friends, unaware that he had potentially added fuel to the flames. Yet, no one could deny it. Each remembered the volumes of blood and the taste of it, wondering if it really had a special quality or whether it tasted supreme because it was forbidden.

Savouring its aftertaste, Jon glared at Daniel who was waiting eagerly for some universal agreement, and said, "Sit down." Promptly, he did.

"The fact is," Liam said to Jon, "you did enjoy it. It's been the best you've tasted in a long while. It's damned blood. It's bad fucking blood. It's closer to our hearts and it's turning us on. - You're pissed because you know I'm right. Except now your conscience is telling you you've been a bad boy. You're losing control over us."

"Fuck you," Jon snapped, sitting forward, itching to stand. "Don't patronise me. You don't know me; so don't tell me what's going on in my mind, okay?"

"I know you," Liam nodded coolly, "probably better than you know yourself. Hell, I've been with you long enough. Most people get out of marriage sooner."

"Well if you don't like it, fuck off. Move out."

"Perhaps I will. I could go it alone. There isn't anything or anybody able to stop me. I could walk out of here - go on a rampage and bollocks to the lot of you - because right now I couldn't give a toss."

"Oh, yeah, that'd be right," Jon said sardonically. "That would be you. Think of number one."

"Yeah, well, what's wrong with that? Just because you're under the thumb: dutiful servant to your precious Sophie. Shit, she's practically got you eating out of her hand." Liam slurped and smacked his lips together. Taking a drink from his can, he missed the swift actions of his friend as Jon sprung up, flew across the table, landed, and grabbed him by the throat before jerking him so vigorously his drink spilt.

"Take that back, asshole," Jon hissed, glaring into dead astonished eyes and throttling him harder.

"No," Liam gagged, refraining from kneeing his friend between the legs. "It's right," he spluttered. "You're a complete jerk, a royal pain in the ass since you've been going with her; Miss Love and Peace; makes me want to puke."

Jon released him. "You're jealous. You envy me."

"I pity you. Two years ago we were drinking from humans. You know – the good stuff. Remember *that*? Damn it, Jon. You're becoming a fucking bore; a constant fucking nag. You're turning into a right bitch of a woman."

"You're twisted. You're so contorted you can't see straight."

Greg said, "He's sexually frustrated."

Jon and Liam shot him a glance. Liam asked, "And who asked you, Dr Greg?"

"Well you are." Greg shrugged casually.

"Yeah," Jon agreed, studying Liam. "That would explain why you nearly got staked."

"I didn't nearly get staked," Liam protested. "The prat wanted to wrap it around my head. He wouldn't think to drive it through my heart. Why would he?"

"Yeah, man," Daniel joined in. "But he could have if he'd thought of it."

"But the geezer never," Liam said, astonished at the stupid conversation.

"Anyway..." Jon said, feeling jittery, "That's not the point. The fact is you put us in jeopardy; the whole sodding pub for that matter all because you fancied some skirt."

Liam glared at Jon. "You've got it on tap so stop squeaking. I'm a red-blooded man. You're too wrapped up with Sophie to think about us; sex-starved and agitated."

"Little man ready to explode, is that it?" Jon teased.

"Can you blame him?" Liam said, addressing his crotch. "The poor bastard hasn't seen the moon at night in two weeks."

Greg said, "That's settled then, we're off to the coast. Party-time."

Liam said, "Shall have to or my dick's going to fester."

"Can we go and see that castle again?" Daniel asked.

"Whatever, mate; if it does it for you." Now Liam realised why, subconsciously he had acted the way he did, and the evening's events had been worth the hassle.

Under the mask of night, the three vampires would fly south over rural countryside to their regular retreat. They would sleep all day in a disused partially boarded up railway tunnel. By night, they would visit the neighbouring towns and villages, seeking female pleasure. Then Daniel would have his own brand of fun.

Visiting the castle in the dead of night, Daniel would keep his vision lowered and run riot. He would jump about amongst the tall, meticulously pruned hedges of the maze, and get lost in the moonlight. Only after the conundrum had won, when Daniel had exhausted all natural efforts of finding himself would he then fly out.

Greg would lie on the grass, stare at the moon, smoke weed, keep the devil from his door and philosophise, become dreamy and poetic with thoughts of Jim Morrison.

Liam would fly to the highest turret. Standing close to the edge with eyes shut tight, he would propel himself off and free-fall to the ground. When sensing he was inches from hitting it, he would open his eyes and swoop upwards, laughing crazily with the adrenaline rush.

To survive they fed off animals. For sex they would pick up local girls. They would steal money, petrol, cigarettes and alcohol, and above all, they would enjoy the freedom from Jon's nitpicking.

"Why don't you come with us?" Daniel asked Jon.

"We're going there to have fun." Liam answered for him.

Jon said, "Because I don't want to know what you get up to."

"Fucking hell," Liam stated. "We don't get up to anything, as you put it. You know, we can survive without you holding our hands."

"Yeah, but can the female population?"

"Oh and here we go again," Liam sang.

"No, no." Jon tutted and sat forward. "You wonder why I nag after you go and pull a stunt like you did earlier. You could have gone off with that girl if she'd been up for it. You could have got carried away on some whim and the next thing you've got a dead body on your hands. We live here."

"It wouldn't have happened, mate," Liam said.

"Why?"

"Because..." Liam sighed. "Anyway, you trust yourself with Sophie."

"Yeah, that's because I love her. But you don't love your one-night-stands. You don't care what happens to them."

"I love them - for the moment," Liam said dreamily.

"Just for a moment; is that it; is that all you can manage?" Jon teased with raised eyebrows.

"You know what I mean." Liam stood up, grabbing his crotch, "Anyway. It's going to be someone's lucky night. I'm loaded."

"Better go and get rid, then." Jon resigned. As the others stood to leave, he said to Greg, "Mind what you're doing. Feed before you screw."

"You worry too much, man." Greg reassured, patting Jon on the shoulder before following Liam and Daniel out of the cavern.

From outside, Jon heard the three vampires chanting, "See you later, mum." He wanted to go with them and protect them. Protect the nation. But he couldn't leave his Sophie. Not even for a night could he travel any distance from her. He wanted to be here where he could stand at the mouth of the tunnel and look across at the town.

The town would shimmer on the horizon, orange and white lights as though it had a hold on him. Fixated, he would believe Sophie's saintly essence was beckoning him. Whether it was an illusion or his own wishful thinking, he found her geographical closeness of comfort.

⁂

Into the otherwise dark bedroom, the orange glow from the streetlight and the silvery moonlight shone in. The opened curtains waved gently in the breeze wafting through the gaping window.

Sophie slept, dreamlessly. Her mind was blank of all images that had tormented her upon falling to sleep; her blacked-out mind empty of Callum's kiss, the hunger of lips. In the depths of a darkest sleep, she remained unaware of her physical surroundings: the pale light casting looming shadows of her bedroom furniture along the walls: the distant engines of the occasional late-night driver, and the mild exhaust fumes drifting in through the window. She was oblivious to it all; oblivious of the darkened figure crouched on the outside window-ledge, gazing in;

unaware of the haunting shape of his shadow on the opposite wall. The shadow was lifeless. The figure outside was lifeless.

The vampire remained deftly still. His heart thumped so loud it could wake the dead.

She was lying on her back facing the ceiling; a picture of serenity. Her hair was fanned out on her white pillow in waves of tumbling dark curls. Seeing more than he had otherwise been privileged, a white slender leg was slightly bent and jutting from beneath her covers.

This sight caused the vampire's heart to surge higher. He had been there a while, yet had no intention to enter. He indulged in the pleasure to watch, only. The vision of her filled his senses. Conflicting emotions took possession. They engulfed him, overwhelmed him so he could no longer banish the reality of his desires. He needed to stay in control, stay sane, use logic yet these feelings were governing him stronger than any he had felt in a long while; much as he tried not to be ruled by them, they were growing too intense to ignore.

For much of the night, her image had remained haunting him, beckoning him, calling him by name. Helplessly spurred on by a gullible and romantic heart, or brainwashed with a sudden and mysterious insanity; he had come. Say jump, he'd jump. Say die, he'd die again, so long as he could once more admire the subject of such love, feast upon her beauty, and, above all, wonder at her innocence in this not-so-idyllic world.

Only after another two hours had silently slid past, and sensing the impending sun threatening to break the skyline, did he reluctantly leave; flying upwards into the tangible dark and dusty pink sky.

Six

SOPHIE OPENED HER EYES. THE white ceiling blazed through the daylight. She bolted upright and turned to the window, expecting a figure to be crouched watching... Nobody was there.

Hadn't someone been lurking whilst she slept? She supposed Jon could have paid her a visit, though he hadn't entered. Knowing her sleep was important to her, he seldom visited during the early hours. On the occasions he did, he couldn't resist venturing in, snuggling down and stroking her until, inevitably she would wake and lovemaking would begin.

She had a good hour to spare before leaving for work. She went to the window. Beneath that streetlight she had kissed Callum. They had kissed furiously. Holding each other; wanting each other. They had kissed hungrily with incredible passion. She had sat behind him feeling the closeness of his body, his blond hair lapping against her cheeks, her hands clutching his waist. She had wanted to ride with him on through the forests, on through the night.

"Damn it," Sophie cursed, seldom swearing. She mustn't think of it. She should push it aside for everyone's sake. She needed balance; harmony in her life. She cared so much for everyone that she lived with a constant headache. Jon and the boys were wayward-leaning on the best of times; it took all her strength to keep calm when they always seemed to wreak such havoc. Roz was like a butterfly, flitting on a constant changing whirlwind. Everyone close to her was reckless to the point it made her head spin – and now she had joined the ranks with a simple kiss.

She made her way across the hall to Roz's room.

Roz had stayed out all night. Her bed hadn't been slept in. The room was a mess, a complete shambles. Clothes, magazines and shoes cluttered the floor, leaving no space to tell the colour of carpet.

A few minutes later, Sophie was relaxing in a warm, luxurious bubble bath. Her mind drifting, she gazed though the haze of rising steam. Callum manifested before her. His smiling lips had softness; a generous quality that she knew the gentleman was kind. His manner was one of patience. Behind his glasses, within his icy-blue eyes, she had glimpsed wisdom beyond his years.

She traced her lips with her fingers. What was his impression of her now? She slid down through the bubbles, totally submerging herself from head to foot. She stayed there, wanting to rid the memory; rid the shame.

Callum had seemed so pleased when she had approached his table. He had changed from seeming deeply troubled to a mood of joy.

Waiting longer than intended, she resurfaced with a splash and dragged her hair back. The memories and shame remained. Callum wouldn't leave her thoughts.

She dried off with a fluffy towel and wrapped it around her then went to the kitchen where she made some herbal tea and toast for breakfast then sat at the table.

From the hall the telephone rang. Sophie answered it, mouth full of toast. "Hello?"

"Hi, Soph, only me," came the apologetic voice.

"Roz, where are you? Is everything alright?" Sophie asked, sitting down in the leather chair next to the table.

"Couldn't be better..." Roz hesitated. "I have a favour to ask?"

"You want to skive off work? Sorry; no can do."

"Sophie, come on, I'm desperate here. I've had a real wild time with Alex and I haven't had any sleep. Lie for me one last time?"

Sophie heard kisses planted on bare skin. "If you haven't slept that's your fault. You can phone Mr Lucas and tell him yourself. I'm not doing your dirty work any more."

"He'll tell me to get my ass in there. Please, Sophie, he listens to you? I shan't be able to function properly. I'll probably make a balls-up and get fired. - I'll make it up to you."

"This is the last time. I mean it. I detest lying. I'm off to the Crypt later. Be there."

After breakfast, dressed in a long, cool summer-dress, Sophie went to the living room to dry her hair. She switched on the stereo. The radio station was playing Madonna's Ray of Light - not her usual choice, but then this wasn't a typical day.

She began moving her hips. She could feel the rhythm, hear the song over the whirling motor, and although she couldn't dance as well as Roz, she began emulating her; swinging her head so the blasts from the dryer caught under her hair, blowing it in waves of wildness. "She's got herself a universe…" she sang but that kiss rose again; came charging to disrupt. Physically it grabbed her so not to forget her atrocity.

Deflated, Sophie snapped off the drier and stereo and fastened her hair in a high knot with yellow lace, letting a few tousled curls escape to frame her face. She needed to rationalise. The kiss was tormenting her. After all, it was only a kiss, wasn't it? In itself, it had no real power. It only had power if she allowed it. She would have to fight harder. No one need know. She could function normally, so long as the passion stopped plaguing.

Doubt intruded. Callum had enticed the woman from out of her. With one kiss he had proved the strength of her sexuality. With one hand on her thudding heart he had possibly sealed his death warrant. She had a feeling that nothing would be the same again. There came more foreboding: the eerie sensation that something more imminent was about to happen. For better or worse it was inevitable. Something stronger than her was at play. Fate was dealing its hand.

⁂

Sophie arrived at work to find Mr Lucas waiting at her desk, acting jittery.

"Sophie..." He faltered. "Where's Roz?"

"She's practically dying. Her head's throbbing so much she's been sick."

"Lying doesn't suit you, Sophie, and she's probably not worth the trouble. Perhaps it's best she stays away. We all need time to ourselves, I feel. You would do well to work here alone today."

"What is it, Mr Lucas? You've been stressed for weeks."

"Burdens beyond my control, my dear." Mr Lucas studied Sophie hard. "I need time out and I'm leaving you in charge."

"Can I help?"

"You're too generous; but I have to decline. I don't know when I'll return but if I don't see you again, you need to know I have a deep level of respect for you. You're a pleasure to know. You're hard-working unlike your friend. You've always helped others. You've helped so many in Sanctuary; more than you'll ever know. You're a little gem."

"I'm a glorified receptionist."

"Don't underestimate yourself. Stay strong. I must leave you to it. Look after the place. You know how I love books." Mr Lucas was sincere and so sad. Sophie was lost. He had never opened up like this before, although he had always shown her gratitude for her work and he had shown Roz contempt; never before had he been so forthright. She wondered whether he was having a breakdown.

"I need to know what's going on? What troubles you?"

Mr Lucas was agitated that she should enquire so much from his secret life, but offered feebly, "My elderly mother is dying. Here are the keys. Use your head, Sophie. In this crazy, mad world, stay sane."

She had no idea what he was talking about, but she couldn't agree more.

⚜

At the end of the day, Sophie prepared to close down her computer. She had been tempted to leave early but better judgement wouldn't allow her to be dishonest. She took a pile of books and began placing them on their shelves.

From outside, she heard the familiar rumble of a motorbike as it drew up. Panic stricken, she ignored the biker climbing the steps; the man who had forcefully returned her kiss; the very one who was causing emotional chaos. She hoped that by ignoring him he would leave.

Callum entered the library and lifted his visor. There she was alone, standing awkwardly. Her bare arms were supporting books. His acute attention ran over her body. Her long dress with buttons running the length, her petite waist and delicate shoulders, the odd tousled curl springing down to touch and veil that oh-so-delicate neck. On her pretty face was a curious expression of what? He hoped it wasn't annoyance. - Shame; he dreaded more. It was almost like returning to a crime scene. He couldn't get enough of her. He couldn't stay away.

"I've come to return the book." He walked past her away from the doors with its faint daylight casting dreaded squares along the floor. He went to her desk, took off his crash helmet and gloves, and turned to catch her scorn. "You are annoyed that have I come to you? You would sooner I leave Sanctuary, never again to caste doubts in that sacred mind?"

Sophie went to him in desperation. "I'm annoyed, I admit, but not with you. I kissed you. I started it, remember?"

"You ask do I remember as though I could forget," he stated bluntly. "I'll never forget. You've affected me in such a way I feel compelled to tell you. The incident may have caused your revulsion, caused your pretty eyes to fill with tears, but I haven't the same regret. Your kiss was a tonic to my long-suffering heart. I apologise for your burden of shame. But I thank you for awakening me to my emotions."

"Then I should apologise." Sophie dropped the books onto her desk. "I've led you on. It wasn't my intention. But I've given you false hope. I've been cruel. And if I were to cry for another year, it would be punishment enough."

"Dear, Sophie. You are too kind. How could you be cruel? You are too serene, too compassionate for the world in which we find ourselves."

Sophie stepped back. "I am none of those things. And you should be advised not to pester."

"You say such things to wound me because of your boyfriend?"

"My long-term lover," Sophie corrected, hurting as he flinched with pain. "He is my world, Callum. He is one in a million."

Knowing Jon to be possibly one in four million, Callum moved closer. "If that's how you truly feel then I should leave you this instant.

But your kiss conveyed your cravings. Your lips delivered your desires. Your tears were merely a conflict of turbulence."

Sophie was overthrown; unconsciously leaning gently towards him; his lips were drawing her closer still. The explosion of tiny fluttering endorphins erupted. "If you are aware of my conflict, why come here? Why cause such pain and anguish?"

Callum fought not to acknowledge the need in her amorous expression. "Sophie, I balance on the edge while you drive me to insanity," he blurted desperately, taking hold of her eager face to disable her from moving ever closer. "You say such things with your tongue as your body dictates otherwise, until I'm unsure what goes on in that pretty mind. I fear you are a kind yet unpredictable creature."

"Yes," she whispered, her hormones stealing her voice. "I'm a woman."

Callum couldn't agree more. He had seen many women in his time, and had taken many lovers. But, besides one other he had never been seduced emotionally by a lady so fair. And this lady remained gazing up at him with wondrous eyes that stole his heart so he would assume it no longer beating hard against his chest if it wasn't aching with want. He whispered, "Let me keep my sanity?"

"Kiss me," she breathed.

Anguished further, Callum shook his head; he had thought of nothing else. He could think of nothing he would rather do besides caress and love her flesh, feel those arms and kiss her fingers, her neck...

He took her round the waist and grabbed her to him. His kiss was firm. Masterfully he roused her desires to equal his own. He sensed her endorphins, felt her heat burning as she returned his kiss and sough out his hungry tongue.

Callum released her and went to her desk. He pulled down the front zip of his jacket and removed the book. She glimpsed red material as he fastened his zip. He picked up his crash helmet. She was astonished and wounded. "You're going?"

"You leave me no choice. Our yearnings are too great for either of us to handle. I shouldn't have kissed you. It's all too electric. To stay would prove fatal. I would rather you remember me with high regards than with pain for the actions you may later regret."

"Fine." Sophie went to him. She snatched up the bunch of keys from her desk and sauntered to the back of the room to lock the office door. She had to keep moving. "You think I'm easy," she called. "You presume that I act first, think later. That I am incapable of doing both simultaneously? Well fine."

"Not at all," he called. "Where there is passion, logic escapes even the saints amongst us."

Sophie pushed the key into the lock, thinking of his words. He considered her a saint yet susceptible of losing her inhibitions to passion. As the key refused to turn to her shaky guidance, she considered he might be right. His kiss had again ignited terbulance in an otherwise calm sea. Hot blood was underlying, simmering in every womanly sinew; and the cause of this awakening was approaching from behind.

"Damn you," she cursed desperately. The keys jingled. The bolt refused to budge.

"Let me assist," his voice whispered near her ear. He was standing so close; his body lightly pressing against hers as he took her hand and guided it. The bolt shot into place.

"It was not in far enough," Callum informed against her hair, aware of their bodies touching. Her shoulder allured him; was bare except for the thin strap of her dress, and was tantalisingly close to his mouth. Her skin captivated him. The light pulse in her throat seemed to spring to life and beat faster; mirroring the reactions of her heart pumping blood, hormones, adrenaline… Lazily, his eyes wandered the length of her long, slender arm down to her delicate hand. He noticed his hand was still covering hers. "Sorry," he said, swiftly retracting it. But much as he knew he should move away, he hesitated.

"Don't be. We are both fighting a bigger force," Sophie whispered. Gently leaning back against him, she anticipated that he would again move from her. He stood his ground like he was frozen to the spot, unable to move if he wanted. "We can't beat this desire, Callum. Neither of us is strong enough to overthrow the chemistry, and ignore it." Sophie was breathless, gently rubbing against his hard penis. He gasped a warm breath smouldering against her shoulder.

"Still I'm unsure of your intentions," he whispered, lips cautiously hovering.

"I want you to take me, Callum." She pressed into him, resting her head sideways.

Callum saw her invitation, her skin; her delicate neck extended so close to his mouth, her pulse beating ferociously, veins gently bulging and tendons jutting. He lowered his lips to greet the soft skin; so warm, so alive, and against it, he said, "I am a prisoner to my emotions and I no longer wish to escape. I fear I may not be able to walk away."

"Sir, I have no intention of stopping now," she gasped, as his tongue slid out and licked the nape of her neck. "What we feel is lust. Perhaps the only remedy is to allow ourselves these moments? Then perhaps, we can put these feelings aside?" He pulled lightly on her neck, sucking in her flesh and teasing it with his tongue. "Don't mark me."

"Trust me," he reminded her, knowing the concern of her lover. Jon would recognize such marks of love; such bites.

Sophie turned and faced him. His biker jacket shrouded him with a manly prowess; behind his glasses, his blue eyes were intense.

He said, "It's been my wish to take you slowly. I find this situation moving too fast; I have dreamt to romance you."

"You, dear sir, have romanced me more than you know," she informed, drawing him down for a kiss. Against his lips, she said, "I'm not normally this impulsive, you must believe me. I need to get you out of my system. I want you to take me as you see fit."

Her words struck him, jarring his every fibre. Callum surrendered to fate. He kissed her hard, pushed her back against the door; his firm torso pinning her there, he grabbed her wrists, drew them above her head and pinned them to the door, rendering her helpless.

He deepened the kiss. Mouths locked in savage hunger, desperation grew. He wanted to taste her, eat her, to always remember this moment, but he wanted her to remember it also. Never let her forget him. Let this haunt her, as she, herself had haunted. And let her desires grow so she would return to him yet again, begging for even more.

Holding her wrists with one hand, he began tracing a line down her arm towards her breast. He cupped her breast, feeling the soft material of her dress glide over her silk bra. The protruding nipple sprang in attendance to his persuasive touch. He encircled her nipple with his thumb and massaged it hard as a bullet, and then he enticed it some more. Expertly, he unfastened her buttons and slid his hand inside her bra. He felt so urgent he was scared he would break her. If he were too harsh he could snap her ribs, he was sure of it. She was delicate, vulnerable and fragile. Her wrists beneath his mighty grasp felt as though they would break if he were to loose himself completely.

He wrenched her bra from his way and lowered his blond head, his tongue teasing her nipple then pulled at her breast with deep surging sucks. Sophie was spinning out of control. The pressure from his grasp on her elevated hands was causing her hands to tingle. Her entire body was tingling. She was glad he was holding her in case her legs gave out and buckled.

His free hand went to her legs, and whilst he sucked each breast, his hand crawled slowly back up her thighs dragging up her skirt; feeling the firm muscles of her inner thighs, all the way until he was between her legs, and softly massaging the gusset of her pants. She was soaking wet as she throbbed wantonly against his caressing fingers.

He pulled away from her breast and let her skirt fall. His gaze was fixed on her as he reached behind. Unsure, yet excited by his intentions, she heard the bolt.

Eyes locked, he forced her backwards into the awaiting room and grappled along the wall for the light switch. The fluorescent light flooded the small office. Her breasts were shimmering in yellow, her lips slightly parted, quivering to pent up desires, her eyes burning his before they dropped to his lips, to his jacket, to his leather trousers. He kicked backwards, slamming the door.

"Sophie." He searched her expression but could see no conflict, no doubt - only longing. Her eyes seemed more innocent to him now than ever. Yet still her actions were all woman as she reached to his trousers and pulled down his zip. She took hold of his penis and massaged up and down its firm extent.

"You blow my mind." He gasped. "I'm in fear of losing all sanity to you that I may never again find."

"Passion is a powerful emotion and desire a dangerous tool," she said, with a glint in her smiling eyes. She moved closer, rubbing herself against the one side of his body. "Many people have died because of it."

"Yes, but love is the greatest of all killers."

"I grant you that, sir," she agreed, reaching her other hand to his hair and tenderly stroking it. Her expression was ardent as she studied each golden strand. Each strand glistened healthily in the yellow light flooding down, each one a different degree of yellow; and for a moment, she forgot her other hand working on him, until he grasped her wrist.

"No more." He bent his head and made to kiss her. He remained not touching; her lips quivered in anticipation. He teased with absent lips. But then she felt his hands reach down her legs, gather up her long skirt, and haul the last of her skirt from his way as though he had done it a thousand times before. He paused, teasing her with abstaining lips, with abstaining hands, and burning eyes of passion. He lifted her and rested her against the door where he held her with no effort.

Sophie wrapped her legs around him, locked at the ankles. She rekindled the kiss; tongues gliding over each other as Callum reached under the back of her and pulled her pants aside. He lowered her onto his penis.

Orgasms threatened to explode then, but neither did. Desire escalated more fervently to torment. Holding her eager hips still and taking control, Callum moved slamming deeply into her end, while deepening the kiss. She clutched one hand to the back of his jacket, the other to the back of his head, feeling his soft hair, his body pressed to her partially exposed breasts, his hardness filled her completely; surging forwards, retracting back, tempting her more before slamming to her end again. His movements remained regular, slow and forceful, that she was awake and in tune with him. Her every inch was begging for more force. Her mind was crying out as her insides screamed. The flitting between her legs was succumbing to the intensity and growing to a pinnacle deeper within that would overwhelm her.

Sensing this, Callum broke free from her hungry mouth and abruptly stopped all movements. Their gaze fixed deeply. Abstaining no longer, he began moving slowly at first, then, gradually faster, sharper, deeper; the door rocking and slamming rhythmically in its frame.

Sophie gasped between gentle squeals, her insides wreaking havoc. Warning currents sparked threateningly, promising her of what was to come. The fluttering exploded in deep pulses and grew to crescendo in horrendous throbbing against him, sending shockwaves throughout her every muscle; electric shocks which jolted her whole body. She was crying out, screaming; in need of help…

Someone needed to collect her body parts and piece her back together. She came back from oblivion enough to realise Callum, more quietly, had found his own pleasure. Buried deep and pushing against her end, he shot his seed. He sacrificed his sanity. Both gripped by ecstasy, they remained gripping each other. They stayed entwined, weakened, shivering in the aftermath.

Resting her head on his leather clad shoulder Sophie trembled. The aftermath of her orgasm was greater than ever. The intensity of her pleasure had overwhelmed her that she mourned its fading while equally she delighted in the experience. She felt ceremonious that her body could feel so alive; so in tune with her emotions; so in balance with her mind. Weak and completely spent, she felt ecstatic both physically and emotionally, until releasing more pent up feelings she began to chuckle.

Callum's concern grew as muffled laughter escaped her. "Why do you laugh?" he asked, but as she lifted her face, he saw her happy expression behind tumbling tears. "You're weeping?" Callum was astonished. Again he was receiving mixed messages. Again he failed to understand.

"I can't help it. I don't mean to cry or laugh. I don't usually act like this."

Callum thought of her lover, Jon; of their shared experiences, and as annoyance swept through him, he pushed all thoughts of the obnoxious vampire from his mind.

Hand trembling, Sophie wiped away her tears. "I suppose it's just another form of release."

Callum was unsure whether to believe her, since none of his previous lovers had responded in such a manner, though he made no remark, and gently lowered her to her feet. He tidied himself as she straightened her bra and fastened her buttons. Her hair was in disarray. The bundle of curls, which had been held high by a yellow lace was so loosened she almost looked like a lady in fashion from a previous century; a familiar century. He stepped closer and pulled the lace gently from her hair. The lace of shimmering sunshine floated to the floor, her curls tumbled, falling about her shoulders. He toyed with her curls between his fingers while studying the smooth contours of her collarbone; the soft indent that gently pulsed, her white skin against delicate protruding bone. He rested his hand to her throat to feel her bursting pulse: he had caused that. He was mesmerised. Using extra sensitive fingertips, Callum traced the contours of each shoulder.

She had no means to know what he was thinking, but Sophie saw his expression intensify as his fingers moved slowly down each bare arm, reaching down to her hands. He lifted both her hands and, turning them in his, he studied them. Unexpectedly, he drew them up and began kissing the back of each hand. Sophie flushed. Her face was warming, her body tingling in delight at his gracious manner.

"For a biker, you know how to romance a girl," Sophie sighed as he continued to plant more feather-light kisses to her hands.

"I come from a place that seeks respect," he stated, kissing her palms.

"You come from a respectable home."

"I have a fine home." Callum planted loitering kisses to her inner wrist, the branched course of thin, blue veins; so delicate; only a thin membrane separating him from her lifeline. His kisses wandered to her inner elbow and over her muscle, planting more kisses to her shoulder so her head felt faint with growing rapture. Deliberately, he moved closer still. Pressing against her, holding her head cautiously to one side, he began delivering faint, teasing kisses to her neck...

"Callum, this has got to stop. I thought once we'd released the tension we would recover our senses. Yet still you make love to me." She gasped deliriously. "Callum, please, I've got a boyfriend."

"So you say. But do you love him?" he asked, distracted by her delicious skin that was begging for his mouth.

"What?" Sophie shot, torn between loyalties. Callum planted more nerve-tingling kisses to her neck. "Yes, I love him. He's my world, as I've said before. And more to the point, he needs me."

Callum left her alluring flesh to regard her more closely. "If he were no longer here would I then stand a chance of winning you over?"

"Jon is a complex sort of person, and is very much here to stay. I trust you not to mention what we've done - not to anyone. If Jon finds out about this there'll be hell to pay, believe me."

"You presume that I would kiss and tell? You presume that I have no honour? I am many things, my dear sweet Sophie, but a blabbermouth isn't one of them."

"I was just warning you."

"My integrity where you are concerned will always remain intact. You must believe this."

"Sorry, Callum, but if Jon were to discover what took place here he'd be murderous. I am merely trying to protect the balance. Keep things in harmony. I feel no shame; I adore you."

Callum relaxed. He understood her concern. She was naive. Callum knew he was under no threat from the loathsome Jon. "Would Jon use violence towards you?"

Sophie went to the office door. "His love for me goes beyond reality. He respects my life more than his own in a sense. Jon is incapable of being cruel to me; he can't hurt me. Don't make an enemy of him; he would hunt you down, he would catch up with you, he would..." The romanticism of their affair was lost. "Oh God, what have I done?" Immediate tears glazed her eyes.

Callum was dismayed. Swiftly he was before her. "You have done nothing that could harm me, I assure you."

"Oh, but I have if you did but realise. I have done irreversible damage. It's dreadful," she said, clutching her hair, trying to think clearly. "If he ever found out about you and I, who knows what might happen. You don't know him or his capabilities as I do. Callum, I have been lost on a whim of fanciful notions without a care of the consequences. And they could be astronomical, believe me. I have been reckless. I enjoyed what we've shared, but this can't happen again. We need to stay well clear of each other."

"Again you show concern for me? Your true feelings are as apparent as those felt in your kiss. The emotions you possess for me are more than a fanciful whim. Admit it to me, Sophie?" He grabbed her arms, desperately searching her eyes for the truth. "Tell me your feelings are more than lust, more than the desire which remains reigning over us. Please, Sophie?"

"No." Sophie struggled, desperate to break free from his clutch. "I'm not falling in love with you, if that's what you're asking. I don't know you, sir. My loyalties are with Jon. I love *him*."

"Repeated often enough you might convince yourself," Callum said, not wanting to hurt her, he was unable to loosen his tightening grip. "But I sense otherwise. You do love me. I'm sure of it."

"No," Sophie retorted. To his astonishment, she found an inner-strength to break free from his hold. She had to keep the balance. She lied. "I don't love you! You could leave this town now; I really wouldn't give a damn! I'm a tart, a whore. I always do this. I've slept with countless men behind his back. I love it. I get a great kick out of it, and then, like I'm doing now, I dump them." Tears streaming down her cheeks she fled to the library.

Callum let her leave, knowing how much she must be hurting to have lied so barefaced. Because she wanted to protect him from Jon, she had risked her own morality, her reputation, and his respect. She had said such vulgar words for his safety's sake. Indeed, she was a saint, a goddess; so kind, so intoxicating.

Callum approached Sophie at her desk. The intensity in his gaze was somehow deeper and it tore her to shreds.

"I have locked the office." He handed her the keys.

Sophie looked vacantly down at her desk, too afraid to speak should her voice betray the threat of more woeful tears.

He reached across and took a gentle hold of her chin, lifting her face. "Please, Sophie, I beg you not to weep; for those pretty eyes to cry. I'm a man of honour. I promise faithfully that Jon will hear nothing of our precious time together. Although I hope we will meet again, some day, some night; if our paths don't cross through a twist of fate, I would like you to know that I'll relive our loving moments a hundred fold in my mind."

Sophie lowered her eyes; scared he would read her thoughts. Her heart was bleeding, pleading for him to stay as he prepared to leave.

Callum pulled on his helmet and fastened it securely. He pulled on his gloves, checking the leather sleeves of his jacket covered his bare wrists.

Sophie whispered, "Goodbye, Callum."

Gentlemanly, he bowed his head. He flipped down his tinted visor and turned to the doors. As he walked, again he checked his wrists were concealed before entering the sunny September evening. As always he held his breath as the daylight hit him.

Callum sat astride his machine, engine running. Sun dazzling so bright, he knew fear. He looked towards the library doors. His heart was heavier now than when he had arrived. It ached with yearning; was physically gripped with the intensity of his feelings for the lady behind those doors so that breathing in the warm air was a laboured struggle more so than ever. Although his visit had been met with the highest sexual satisfaction it had not been the tonic she had suggested.

He knew of her plight, of her lover's capabilities more than well. Yet he couldn't convey his own innermost secrets to assure her of his safety. His mission was more important. To disclose his inner-self now could prove fatal. Usually he was patient, tolerant and focused. He would use these attributes and complete his crusade, starting this night; and concentrate all his efforts to survive. Only then, with due respect for fate would he again approach the lady who had captivated his heart and stolen his sanity.

After locking the library, Sophie dropped the keys into her handbag and made her way home. A cool evening breeze blew gently about her; tugging at her dress and pushing her hair onto her face, it whispered but she failed to notice. She couldn't hear its mocking, nor didn't want to. Dazed in rapture of their lovemaking and confused by her conflicting emotions of being torn between men, between worlds, familiar tears welled in her eyes.

Seven

FROM THE BALCONY, CALLUM PEERED down through the flashing colours and white strobe lighting, watching the antics of the Crypt. He had only a modest experience of nightclubs and rarely mingled with today's generation so intimately; so many of them in one place. But he had observed this generation enough to know the clientele in this place was different. The heavily tattooed, the body pierced, the pink hair, the green hair, the every shades of blue hair; and the most intriguing of them all: the devout Goths. The Goths, wearing outlandish yet fascinating clothes were shrouded in a black morbid fashion with silver crucifixes about their necks, and seemed to revel in a mysterious fascination with face-metal and death. Why? Callum tried to fathom. Why celebrate loss and misery as though every day's a funeral? How little they knew. They should appreciate their souls, nurture their spiritual side and protect their chances of eternal peace but he couldn't warn them. What could he say? Souls without bodies haunt this earth. Bodies without souls roam this earth. He wanted to remind them just how complete they were; how intact, how blessed: these mortals. He was staring at a crucifix; he looked away.

The crowded bar was below. Surrounding this more social, well-lit part was the apparent reason the club was called the Crypt. It resembled ancient burial catacombs. All seating was set back in dimly lit, arched stone alcoves. There were low tunnels and miniature caverns intermingling.

Callum liked the place and found it welcoming. The entire room seemed mystical, steeped with hidden secrets; it felt as though it openly accepted him. There was an atmosphere of understanding amongst its people. The unity felt was vibrant as individuals acknowledged each other with nods of heads and a certain politeness as they moved underground in solidarity against the outside world, albeit for this night, anyway. Having to be different to enter this belowground place; Callum felt reassured, no longer so damned isolated.

He had discovered the club while walking along the southern side of the high street, and followed a bunch of Goths as they entered a side door next to an Electrical Retail store. At this point it felt he truly was walking shoulder to shoulder with vampires. He appeared the most normal, a mere biker dude; too pretty to be dead. After being mildly observed by two gruesome doormen whose jobs were to check no one was wearing suits and to ignore all suspicious packages, he had descended a narrow staircase to the basement, paying at the kiosk before entering.

Knowing Jon and his gang had arranged to meet here after overhearing such plans through the crowded pub last night, Callum waited patiently. Sooner or later they would turn up. Like bad pennies.

Unfortunately, he needed them. He had been in Sanctuary for a third night now and still he had no definite leads. And he needed to be definite. He needed to befriend others like him: to befriend Jon, the leader of the pack: Sophie's lover.

Callum didn't need her squeals of pleasure echoing in his mind. She would be here. The situation was unavoidable, and her slovenly, unkempt lover would drape himself about her.

Callum took a long, cool drink from his bottle of beer while scanning the increasing crowds below. A familiar figure with long, blonde hair caught his attention. She was Sophie's friend, Roz. He remembered her name from the library. So long as he remained vigilant, the others would eventually swarm.

Callum relaxed. She was dressed sexily yet he felt appalled. Her black, silky chemise dress with buttons running the meagre length left nothing to the imagination. Although he felt embarrassed, he couldn't help but notice she had a nice pair of legs, the length of which most of this generation seemed to genetically possess. He wanted to protect her; had an urge to jump down to the floor below with a blanket or something and wrap it about her. Then he supposed he was being old-fashioned.

While waiting for Alex to return from the bar, Roz spotted Sophie entering the club. She couldn't believe her eyes. Sophie walked towards her, skirting the dance-floor. The hippie Sophie was gone and standing before her was a new, transformed Sophie. Her hair was fanned out and wild, her face was made-up in dark, enhancing eyeliner and blood red lipstick. She was wearing Roz's red, skin-tight, PVC dress and black knee-length boots, the extents of which were intricately laced.

Roz spluttered in amazement, "You look... vampie."

"No shit?" Sophie giggled, causing Roz to study her more suspiciously.

"Have you been drinking?"

Sophie hiccupped. "Half a bottle of white wine whilst I got ready; good, isn't it?"

"Fucking hell, girl, yeah, it's good. But why; you don't drink? And my clothes look almost as good on you as they do on me. Borrow whatever you like, you sultry diva." Roz couldn't stop admiring her new friend, shimmering in the devil's red dress. "When you do something, you do it well; you've so exploded out of that pent up closet."

Sophie struggled. The alcohol had loaned her the confidence to wear the clothes and walk into the room, yet she felt the conviction failing her now. Callum had awoken a deeper part of her that had lain dormant and well hidden yet had been bursting to escape. He had demanded her body to react with such vigour and please her so powerfully that even the memory put her to on high. Inwardly, she was smiling. He had divulged to her a greater secret of her sexuality, of her ability to manipulate men. She wasn't just capable of powering over them; she was capable of finding incredible satisfaction of equal reward. Now, she understood the yearning to find such great pleasure again. Sophie looked at Roz, and although she still felt her confidence flagging, she understood her friend for the first true time. She understood the driving force behind human nature. Sex wasn't only powerful; sex was power.

"I think I should go home and change," Sophie blurted.

Roz grabbed Sophie's arm. "No way are you going back to that wardrobe, Narnia: you look great. Honestly. If you've got it, flaunt it."

"It's not me." Dismayed, Sophie glanced down at her attire. "It's not me, Roz. I feel a complete idiot. And what's Jon going to think when he sees me?"

"He'll flip," Roz stated, suddenly looking forward to seeing him. "But, he'll get over himself." Panic flitted across her friend's face. Roz reassured her, "It's only clothes. You're still you. If he can't see past that then he's a bigger jerk than I thought."

"Thanks a bunch." Now Sophie was feeling more trepidation at facing Jon since her infidelity. She was going to give it away. He would take one look at her and know she had betrayed him. It would be written all over her.

Alex joined them, holding two double whiskeys. Roz decided to help her friend further. Sophie was looking her best, totally horny, and she was definitely not fleeing to change into a sedate, ankle-length dress. Sophie was coming out to play. Out of that shell of misguided innocence and into the real world; and Jon could get lost.

Roz smiled sweetly at her new lover and, taking both drinks from him, said, "This is my friend, Sophie, in need of a drink. I hope you don't mind?" Handing Sophie her drink, she ordered, "Get this down your neck. Everything will feel better." Roz took a large sip from Alex's drink, and said to him, "Go get some more in." As he was about to protest, she leaned closer, whispering, "I'll make it worth your while: in the toilets in ten minutes?"

"Fucking hell, Roz, the bloody bar's packed. It took me an hour to get these," he exaggerated.

Not letting up, Roz whispered, "I'll unbutton your jeans real slowly like, and pull down your boxers with my teeth. I'll make you come."

- Fair shout. - Alex made his way back through the crowd.

Roz had persuaded him to buy her a new dress and boots to wear, and now he was buying the drinks. Although he wasn't her millionaire he had money to waste. And it wasn't his money; it was the devil's money. As others got wasted on the drugs he supplied, she would manipulate his spending on her. Suddenly she became aware that Sophie had downed her drink in one and was, more bizarrely, making her way onto the dance-floor.

Callum leaned against the balustrade, entranced by the vision below as the two women danced to U2; Hold me, Thrill me, Kiss me, Kill me. Sophie seemed to loosen up. The raunchy rock beat was now moving her suggestively. Eyes closed, she began swinging her hair sexually as though in the throes of a familiar orgasm. He threw fleeting glances about him to check if others had noticed the spectrum dancing amongst white smoke at her feet; slicing the beams of light with arms as pale as milk. Most of the men were staring into pint glasses, talking to friends or ogling other women. At their ignorance, Callum stared again at his seductress. Still she intrigued him, confused him since his everlasting, undying impression of her was one of innocence and shyness like an angel trapped in a woman's body. How he longed to protect her, to preserve that such rare innocence in this modern age. Although he found the skimpier of ladies fashions unpleasant, he watched her admiringly while patiently waiting.

Several dances later, Callum caught a glimpse of dark, spiky hair meandering through the crowd. Jon was alone? Callum scanned again. His friends weren't accompanying him? He had no time to ponder reasons. He held his breath, not wanting to witness Jon approach Sophie as though he belonged by her side; yet he couldn't ignore it. Perhaps he was a masochist as the cruel blades of jealousy stabbed, inflicting physical pain. This caught him by surprise. He hadn't realised until now how much he had fallen for the goddess dancing. He needed to look elsewhere and fast. Jon was drawing closer to finding his girlfriend, as he scanned the room. The pain was now torturous. He demanded his eyes closed, blot it out. But, as Jon skirted the dance-floor ever closer to his Sophie, the torment concentrated its hold, grabbed Callum by the throat and restricted his airway. Completing this mission meant more to him than breathing. Existence as Callum knew it, relied on him not messing up. Absorbing more grief and holding his nerve, Callum watched without as much as a blink.

Jon was late, having overslept, which was his friends' faults for abandoning him. Now, he had the worry of their misdemeanours to fret over. He made his way through the crowd towards the bar. She wasn't there.

Agitated, he scanned the dancers. If his friends had been with him they would be there jumping about and knocking into each other haphazardly to prove their affections. Or Liam would be instantly drawn to some Gothic chic in mourning, hoping she would be emphatically drawn to him. But his friends weren't there. They had gone on some bonking-spree never minding him. And what if they accidentally killed someone in the process? What would Sophie think of his kind, then? What would she think of him? Desperately, he had to lose the insecurities; he needed Sophie.

Then, through the moving bodies, he caught a glimpse of *her* and was repulsed, though strangely, his heart jumped. He checked his reaction. His heart had quickened, and seemed to be pounding in his mouth. His penis had responded in total involuntarily hardening. Oh, shit. Now he felt sick. Yet his eyes remained searching the short, black dress, the long, perfect legs all the way up that could wrap around his back as he banged her... Roz? - It shouldn't have entered his head. Shocked as he was, he then saw Sophie.

He froze. The world had gone mad. She was holding her wild curls high on her head. Her body, wrapped in red was swaying with hips gyrating as she dropped the bundle of curls and raised her hands over her head, rotating arms like snakes in the mist.

Jaw locked open, eyes as wide, Jon surveyed the room. Through incensed delirium, he realised vaguely that other males were oblivious to the bewitchment. Aggravated, Jon pushed past the barrage of bodies without hearing their protests, and swiftly he was there, glaring daggers at the slut.

"What the fuck do you think you're doing?" he hissed, giving Roz no chance to explain. "What have I told you about influencing Sophie, hey? Are you totally fucking brain-dead?"

"What?" Roz asked, more or less on his height while wearing heels.

"You must be gone in the head." Jon nodded sarcastically. "Must have a screw loose in that empty, bimbo brain of yours, bitch. You think you can dress her like a slapper and get her pissed, and I wouldn't rearrange your face?" He wanted to lash out, hit something and hard. Adrenaline was rushing; her sudden smirk riled him until his fist began shaking by his side.

"Fuck off," Roz blurted in amusement.

"Jon, it wasn't her doing," Sophie pleaded. "I wanted to dress like this. I borrowed her clothes and had a few drinks whilst Roz was at her boyfriend's place. I met her here." Sophie grabbed his arm and drew his undivided attention away from her friend.

Sophie's words began sinking in. "What?"

"I wanted to wear this. I never asked her permission, her opinion; it was me."

"Why?" he asked, anger subsiding as her blue eyes began welling with tears.

"I don't know," she lied through a haze of guilt. "I love you, Jon. I'm so sorry. Forgive me? Say you forgive me?" she begged, grabbing his other arm and gaining his full attention.

"Yeah." he nodded, perplexed. Not being able to handle tears, especially hers, he added, "It's only a dress." To convince himself, he repeated, "It's only a dress. I overreacted. It's just a shock, that's all."

"Perhaps you should also apologise to Roz? After all, it isn't her fault."

She had him over a barrel; he could deny Sophie nothing and reluctantly he turned to see Roz gloating, and mumbled, "Sorry."

"Well wonders never cease." Roz grabbed her ear. "Say it a bit louder, I didn't quite catch it."

"Slut."

"Jon?" Sophie gushed.

"Okay." Again, he turned to Roz. "I'm fucking sorry. Now, go run along and play somewhere else."

"Well, I'm charmed," Roz sneered. To Sophie, she added, "Where did you say you dug him up from?"

"Psychos anonymous," Jon retorted. "Now take the hint..."

Despondently, Sophie said, "I've got to get a drink." Leaving Jon and Roz, she made her way towards the bar. She needed alcohol to numb her mind and give her a few hours respite from her confusion. Jon and Roz had agitated her with their feuding, and all the day's stresses were mounting so high sooner or later something was bound to topple. As she joined the queue at the bar, blue twinkling eyes and the smell of leather barged through her mind and barricaded themselves in.

"What's wrong with her?" Jon asked Roz. Thinking Roz hadn't heard, he repeated, "What's up with Sophie? Why's she acting so weird?"

"You, Jonathon, are asking me?"

"You're a woman, ain't you? Why's she so uptight?"

"I'll be fucked if I know."

"Probably," he jibed, though he remained solemn that Roz almost felt sympathetic.

"Why not go and ask her? You know, find your feminine side; be sensitive, if that's at all possible?" Roz said, dancing.

"No. She'll be sweet. It's probably hormones or something."

"You men have no idea, do you? Everything is put down to hormones. Little lady is crying; it's her hormones. Little lady gets tetchy; it's the hormones. - Fuck."

"Well that's your answer to everything. Everything you do is hormonal as you screw everything in sight. You know, you should watch yourself or one of these nights you're going to catch something," he stated, aware her breasts were jigging to the beat.

"I didn't know you cared," Roz teased over the top of the music.

"I don't. But if you get something half of Sanctuary's going to get wiped out."

Roz glared her aggressor up and down wondering why, besides her father, Jon was the only man who could verbally wound her. Why everything he said, she hung on to as though she gave a shit. Jerk. Shrugging, she said, "Well at least you'll be safe."

Jon was taken aback by her forwardness, by his hurt. He threw his hands to his chest in mock agony. "You mean; you don't fancy me?"

"I wouldn't go with you if you were the last man on earth."

Jon regarded her more carefully, picking the best insult from the ones unravelling in his mind. Leaning closer, she instinctively leaned back, and as always, her confounded weariness baffled him. Not that the hardened bitch would be wary of his words, but it seemed a more physical thing. Like she knew what he was or sensed his capabilities. He straightened up, no longer enjoying intimidating her. "Crazy as it sounds, I think underneath it all, you're probably capable of being clever."

"Thank you." Roz smiled, ignoring the insult. She made to walk past him, dared to brush shoulders and stopped, daring to hold eye contact. His dark eyes were alive and twinkling with intrigue. She whispered close to his ear, and although her words were drowned in music, his keen hearing picked up every syllable, "You can watch out for me; I'm in the shadows. I have a brain. I'm sex on legs and I've got your number." She leaned closer daring her lips to brush his ear. "Love is a myth."

Jon allowed her this shining moment. She went to her lover who was loitering by the dance-floor. Taking her drink, and leaning to kiss him, her dress lifted slightly, revealing more leg. Jon had a tantalising glimpse of her buttocks. - Sex on legs. - For the first time, he happened to agree with her. Then, crazily, stupidly he remembered his murderess: Destiny. It hadn't occurred to him before but he could put waist-length, red ringlets on Roz's bleached head and beads about her neck, and she'd be that devil's own hippie bitch: the bitch with the eternal purpose that if it moves, breathes, with veins and organs pulsating; shag it, and then to hell with it. Then it hit him. And it wasn't so crazy. He realised why he loathed Roz; she was a cold and calculated man-eater and all men were easy targets. So why did he hate all her lovers? Why did he want to mutilate them, rip out their weak hearts or smack them dead? Was it because they were weak and gullible just like he had been back then? Perhaps he longed to put the suckers out of their misery?

Callum had watched Sophie drink two large whiskeys before ordering more. He watched Sophie and Jon find a table for two in an alcove, where, sitting closely, they proceeded in talking and canoodling.

Through the bright appearance of the room, Callum could see Jon holding her. Although the alcove was dark to others, he saw the tender way Jon kissed her. The tender way Jon placed his hand on her bare knee with fingers curled against her inner thigh, moving slowly on up to red plastic then gratefully down.

Callum placed his empty bottle on the wooden handrail and clutched the balustrade for support. Unsure whether the room had begun spinning, or whether he had begun reeling in the still room, either way he felt faint; unnaturally tempestuous. With his heart pounding and breathing gusting in shallow fast breaths, he managed to search elsewhere for a focus of attention.

Roz was sitting astride her lover, kissing his neck as he awkwardly gave a guy towering over them a cellophane wrap, and more curiously, exchanged it for money.

Inevitably, Callum's attention drew back to Sophie. He remembered the smell of wild flowers, the softness of her skin, her delicate hand massaging him, her vulnerability, her fragile neck. All the while watching some-one else give this fair lady pleasure like it was his right. Callum encroached on their privacy for minutes that felt like an eternity. Although he had all the time in the world, he had seen enough. - Definitely. - With the room revolving and speeding up, he had seen more than enough.

In the alcove, lit by one softly yielding wall light, was one other couple. They were huddled close, whispering and playing footsie beneath their table as the lady ran a dampened finger around her wine glass.

Breaking off from their kiss, Sophie began toying with a beer mat trying to focus on it through an inebriated haze.

"What's the matter?" Jon asked.

"I can't help worrying about your friends on their vacation."

Jon ignored her tilted slur. "It bothers me, too. But what can we do? They've gone to get laid. What can I do to stop them?"

"But Liam's so wayward and the others are so easily led. They really need you there, Jon. You should go with them next time and keep an eye on things."

"To tell you the truth, I think they go to get away from me. I bring them down. Anyway, I couldn't go and leave you here by yourself."

"But I worry about them. Who knows what they might get up to? You are alone for most of the night. It's not right. They shouldn't leave you," Sophie slurred and hiccupped.

"Don't worry about me; I'm fine." Jon tried to convince himself. "They promise they don't harm people, and since I can't be in two places at once, I have to believe them. Shit, it's either that or lose my mind. Just don't ask me to go with them. I can't."

Despite the alcohol, Sophie fought to change tact. "Would you like to come and visit me later after you've fed? I could leave my window open, and you could spend the remaining night beside me; instead of sitting outside like you did last night."

"I didn't sit outside yours last night. What made you think that?"

"I had a sense that you did. It seemed so real…"

"I missed a treat," he whispered, kissing her again. He felt her soft leg stirring his anticipation for his visit, but as he ran his hand further up, it grew warmer. Perplexed by her sudden heat, he broke contact.

"What's the matter? What is it?" Sophie saw the intensity in his expression as he scanned the room, seeking something or someone. "Jon, you're frightening me." Could he somehow sense that another man had touched that leg; gone higher? She had bathed. There could be no smell of Callum remaining; no odour could delude her pink bubbles. So why was Jon now staring at her leg in a state of inertia?

Jon was alert to the nearby table, to the wine glass; aware of a finger screeching round and round, the bubbles breaking free, fizzing to the surface and popping to freedom as the hushed conversation developed into harsh whispers. The conversation was smutty, interesting. Disconcerting panic plunged into Jon's subtly fading mind. "I'm changing, Sophie. My five senses are growing sensitive and I don't know why. But I can't control them. Shit!" he exclaimed, running his fingers through his hair. "What's happening to me? This shouldn't be happening. Not now. Not yet. Goddamn it, I've only just got here!"

"It's your friends. They've upset your body clock, obviously."

"But this doesn't make sense. They're always going off. Shit, Soph, I'm telling you this is freaky." He checked the brightening room again, unsure what he was seeking but he'd know if he saw it; dull eyes staring at him, manipulating him, perhaps? Fangs mocking him to join the unknown devil in some masquerade and partake in some blood-lust ritual right here in this room full of energising bodies?

Although he feared no mortal, fear of the undead was another matter. Fear was not a stranger to him. He feared himself, because of his potential strength. He feared the emptiness; the astronomical thought of eternity – forever without end. Paramount to that he feared losing Sophie, and equal to that, he feared fear. Other than that he supposed he was sane.

"I've got to go." He stood up. "I'll be back to walk you home at this rate. Find Roz and stay safe." Hurriedly, he lit a cigarette.

"Are you alright?" Hiccup.

"I will be. Give me time to feed, and I will be." He headed for the door, leaving Sophie swaying; leaning to his glass to finish off his drink before concentrating on slurping her own.

The nightclub door swung closed. Jon stood between the two doormen and scanned the street. Everything was normal except for a biker sitting on the pavement opposite, head bent to risen knees. Although Jon couldn't see his face, his long blond hair seemed familiar. Then he remembered he was the ponce with the snobby voice that had inquired about Sanctuary's nightlife several nights ago. Indifferently, Jon pushed his hands into his pockets, spat out his cigarette butt to the pavement and nodded at the doormen.

"Goodnight," said one.

"Is it?" Jon uttered.

His car was parked close by. He decided to return later and drive Sophie home, so began walking in the opposite direction towards the nearby southern forests. Desperately, he rationalised that he was neither feeling insecure nor paranoid without his friends when he thought he heard his name being called from somewhere behind.

The biker dodged a passing car as he crossed the street to him.

"Jon," Callum called to the lone vampire.

"Do I know you?" Jon wondered how the hell this guy knew his name.

Callum regarded Jon's appearance, his unkempt hair. No excuse. No need for it. "I'm Callum."

"That's nice. But I'm a bit busy so push off." Jon resumed his journey. Astonished that Callum should follow, Jon stopped. "Look, mate, there's a gay bar in the city. You might get better luck there."

"Give me a moment to explain," he called to Jon who had sauntered off.

"I'm not interested. Now crawl back to your beer. I'm late for an appointment." Jon's senses were heightening rapidly. He walked faster.

"If you so choose, I could go with you; participate in your intentions?" The biker was suddenly walking alongside him.

"For fucksake," Jon cursed. "Don't you know when to quit?" He studied Callum with his trendy glasses, his long hair and diamond earring. Blood was blood. He could grab him by the hair and drink from his neck. He was tall, possibly muscular beneath the black cowskin. It would take some drinking to leave him dry. Subtly Jon realised the images were having no detrimental effect on his conscience.

He swirled around, grabbed Callum and pushed him backwards, slamming and pinning him against a shop wall. "Get off my back." Jon seethed, face against face. "I've warned you to leave me alone. I don't know what your problem is, but if you carry on you'll get a piece of me that you won't like."

The biker smiled. Coolly unaffected by the aggression and the tight grip on his throat, he pushed effortlessly against Jon and sent him staggering backwards.

"Perhaps now would be a good time to introduce myself properly?" Callum was amused as Jon reeled and straightened in astonishment. He raised his hand slowly to his face, and saw Jon's bewilderment grow as he pulled off his glasses.

Jon gawped at the biker; at his blue eyes of mischief. They were empty. His pupils were matt black and not glistening healthily alive as before when he had been wearing his glasses. His eyes were dead: soulless. The biker was soulless? - Undead? Jon's brain tried to reach solid ground. The biker was a goddamn bloodsucker? Inert, he uttered, "Fuck..." His attention swaying down to the glasses Callum was holding, then back to his dull blue eyes and the haunting black chasms of his pupils.

"Now, my friend, it seems I have your attention."

"How the hell... what are they?" Jon addressed the glasses, wondering how they had managed to mask his eyes and make them glisten.

"I'm unsure," Callum stated. "These are the reason I have come to Sanctuary."

"Is that so? And what's that got to do with me?"

"I seek your support. I'm looking for something and, if I'm not mistaken, it should be here." Callum surveyed the empty street with growing concern. "But right now, we need to get away."

"*We* aren't going anywhere." Stubbornly, Jon walked off.

"You're growing in rapid need of blood."

Jon spun around. "It was you? You caused me to change. It was you in the club?"

Callum walked past Jon feeling elated. He had succeeded in unleashing Sophie from this obnoxious vampire. "I needed to ask your advice. I grew impatient and would apologise except I'm not sorry."

"Is that a fact?" Jon was astounded by this vampire's nerve.

Callum shot Jon a resigning look. "I admit I may have accelerated you a touch too hastily. You are obviously inferior, and have found less control over your body than I had first presumed."

"Fuck you," Jon retorted.

"Thank you, but I must decline."

Jon jumped in front of Callum, vampire or not. "I don't know who you think you are and I really couldn't give a toss. But you need to climb down out of your arse or you and me are going to fall out."

"You and I," Callum corrected. "And you're very definitely right. But, as I can tell; you are losing sense of true judgement. I will suffer your ignorance and wait until you are full, then perhaps you'll become intrigued enough to help?" He waved the glasses in front of Jon's face before gently sliding them into his jacket pocket. "I suggest we go now?"

As they walked, Jon's thoughts became vague. He could no longer wonder of the vampire beside him or the mysterious glasses. He concentrated on getting safely away from the town, away from human blood before his rising senses stole his conscience. But as his senses grew sharper, the black jacket rustling by his side agitated him.

"You may hazard to wonder what blood I have taken since my arrival?" Callum queried.

"No."

"Rest easy, I have been drinking from animals in the northern forests. And they are quite spectacular."

"What, our animals?" Jon asked, battling to care.

"No: the forests." But Jon glanced at him more blankly, and Callum refrained from speaking further, silently delighting in the fact that Jon, Sophie's lover, was indeed lower than a toe-rag.

Ahead of them was the road that led along the perimeter of the southern forests. The shops were beginning to grow more sparse and during this time, the inevitably began occurring. With taste buds heightening, their sixth sense and instincts turned to warm, luscious blood. Both vampires equally felt the usual tingling in their gums as their fangs began extending and their consciences began to escape.

Eight

"DEAR GOD." PAULETTE SOBBED, TRYING to gain her bearings through the blackened night. The trees looked the same in front, to the left and the right; like formidable monsters towering over her. Lurching, leering at her stupidity.

Her head spinning from disorientation and fear; her podgy body weary, she staggered to the nearest tree and retched. Bile alone escaped her.

In retrospect, she shouldn't have argued with her friend, Julie, or at least she should have swallowed her pride and used Julie's telephone to phone her father, her mobile having no signal in the forest. He would have come to pick her up from the failed slumber party. But no, Paulette was headstrong and spirited, she had left her friend's house without her bag and without regard for her safety in this dead of night.

Oh God, pride comes before a fall. "Shut up, brain," she demanded aloud, wondering above all else why God kept appearing in her mind? She wasn't religious. She wasn't an atheist either. She believed in something: fate, guardian angles. If asked, she wouldn't be able to replicate a delicate flower, paint its frail petals and mass-produce it. She felt all these wonders didn't just appear with a big bang. But she had never approached the creator. Her brain was too complex. It scared her in the small hours until she would lie ridged, clutching at the covers.

Brushing her fringe from her face, it clung to more sweat. Paulette straightened up and wondered where her guardian was now? It must have a warped sense of humour, allowing her to eat and then eat some more for all her sixteen years, and then see her, this night, leave the desolate road and take a short cut through this labyrinth to her parents' remote guesthouse in the woods.

Tears streaking her dirty face, Paulette cautiously walked forward. Snivelling in self-pity for her aching legs, for her mum to come and find her, for her cosy bed. Perhaps if she closed her eyes and wished hard enough, she would wake up there like Dorothy returning from Oz? But this wasn't a film or a book or some daydream picked out from her vivid imagination - this was reality. She was lost. She was going to die: to die a virgin.

She would be found months later, half a mile from home. Her body decomposing and smelling repugnant, the creatures would tear at her. Crows would tear at her eyes, picking out eyeballs on red elastic. Her parents would wonder what the stench was drifting in through their opened windows, and it would be her; their long-lost daughter; their only child. They would cry. It would be sad and pathetic. Her mother would announce that she had always loved the forest; how ironic that the trees should claim her.

"Oh, belt up, brain!"

It's only the fear of the dark, fear of the unknown and unseen. - And fear keeps you safe.

"Fear keeps you safe. Fear - keeps - you - safe," she recited.

But then she had known fear in the sunny light of day.

The ground rising to each welling tear, she shifted forwards, the twigs cracking underfoot. The trees thinned out and she entered a clearing. A familiar clearing! Hope surged as she knew where she was.

She glanced up at the star spangled sky through the circle of foliage. The trees leaned in. A cool breeze blew up from nowhere, stinging at her salted cheeks. The trees began to leer, their leaves whispering, "You've been here before, stupid. You've been here before." A crow cackled. "This night, silly girl: this night."

Taken on the next breath, the trees lurched inward at her. Mocking, hissing in hushed whispers amongst themselves, they swayed back and forth, jovially sneering.

Her mind jolted. They were right. She glanced about, shivering as cold dread adorned her like a robe. She had been here already. What, half an hour ago? Had she been running in one large circle?

The labyrinth sneered.

Panic jarred in her head, escaping to yank at the fine hairs on her neck and stand them to attention. Although she needed to swallow, her larynx refused.

About to turn tail and run to anywhere, she heard a noise. It was the distant sound of a car engine. Guessing it was coming from the road at the forest perimeter, she turned to face it. If she could just get back to the road, she could follow it to the track, which led to her parents' long driveway. She'd be home.

Walking briskly, Paulette focused through the dark at the tree in front. Reaching it, she focused on the next, mapping herself away from the infernal circle. She may be scatterbrained, but she wasn't totally daft.

From behind, flapping wings startled her. She turned in time for her frightened eyes to catch a wood pigeon rising from a gorse bush and flying upwards to the night sky. The bush stood still, not uprooting itself and sneaking to follow. There were no ghosts or shimmering skeleton bones dancing in the moonlight. Death's hands fell on her shoulders. The ice chill of its grasp ran like liquid nitrate through her veins and froze her brain. Momentarily paralysed, death violently shook her, and, freeing her mind, she began to run.

Seeing her endeavouring to escape, the trees turned more malicious, sending signals in a chain-reaction from their bows to their roots and onwards through the earth to their neighbours. Frantically, her chubby legs carried her. Suddenly, she was aware of the conspiracy. The woodland floor, taking its part in the masquerade, grabbed at her ankles, tearing, scratching at her bare legs. Sturdy roots and sprawling woody vines threatened to trip her and pin her down.

She knew the slithering tentacles would entrap her. She had lived here all her born days and respected nature. She wasn't a tourist, some fly-by-night. She was loyal to the forest. She admired its changing colours as it past through each season. Yet, the forest wouldn't care of that; of any of it. Its vine fingers would search her face while she lay struggling. Sucker pads would pull at her skin and realise she was plain.

Then, with whip-lashing vigour, thick viny arms would swoop about her whole body until she could no longer breathe or scream out. She would drown in sap, be impaled by huge thorns, or be asphyxiated by a mouthful of leaves; disgusting, putrid tasting leaves.

She would be lost forever, staying ultimately loyal to her surroundings because that was their objective. The forests demanded loyalty, and so too did the natives.

Her imagination in overdrive, she ran faster. Stumbling, jumping awkwardly over roots and branches lying in her wake, until her muscles were burning and her raspy breath was stinging in her chest. Just when she thought she could take no more, she saw the break in the trees. The trees shivered and leaves rustled to keep her hidden.

⁂

Side by side, two figures walked in silence. They had made it to safety with no time to spare. Having reached the southern road, the perimeter of the forests, their intuition told them to enter through the trees, but their keen hearing detected otherwise. Fast and haphazardly, the irregular footsteps sounded more like a stampede. They could hear twigs breaking, small creatures scurrying. And with heightened intuition and a keen sense of direction, they knew fear to be out there already, and more importantly, heading straight for them.

Two smiles developed: eager fangs glinted in the moonlight. The vampires, whose consciences had faded, drew to a halt. And silently waited...

Thanking God, Paulette reached the break in the trees, and stumbled down the grass embankment and out into the middle of the narrow road. Leaning over, hands on knees and body heaving, she fought for breath. She had made it.

The vampires were transfixed by the vision. Ahead of them, the girl's heart was pounding like a heavy-duty road-drill. The girl was exhausted. The girl was bleeding: red trickles seeping through torn skin about her legs; lashings of the stuff drying on wrinkled socks. The vampires drooled.

Keeping his attention fixed on the prey Jon turned slightly to Callum and whispered, "Virgin."

Paulette looked up. In the moonlight, she saw two guys standing in the darkened road. Immediately, she sensed danger. She couldn't pinpoint it. The manner in which they stood like statues; not moving or threatening to approach was of no comfort. The way they stared at her without comments to each other was downright weird, almost intimidating as though they were telepathically linked. Although, from this distance, she could establish no features and could see no oddity, again, her first and only instinct was to run. She turned away from them, in the direction of home and ran as fast as her weary legs would allow.

Further along, a twisting cramp in her side threatened to halt her but fear was driving her. She ran. She ran so far and so fast for her life, her long-suffering P.E teacher would have been proud. Through blinding tears, she glanced over her shoulder. The road behind was empty.

It had been her imagination. Of course, it had to be – everyone had mocked her for it in the past. She was the original daydream girl. – Only now it was a nightmare. The two men were mere figments of her frightened mind. Or perhaps they had been ghosts trapped in time?

- Imagination overload.

Her legs failing and her whole body aching with exertion, she willed herself to keep going, she was almost there. But her overweight torso and unfit legs were giving in, her knees giving out. The stinging in her chest had diminished and was superseded by a raging inferno which persisted in spreading through her ribcage to burn her lungs, snap her spine, and stab between her shoulder-blades. Then she saw the track. Hope filling her again, she stumbled towards it, cursing her parents for living in such a godforsaken place as relief swept over her.

She stumbled frantically towards the dirt track ahead, willing her legs to keep moving, ignoring all pain.

She was almost home. - Almost.

The vampires flew in from above. The girl changed course, running clumsily, panic-stricken towards a gate with its long driveway the other side. She was like a preyed animal scurrying for shelter but with nowhere to hide. Side by side, they flew soundlessly over. But she never noticed. With synchronised movements, they turned a summersault in mid-air and dropped to their feet.

Paulette gasped in horror as the phantoms fell from the skies. As the solid men landed, she fell to her knees. "No," she gasped, despair throttling her.

Imagination overload: malfunction! SOS…

With powerful strides, Jon walked to where the girl was; crumpled, broken. Towering over her, he demanded, "Get up." The trembling virgin girl gasped for breath; cowering with her head lowered, she refused to look at him. Sweet, captivating blood still oozed from her hidden wounds. Deep within him something dictated he must stun the prey first. "I said; get up."

Keeping her eyes on his trainers, Paulette shook her head uncontrollably, let out a gasped sob and tried breathing back in. It caught in her throat. Sensing the executioner's intentions like his gun was pointing at her head, she sobbed again. She needed saving. Was there nobody in the universe who could save her? - Reality. - She was going to die! She hadn't grown into a woman yet. She was too young to die. She wanted to live.

Jon was about to drag her to her feet, when her lips started moving. But even though his hearing was focused, she was saying nothing. The uttering grew louder, audible.

"Hallowed by Thy name…" Sob. "Thy kingdom come, Thy…"

"Shut –the- fuck- up!" Jon bellowed, mesmerised at the child's strength as, ignoring him, she continued,

"…Earth as it is in Heaven…" Then oddly, almost serenely, she looked up, and taking a sudden deep breath, blurted, "Though I may walk through the valley of death, I shall fear no evil. You can't hurt me, whatever you are. I've asked for protection." She lowered her face.

"I've had enough of this. Shut up, you crazy bitch!" Jon stooped towards her through the hazy odour of pure nectar. Her words were annoying him as she continued. There was something menacing in them. But his transgression was complete, and without true thought he had no control. Without conscience, he had no empathy.

Having heard enough and his taste-buds anticipating the virgin blood he hadn't tasted in over two years, he raised a clenched fist high above his head and focussed on her skull. Stun the prey.

"Deliver us from evil. For Thine is..."

Jon swung his fist down hard. A more powerful hand grabbed his arm from behind, stemming the swipe. Shocked, he swirled around to the blond vampire who was gripping his arm tightly.

"Let her be," Callum stated.

"Are you out of your fucking mind?" Jon exploded, shaking free from his grasp.

"I didn't come here for this, my friend, and I want no part of it."

"Piss off then!" Jon shoved Callum backwards and turned to the praying girl.

"It's not my wish to fight you, Jon. You won't win." Callum stole a quick glance at the virgin who remained with her head bent. "I will ask, however, what do you suppose your girlfriend would say if she knew of your intentions?"

Jon stared at Callum blankly. The last virgin had tasted so surreal it had practically blown his mind and he hadn't needed more blood for a week. But the dull blue eyes remained questioning him, and who was this vampire? Who was this girlfriend? He turned to the prey - to her neck.

"Stop that chanter, wench," Callum demanded to the girl. "Tell us your name."

The girl fell silent then uttered, "Paulette."

"Makes no difference how you dress it up." Jon shrugged. "Who cares? Paulette, Pauline, Polly-puts-the-fucking kettle-on. I'm still going to have her."

"Your girlfriend has a supreme quality of sweet nature and kindness," Callum pleaded, no longer prepared to look at the virgin girl. The smell of her was intoxicating the air and his teeth were sharp.

"What?" Jon shot.

"She's your love. You adore her, remember?" he lisped flatly. Jon turned again to the quivering girl. Callum added, "You want to break your love's heart?"

Trying to comprehend the vague meaning, Jon kept from stepping closer to the virgin. In a hushed voice, he said, "You so much as utter this to anyone and I'll find you; when I do, you'll consider this moment a picnic by the seashore. Understand?"

Paulette nodded, feeling more fear with the quiet way the threat was spoken than the ranting before. Shaking from head to foot in terror, she heard no more. No conversation. No footsteps.

After a while, she looked up at where his trainers had moved to, but they weren't there. She surveyed the dark lane, but mysteriously, whatever they were had gone.

Wiping her wet face with trembling hands she staggered through the gate, knowing she was lucky to be alive. Everything she had experienced had been reality, yet she wouldn't tell a soul. No one would believe her. They would blame her overactive imagination and pack her off to some loony-asylum where she would be locked in some padded cell, be wrapped in a straightjacket and tortured with electricity until she keeled over.

But above all, she wouldn't tell a soul for fear of seeing them again, knowing the promised repercussions. No. She wouldn't even write it down. Not in an essay or in her diary.

⁂

Callum's arms were sprawled across the width of a deer holding her still. He sucked hard at the red stream and drew in more sweetness until his stomach was filled, then stood up. The deer lay with limbs convulsing, head twitching, eyes rolling and stomach rising and shallowly falling. From four small holes, more blood oozed to beads and balanced to congeal.

Callum could neither think in words nor rationalise. But as always, letting his intuition govern him, he felt that death was part of life, so he left the feed to die slowly and began to walk back to where he had left Jon. He retraced his flight-path that the animal had galloped. Upon reaching the clearing where the deer had been found grazing, he stood by the last tree and waited.

Jon's stag was dead. The fine animal had been brought to the ground in carnage. Had there been a need for it? Callum wasn't coherent enough to decide. The scene was grotesque and deplorable to his eye. The stag had two holes in his head where the antlers had been plucked from their roots. The antlers had been used like a butcher's knife to rip through the stag's stomach from front to rear and were still impaled there, propped upright like branches. Jon was kneeling beside it. His face was lost in the deeply gorged hole and his jeans were saturated in wasted blood.

Jon rose from his meal. Sombrely, he said, "You'd better follow me."

They flew, Jon taking the lead. Diverting course and staying low to the trees, they headed south. Callum's thoughts began returning, and he wondered briefly where they were going. He wondered if the inferior vampire had returned to true thinking yet. His thoughts turned to the virgin in the woods, and he remembered his unconscious words about Sophie. He had spoken of her kindness. He had reminded Jon of his love that had helped save the virgin blood which both had wanted.

"I'm not angry with you," Jon called. He slowed up becoming level with Callum. "The virgin; if I had taken her I would be in deep shit and regretting it by now."

"It pleases me to hear it," Callum said. "I'm unsure how I didn't succumb to such a feast myself; suffice to say from deep within something governs me away from such temptation. Although I have, in several cases during my past, taken that of a virgin and enjoyed it profoundly."

"Do you know Sophie?" Jon asked the dreaded question.

"I observed her in the club and the pub and upon visiting the library once or twice. I neither know why I spoke as I did, nor why she should have been mentioned."

"It did the trick; brought me to my senses. Beautiful isn't she?"

"Who is?"

"Sophie."

"I can't say I've noticed," Callum lied.

Must be raving gay not to, Jon thought. He studied Callum suspiciously. "Did you say you've been to the library?"

"Yes."

"What, in the day; in the sun? You went to the library in the daytime, when you should be sleeping - and you didn't fry?"

"Yes. But I think it best to begin from the beginning. So refrain from such queries, my friend, and all shall become apparent in due course."

"Listen, I don't know you so let's get one thing straight. I'm not your friend and I'm not gay." Jon's thoughts turned to the stranger's supposedly other purpose for being with him. "Those glasses; they let you walk about in the sun without meltdown and keep you awake. What are they, magic?"

"If only it were so." Callum sighed. "If only they were."

Nine

"Do you want a beer?" Jon asked Callum who was standing next to the settee, dubious to sit down and scanning his surroundings with what Jon supposed was distain. Callum accepted, and as Jon handed him a bottle from a crate, he said, "We don't stand on ceremony here."

Callum sat down as Jon tore off his tee shirt and discarded it to a box before going to wash the stag's congealed blood from his face. His back was naked. Sophie had touched that back, his skin. Callum supposed she could even have dug her perfectly manicured nails in while the obnoxious Jon did his will. Callum wasn't used to the pit of his stomach churning but since meeting Sophie, he was growing more accustomed to it.

Wearing clean clothes and returning with a can of lager, Jon said, "So? Are you going to spill the news on those glasses?"

"Maybe; but first, are you aware of any other vampires in the area besides your gang?"

"Hang on. Hold it right there, goddamn it." Jon spat, the flame from his lighter hovering before his dancing cigarette. "We don't use the 'v' word, okay?"

"Is that a fact? - It offends you? Then it seems we need some ground rules, for I chose not to use the 'f' word. I'm not accustomed to hearing it casually, and especially not directed at me. So if you could abstain from such vulgarities, I'll indulge you likewise."

Jon sat in an armchair opposite, eyeing the longhaired biker; his fancy leather boots, blue jeans, jacket, and diamond stud. "My mates are going to be so annoyed they missed this little meeting. I reckon you would get on great with them."

"And I think not," Callum stated. "It's been my misfortune to witness their primitive antics. I watched your clowning in the Bat Inn Hand. They are irresponsible delinquents and nearly caused my transgression. I fought hard the hunger."

"Primitive?"

"The way you fed upon the stag was primeval. You mutilated it. And last night, while I took blood from the northern forests, I came across the carcass of a cow. Need I say more? Do you not think blood tastes nicest when it is being sucked in gradually past the teeth so it flows in streams over the tongue? Or have you always ripped your feed to shreds in such a macabre frenzy; like nothing more than mere animals yourselves?"

"Bollocks." Jon bellowed out smoke, his agitation growing.

"So, am I to understand that you don't enjoy being a vampire?"

Jon drew in a sharp breath: *vamp...?* "No. What's there to enjoy about it? I mean, yeah, you've got your better senses, and your flying and all that shit. But what else is there? You walk around, year after year, doing the same old thing in some eternal misery, bored out your sodding mind. I've been like this since the swinging sixties, man, and it's been hell; all because of some crazy bitch."

"Your soul was stolen by a woman?"

"Yeah," Jon blurted. "Damn right. Being heterosexual that would normally be the case. You're going to tell me a man bit you, right?"

"It is of no consequence."

"Fuck," Jon hissed under his breath. "Look. It was like this. - It was the sixties with free love and women wearing braids and beads, with 'come-and-get-it – I know my rights' written all over them. Not that you'd know. Anyway, being twenty-five, virile and horny for anything in a skirt, I suppose I was a sitting target. I went to this music festival and was happily involved with the activities, with the night closing in, minding my own, when this gorgeous chic dances up to me. Fuck, she was so horny; I mean, real sassy, with long red locks and long red frock. Then she said her hippie name was Destiny and asked if I was lucky. I told her she could call me lucky, horny or coming already, and off we went." Jon paused, lighting another cigarette from the stub of the old one, and noticed Callum's amusement. "I know what you're thinking. You think I deserve what happened next because I was a tart. Well, let me tell you; no one deserves what that bitch did to me."

"It's the way you tell it. I'm intrigued. You have my attention."

"We rented a room. Stupid old me staring death in the face, didn't even see it coming. But, she knew. She knew exactly what she was doing. We got straight down to it. I was giving her some, and then some more then she turns me over real sharpish, and takes the lead: which was fine because I was knackered. She was real frantic. - Riding up and down. God, you've never seen anything like it. I thought I'd died and gone to heaven. Then she starts biting me. Little bites. You know the ones. Then they get more painful, and then she goes the whole damn hog and sinks them right in. Shit, I didn't know if I was coming or going, loving it or hating it. It was just sort of happening to me. I was helpless, completely helpless. - Bitch. - Then she looks at me. She leans down and snogs me like nothing else. But the slag had bitten through her tongue and was tickling my tonsils with her blood. Then she raises her head and smiles, though I didn't really notice her long teeth at that point because I was too freaked out by her eyes. They were different: really spooky. Dead eyes which was a shock in itself, but then she starts moving and laughing and screaming. So I began to panic, she reached orgasm and I past out."

"Did she not help you when you woke?"

"Did she bollocks? No, she had long gone; left me to find out the hard way. Then, several months later, I bumped into the others: Liam, Greg and Daniel, all with their dead eyes. They too had met Destiny. So eventually, we tracked her down, and all four of us took it in turns in staking her and not just in the heart. In the two minutes we had before her body disappeared, we had taken away her looks, ripped out her hair and stabbed her so many times we couldn't recognize her. Then we sent her merrily on her way to meet her maker. She's probably screwing the devil senseless right now." Jon pulled in a deep breath. "So, what's your story?"

"I'm one hundred and fifty years old." Callum smiled proudly. "Which just about makes you juvenile. But unlike you, I have the deepest regards for my maker. His name was Tom..."

"Figures: no needs to go into details there, Callum. I've got the gist so get to the point."

"Tom was five-hundred approximately, though he said he had lost count of those wilderness years, and I daresay I didn't blame him. He was older in appearance also, possibly early forties, though he never truly divulged that, either. He was like a father to me. He took me under his wing and let me dwell with him in his fine home in the North of England. And our friendship never dwindled nor faltered. But you must realise I never really knew the man. He was a dark horse that I never dared asked him questions, and always remembered my place. I owed him that."

"He's dead, right?" Jon asked, seeing the sorrow flit past Callum's dull eyes. "I mean really dead; obliterated?"

"You are rubbing in salt, my friend. I'm overwrought with grief, that I'm unsure how I function on times - such a delicate subject. Ah, but alas, the story must be told if you are to help."

"I don't know about that, depends." Jon took another gulp from his can.

"What I seek is another vampire: a vampire with a difference. He's here in Sanctuary, dwelling amongst us. Dwelling amongst you, and has done for a while most probably."

"Look, mate, don't you think we'd have seen him by now?"

"Did you recognize me Wednesday evening when I approached you in the street?"

"No." Jon was perplexed. "You recognized me, then?"

"Think. My eyes were disguised from you, yet I am still able to see death within you. It's the same for another one amongst us; I'm sure of it. This vampire has what I want, and possibly what you would wish for also. I should start from the beginning. - Two months ago, Tom announced he was to journey to Sanctuary on 'personal affairs', which in itself was quite extraordinary since, for the last half-century or so, he rarely ventured far. But I asked no questions and he offered no explanations..."

"God, I hate secretive people."

"Show some respect. You didn't know him so don't judge. By the morning he had returned, and still he spoke of nothing concerning his trip. Then, one week later, after rising from sleep, I went to the dining hall to wait for him as usual, but he failed to venture downstairs, so eventually, I went to his room..." Callum visually shuddered. His memory was alight, his sorrow growing; he desperately tried not to wear his heart on his sleeve and was failing miserably.

"Didn't you guys sleep together – share a room?"

"No." Frustrated, Callum bolted to his feet and stared across at Jon as though he had sprouted three heads. "He was like a father to me. Don't you listen? If I were to tell you I've spent approximately one and a quarter centuries loving the memory of a woman, who married someone else, you would fail to believe me. If I told you that mourning the lost love of my Sarah has very nearly brought me to my knees on countless occasions, you would be sceptical; presume me to lie. You would also presume me to exaggerate if I were to say, Tom gave me the east wing of his home, in which I slept. So believe what you will, I don't seek your approval."

"Alright, man. Just checking; just want to keep up with the facts."

"I went to Tom's room," Callum continued weakly, sitting down. "From the door, I could see his bed, and that it was empty. I went to the four-poster and immediately realised his demise. For, where his chest would have lain was a stake. A beautifully carved stake with one end turned like a spindle, and inscribed along the centre were the words, 'I have come to reclaim that which belongs not to you.' And Tom was gone, gone from me forever. Someone had sneaked into his room and staked him while he was sleeping. He was my only friend: my only source of companionship that I could rely on and respect, an undying friendship that is lost forever. Can you imagine how you would feel waking one evening to find three empty beds with stakes where your friends should be lying; only to then face the rest of eternity alone?"

"No - no, I can't." Jon went to the crates, thinking he'd been a jerk and Callum wasn't so bad. In fact, the more he thought about it, the more he was growing to like Callum, although he was posh. Handing Callum a beer, he sat back down. "What happened next?"

"Nothing; no explanation came to light. For these last seven weeks, I've been perpetually flummoxed as to his death. The wondering alone nearly drove me to insanity. It was so worrying. I thought each day, while sleeping, would be my last; that the slayer would return. Then, this Wednesday, in the early hours as day was approaching, I took courage and revisited his room where I proceeded in tidying his bed. Beneath the bolster, I found these." Callum handed the glasses across the table to Jon. "Lying beneath them were two pieces of parchment with their edges torn, as though they had been extracted from a larger manuscript. I haven't brought them with me for fear of them being found on my person. Both pages described a recipe for a potion. Any glass can be dipped into this potion and in turn bring about an image of life and reflection."

"Are you saying these glasses give you a reflection?" Jon toyed with the glasses more gently as he tried to comprehend the reality.

"Indeed. I believe Tom purchased the glasses recently for they are modern. He picked the herbs and collected the barks, made the potion and dipped the glasses in. They work. When you didn't recognise me Wednesday night, I realised my find was very significant; I was disguised from all immortals. Believe me, they are truly clever."

Callum could see the desire ripen in Jon, the excitement burning. Much as he first thought, and still wanted to believe Jon was an obnoxious and primitive imbecile, he recognized himself in Jon. They loved the same woman. Each spoke one's mind with an honest tongue, though Jon was a little crass. Although Jon seemed to hide behind a smokescreen, a macho image, Callum was fast learning Jon was as equally sensitive and vulnerable. Also, Callum recognized Jon's longing to recapture his reflection.

"I haven't got any mirrors, shit. Do you reckon I could try them once we get back to town later? I've left my car there because I'm taking Sophie home. I could have a look in the car mirror first: check me out."

"Be warned. It's a startling sight."

"Cheers mate. Can't add to that; can hardly recall."

"Imagine not being able to see your reflection for so long, that the years passing are so cruel and the only thing keeping you sane is that your friends don't turn into freak shows when hunger grabs them."

"Yeah, I'm with you on FM," Jon confirmed.

"All these moments collide into one existence of a lower esteem and without the physical it is hard to be complete. Ah, the misery. I lit a hundred candles. I put on the glasses, lowered my sight and drew back the curtains to the night. And then I very nearly died again, my friend. For, in front of me was my very self in the flesh. The image nearly stole my legs; I was so joyously overwhelmed. Yet, I warn you solemnly, the memories you have of discovering your image to be lost forever, is only half as eerie as recovering it."

"I think I can handle it." Jon smiled, delicately placing the glasses down on the table. He stood up. "Better get going then."

"There's more. Be seated." Callum relaxed back in his seat. "You're too impatient. Best things come to those who wait."

"I've waited forever for this..."

"Ah, the luxury of time - another hour or so will make no difference. I promise you shall see your reflection. A gentleman's word is his honour, rest assured. But hear me out. Near the bottom of the second page was the title, 'Stake Survival'. Below this there were no remedies or ingredients only a short theory of wood properties to the vampire's susceptible heart. But alas, that is where it ends."

"Are you telling me, we could survive the stake, as well?"

"If we find the subsequent pages; yes. It's my opinion that perhaps an entire book exists holding remedies for all our failings, somewhere close by. Imagine it; walking in the sun, sleeping during the night, with no desires for drinking blood, and no needs to kill. My friend, we could be cured. We could at last be free of ourselves; be normal."

"Shit, yeah." Jon lit another cigarette; the dancing flame blackening his dead eyes. "But what about flying and stuff: what about our senses? We'd lose all that, right?"

"I'm unsure. I need to find the book. I presume all these would remain with us for they're not detrimental, and if we're cured from wanting blood then we could possibly raise all five senses without transgressing into an inferior self."

"Be like a comic book hero. Have control without our bodies ruling us while flitting on the breeze whenever the mood takes us?"

"Possibly, but until I recover the book, all this is speculation."

"Damn it. Why didn't your mate get the whole book: why only two of the pages?"

"That, my friend, is a question that's ricocheted through my mind since Wednesday, and one I've found no answer to. But Tom did nothing without good reason. He was a shrewd gentleman, one far cleverer than ever he boasted. He did nothing without good reason especially where I was concerned. I can only assume he conveyed nothing to me to protect me from his slayer.

"If this book is as good as you reckon, why didn't he protect his heart? He must have seen the entire book? He must have read it?"

"Damn it, Jon." Callum stood up, abruptly. His mind spinning, he began pacing back and forth. "You echo my thoughts. All this is a mystery. You can see my dilemma: my misery? For seven weeks, I have been in turmoil at losing my friend. Since Wednesday, after finding the glasses and pages, I've been frantic with these same dire questions churning away. Besides all this, other emotions have wreaked their havoc..."

Something flashed across Callum's face as he broke off: desperation sadder than his words, a deeper misery yielding from his core to surface in his dull blue eyes. And then it was gone.

"I'm weakened by it all," Callum gasped, slumping down onto the settee. "I have no leads, no true inclinations as to the identity of the book owner. I'm no further forward than when I first arrived."

"We need someone who wears glasses. That would be a start."

"We must be cautious. Understand that the keeper of the book has qualities far greater than our own. He can walk by day without leather and plastic to protect him from the sun and light, and if he becomes aware that I'm Tom's friend then you too are in jeopardy. He would undoubtedly arrive by day and stake you while you sleep. It's of the greatest importance that you mention to no one who I am, of my home in the North, nor of my cause for being here. Understand?"

"Fuck, yeah," Jon said.

"Not even your lover must know."

"You can trust Sophie, she's sweet. Shit, she'll be ecstatic to know I might be cured of this. I could even move in with her, live normally."

"No!" Callum leaned forward. "It's imperative that she doesn't know. You must tell her nothing concerning my identity. I don't want her to know what I am. This mission is arduous enough. Don't speak of me."

"Alright, keep your hair on. I'll keep quiet."

"Not good enough. Swear to it," Callum said forcefully.

"I promise."

"You must understand to stake Tom was a feat. Tom could be cruel and most sinister to outsiders. Whoever attacked him so mercilessly must have had the courage and strength of a thousand men."

"We need a plan," Jon said. "We could wait for Liam and the others to return; they'll be back tomorrow night probably. Then there'll be five against one. We can all go on the mission, rip men's glasses off and check out their eyes.

"And find ourselves defenceless against the stronger enemy? Are you insane? – I'm afraid the treatment needs to be a little more guarded. This vampire has a heart protected from wood. He can move about in the midday sun, totally naked if he so desired, and he wouldn't burn. He's indestructible. He could stake all five of us and we wouldn't have a weapon for defence. Instead, I suggest we use observation and bide our time since I have a suspicion of the one we seek."

"Yeah: who?"

"He works in the library with your lover and her friend."

"Lucas? What makes you think it's him?"

"I confess my uncertainty, but he works amongst books. He wears glasses and as he walked the length of the room he looked directly at me."

"Wow, must be him then; absolutely, most definitely. I mean if the guy looked at you, then that's that."

"You're mocking me?"

"Yeah, mate. And it better bloody not be. I'm not having Sophie working there with a frigging bloodsucker."

"A cured bloodsucker," Callum reminded distantly. "And why not: her lover is one? She must hold no qualms to our kind, to feel so at ease?"

"That's only because she knows I would never hurt her."

Callum lamented. "The love which binds you together appears to be strong. Yet do you never feel the urge to sink those teeth in? Not even during your most vulnerable, most intimate moments, tracing her blue veins with your lips?"

"Maybe…" Jon found himself confessing to this stranger subjects he could hardly confide in his friends. "In the beginning, the urge was the strongest. But the deeper I fell in love with her the more that desire faded. And now, just the thought puts me off and makes me want to chuck-up."

"Excuse me?"

"Vomit. No. I couldn't hurt her, not one hair on her head. She's my angel. Can you image not having the desire to bite flesh?"

"I can't," Callum said, remembering her pure skin; her delicate neck so close to his mouth, his tongue - his teeth. Jon was in a world of his own, loving Sophie also. Callum added, "I fail to imagine normality since I've been a vampire for far too long."

Jealousy tore through Callum. What had begun as a mission was fast turning into a tormented hell, and he was falling deeper. Instead of finding Jon loathsome as his first impression, he had now discovered a deeper level; an honest, raw level that couldn't be ignored. Instead of despising him, Callum now possessed empathy for his suffering. Against his will he had found affection for his newfound friend. Much as he cursed his fair-mindedness and his stupidity for getting too involved, he feared eternity. He dreaded loneliness with Tom gone forever. And he longed for a long-term friendship. He could see this friend in Jon. Yet he loved Sophie: Jon's Sophie.

Suddenly, it occurred to him that he had stumbled upon hell. His soul wasn't lost to hell, some burning place on another dimension. No, his body, the physically flesh of him had found hell; it was here in this dimension, this earth, this 'so called' existence. Hell was suddenly within; torturing him with burning envy and love, guilt and grief. Torturing him with volcanic lava that wormed its meltdown through his veins as a little red devil stood on lava rock in his brain; tormenting his mind, stoking the fires, poking, jabbing at the lava lakes with his pitchfork. Yes, his heart was in hell. His mind was in hell. So what of his soul? – It was better off away from him by all accounts.

"What's up? You look like shit. You're still missing your friend, right?" Jon queried.

"Amongst all else I miss him with a vengeance. He was everything to me; and not in some sordid way that you might think…"

"I get it. I've been a jerk, a complete asshole. I don't think you're gay. And now that I know you, I wouldn't mind if you were. Not that you are."

"Thank you." Callum managed to smile. "Tom taught me many things. How to wake myself during daylight hours and to combat sleep until the yearning overwhelms me. And he could be so generous, lavishing gifts and dressing me in the finest of latest fashions that the money seemed endless and I'm convinced he had friends in high places. But alas, he was no saint. Indeed, some might define him as evil. He had taken many victims during his time, especially before my arrival. He divulged such things to me, but I couldn't be so complacent. In those early days, I would participate in the orgies of blood lust and then find my conscience wracked with guilt, which Tom found amusing, though I sensed envy. He preferred the company of whores. Although he carried on so, he would always forewarn me of their visitations. Does that not show he respected my wishes, my feelings? Should I not feel entitled to grieve for someone who caused so much misery to others?"

"Yeah, of course you can. He showed you kindness. He took you in. So he wasn't all bad. And besides, we can't help how we feel. No - I mean - Liam's a prick at times and Daniel is a bit slow on the uptake. And we've had our moments, I can tell you. But I care about them and what happens to them. Shit, if someone staked them, no matter what they'd done I'd be livid."

"So strange; I find I'm not angry or seeking retribution. I seek answers. I'm so alone, that I feel Tom took a part of me with him that will surely be lost for eternity."

"When was the last time you got laid? We could go back to the Crypt for the last half hour before closing and get you some female company."

"Much as I now wish it was, that is not the problem, my friend."

"Men are men the world over."

"So it would seem. However, we should make tracks if you're to see your reflection before the club closes?"

"Where are you staying?"

"I've taken a room in town for a week, though I may need to stay longer. And the curtains are heavily lined and meet in the middle."

"You can stay here. There's three beds not being used and the company will do you good. I'll see Sophie for a couple of hours, and then we could share a few beers before dawn and you can tell me all about this Sarah chic."

Callum rose weakly, cloaked in sadness deeper than before. "You're truly a friend; one I'm not worthy of."

"What are you on about? We vampires must stick together." Astonished, Jon gasped, "Shit, I said it. I said it. It actually came out." He stood, reached across the table and punched Callum in the arm affectionately. "See, you're good for me. You're going to cure me; you're doing it already. Stay with us. The others are dicks, but you'll grow to love them. God knows I did."

"You're too kind, but I can't. I prefer to stay close to the town and we should stay separate for the mission's sake." Callum put his glasses on. His dull blue eyes sparkled back to life as though his soul had been snatched back.

In awe at the vision, Jon felt a sudden rush. He was going to see his reflection. The one-and-a-half-century-old vampire was a gentleman, and his word was his promise.

"Remember not to mention anything to Sophie?" Callum grimaced as the devil twisted his pitchfork.

"I won't mention anything. A gentleman's word is his honour, remember? I can be a gentleman if I want. You can trust me. I'll keep it as a surprise for her."

Ten

"ALEX, WAIT UP! THERE WAS something else in it!" Roz shrieked. The doors of the nightclub swinging closed behind her.

"Of course there wasn't." Alex turned. "I thought you said you were streetwise. You said you had smoked Skunk before?"

"I've smoked Cannabis. It's all the same."

"No it isn't. Different process: different part of the plant. You get different effects. Anyway, what's the problem? I had the same as you. Literally the same frigging spliff and I'm fine. Now, calm down. One minute you're laughing, the next, you're freaking out at some metal-head's tee shirt."

Roz tried hard to focus on his words. The tee shirt - yes, the logo of hell and monsters with skeletal fingers reaching out of the material, wanting to drag her into the picture to be lost there forever while the background music woefully warned of sin. And laughter: had she laughed? Had she found anything amusing? She was unsure now, but she had laughed longer than her weak diaphragm could be bothered; and had tried nursing her aching ribs with arms that were too heavy to move. But nothing had been funny then, and it sure as hell wasn't funny now. The devil, the supplier was in front of her and he didn't care. He didn't care that her brain was racing so fast, she suspected it would explode. His speech was so slurred and slow in comparison.

"What else was in it Alex, tell me? Please? This has never happened before. I don't know where I am. I can't control my brain," she moaned in a voice that seemed monstrous and deeper. This inner being was freaking her out.

"I've told you," Alex snarled, quietly. He glanced nervously at the doormen. "It was Class C. Now let go of me. I'm going home."

She clung to him, panicking as he tried pulling away. She needed to come down by clearing it out of her system, but how? She couldn't vomit. Not like Sophie who had drunk herself into a stupor, been ill in the toilets and gone home ages ago to her bed. No amounts of fingers down the throat would save her now. She was loosing her mind to some strange delirium. It was too late. She clung to hell's servant more desperately, yet he broke free and walked away, abandoning her.

"You can't leave me here!" Roz screamed.

"I'll call you."

"No you won't, you bastard. You're just the same as the rest of them. You can't leave me like this. What's happening to me?"

Alex marched back, grabbed her arms and in a droning voice, said, "Look. The reason why you're being like this is because you're brain is fucked already. The drug is just picking up on an anxiety, a guilt thing, and the fact that you've got a screw loose. And if you can't handle the heat, I reckon in future, you should stay out of the party." Determined this time to go, he sauntered off to find his car.

Roz slumped down onto a step in the shop doorway. She nursed her head in her hands to help contain her brain. She began rocking to somehow draw comfort. Images ran by of gliding lowly over desert sands, and hushed, indistinguishable voices rattled inside her skull. In reality, revellers passed chatting. A car accelerated then drew to a halt.

Alex wound down the window. "Hey, Roz, watch out for the paranoia. I've heard it's a bitch."

The car accelerated off, leaving Roz not wondering about his words but feeling somehow relieved. Contentment washed over her. She had found solace from deep within, a spiritual thing, a deeper meaning to life. Her mind sped on. No one had ever loved her, not even her wealthy parents. No one on this dimension gave a shit. Yet she had found a tranquil place within her heart, clarity within her soul. She was filled with love so strong, so peaceful; she could stay there forever.

She rocked. She smiled. - She felt immortal.

She knew all there was to know. She felt as though she had found God, as though he was inside showing her holy deserts, whispering secrets in a foreign tongue that from her essence she could understand. She could jump from the highest building and fly like an angel. She couldn't die she could only go home. She wasn't evil, was she? No, others were evil; the men with their tee shirts, the songs glorifying death.

"I said; where's Sophie?"

Trainers, jeans, black tee shirt, dark spiky hair; a familiar face in the orange glowing streetlight leaned close. "What's the matter; deaf or something?" Jon asked.

"Fuck you," Roz gabbled, her mind still rambling. She wanted to stay watching the desert sands. Loved up, she had better things to contemplate than listen to this cretin.

Beside Jon, Callum looked guardedly at the door, in case Sophie was around. "I shall leave you to it. Remember; not a word to a soul."

"Wait a minute," Jon said, returning his attention to Roz who, seeming to be in some alcoholic stupor, staggered to her feet and straightened up to him. "I asked you where's Sophie? Did you leave her in the club on her own?"

"What was that, cretin? Did poor little Jon lose his goddess?"

"Cretin; is that what you think?"

"Yeah: what's the matter, deaf or something?"

Jon couldn't believe the slapper had called him a cretin. Instead of her usual wariness, she was leaning squarely to him in confrontation. She was ablaze as she stared deep. Her lips, although free from the red lipstick were just as red naturally - real red.

"What are you looking at? I know your game. You're all cretins." She scoffed at Callum then Jon. "I'm using all my brain not just one brain cell like the rest of you morons. Deep down, you still think I'm an airhead."

"Well aren't you?"

"Far from it, you malicious freak. What's the matter, am I scaring you? That's it, I frighten you. You're not quite sure what to make of me because all you throw at me with that hateful mouth I bite back every time. All your empty threats don't bother me. I can see it in your eyes; you want to break my neck like you keep threatening? Well, just try it. I dare you. Go on - be my guest. I'm as clever as God. God is inside me. I'm more than your equal, worth more than a hundred of you, Jonny-boy."

"What?" Jon was stunned. Everything she said was beginning to make sense if he were to believe Callum.

"You heard, imbecile. What's the matter, chicken shit? Does the truth hurt? Had enough now? Want to take off like a bat-out-of-hell, like the rest of them at the first sign of trouble? I'm holy now. God has shown me his path. You're a poor and pathetic loser, Jonny."

Callum stepped closer to study Roz more carefully. Her words were gabbled, rolling off her tongue in some crazed state. In her eyes was madness. They also glistened. It was her words Callum took heed to. The truth was in her words. Perhaps she was cured enough to gain her soul back from God?

Jon felt his temper rise, considering her either brave or psychotic.

The loud mouth started blabbing again, "The trouble is with men like you, you're so shallow you're empty. You don't stop to think about the deeper meaning of life. Well, I've found God. I've found my soul. And from now on I'm going to use my intelligence. Sod all the little games you play because I know them all. And I'm worth more than that. I'm better than you could ever dream possible. So crawl back under your rock, or wherever it is you come from, and leave me to think."

"You are the one? You have the book?" Callum dared to ask.

"Piss off," Roz spat, her words flowing as fast as her brain could produce them. Although she had trouble remembering what she had just said, it must have been good because both guys seemed exasperated. They glanced at each other, mumbling words she could hardly care to hear only to regard her again.

"It was you who staked Tom? You killed my friend so callously?"

"Tom? What?" Roz shot, her brain searching for a Tom. "Oh, Tom was ages ago. He was gagging for it. But what's it got to do with you? I know I was desperate, but I'm not doing that stuff any more. I regret it all. I'm on a higher plane. Like I've told you, I'm cured."

"Fuck." Jon studied her, his anger mixed with horror. "How many have you done?"

Roz laughed. "More than you've had hot dinners. Shit, you lot are so weak. I just take my pick on who I fancy next, and just do them. But you've seen me in action so you'd know that. Anyway, all that's no good for my morals anymore so quit pestering. I've had a moment of clarity. I am truly redeemed; healed, rescued, fucking pardoned. So you can piss off because I've got more soul searching to do."

As Roz staggered off, Jon turned to Callum. "I knew it. That bitch has always known I'm a vampire. The way she's always been towards me makes sense. I just can't believe she's staked loads of us. I mean, how many of us are there?"

"It would appear there were countless. But how can we be sure she's the one?"

"I'm sure, without a single doubt. You should have met Destiny. Shit, I swear, you could put red hair on Roz and she'd be that crazed, psychotic bitch from hell." Jon watched her progress slowly along the pavement. She stopped to rub her head before moving on.

Callum said, "Perhaps we should observe her for a while longer during the course of these next few nights? Then, when we're one-hundred-percent sure, with the help of your friends, we could devise a strategy to overthrow her."

"Please yourself, but I'm telling you, mate, she's the one. We're wasting valuable time, pussy-footing about. She's only a woman."

"A cured vampire; and one mad enough to send you to the devil and ask questions later."

"Then we wait; just to be sure." As a group of nightclub goers walked past, Jon added, "I'm just going to find Sophie. Wait here, I'll be back in a minute."

"No, Jon." Callum grabbed his arm. "It's time I left you to your lover. Not only do you deserve each other, but also you deserve to be left in peace. Now go to her. I'll see you this next night. Perhaps we could meet in the Bat Inn Hand?"

"What about my reflection?" Jon asked, suddenly remembering the promise, above all else.

"I'll bring the glasses with me and a looking glass to suit. Now I must leave."

Without waiting for a reply, Callum bolted across the street, and began heading home to his loyal motorbike. He planned to take a long ride to anywhere. Watch the hedgerows speed past, the black tarmac blur. Go to anywhere that was further away from this place, this Sanctuary where the lady of his dreams would make love to another. How he would love to again crouch at her window and feast upon her beauty whilst she rested in the security of his gaze. To again see that leg jutting from beneath her covers...

His mind jolted. If, as Jon was convinced, Roz were the book-holder, the book would most likely be in that flat. Jon had told him that Roz was Sophie's flatmate when they had approached her sitting in the doorway. His mission could end at that flat. He had sat at Sophie's window, and all the while, hiding in her friend's room was the book of remedies to obtain normality. Even remedies beyond his wildest expectations, to beckon his lost soul back from oblivion like Roz so obviously had by the gleam in her eyes. Had God filled her with love like she had bragged? – A cure indeed.

Callum decided he would wake early and while the library assistants worked their Saturday morning shift, as read on the Library door, he would enter the flat and begin his search for the truth. If his quest concluded there, he would divulge all to Jon, his trusting friend and ally.

Feeling more optimistic, Callum decided to concentrate much as he dare on the mission. He had no choice. To visualise Sophie and what she was doing now, or in ten minutes or half an hour would most likely cause him to crash his Bess. Go headlong into the nearest tree in some blinding state and wrap the grinding metal around the sturdy trunk, until the agony from his injuries and the grief of his twisted machine surpassed the pain in his heart. Although the physical agony would only last two minutes, it would prove a welcomed release.

Tom had given him the motorbike, the protective leather clothing and helmet as a gift. Mourning his lost friend again, Callum wondered if he would dare approach Roz tomorrow when she would be sober. The pages he had discovered beneath Tom's bolster three nights ago were old and course parchment, both frail and yellowed. If Roz was the keeper of the book, she must have obtained it from someone else, through gift or theft. Callum surmised she was a modern woman, not as old as the parchment. She had to be.

Much as he tried to imagine her coming from any bygone age, he could think of none that suited her more than the present. The Victorians were promiscuous, and not as stuck-up as today's belief would grant. The suffragettes, the wars, and the rise of woman's rights were rife in his memory. Yet Roz seemed more than that. She could have lived through it all, evolved in her lifetime into such supremacy. She was forceful, powerful and spirited, not hiding behind batting eyelids and coy 'little woman' expressions. She was upfront, outspoken and seemed to relish every moment. She played with men's affections like roles reversed.

Callum lamented, if he were honest, he wouldn't confront her drunk or sober. She was too fast thinking, too fast talking, and without being ruled by emotions or plagued by compassion was, by far, too dangerous.

⁕

Jon threw his cigarette butt out the car window and accelerated faster along the high street when he caught a glimpse of Roz turning into a loading bay.

The dark wide area led into an alleyway that would take her directly to her road, cutting out a third of her walking distance home.

He slowed the car, watching those long legs stumble in her high-heeled boots. She grappled with a sidewall of a shop to help her walk straight. As she endeavoured to remain standing, he felt an involuntary sense of compassion.

"Roz, get in, I'll give you a lift!" he called. She turned, flipped him the 'v' sign and staggered onwards.

Bitch. Jon switched off the ignition and flung open the door. He had gone in the club, and not finding Sophie there, he supposed she must have gone home. But Roz hadn't helped him to find her, and still she refused to comply. He slammed the door shut and followed after her.

"Roz, wait up! You're in no fit state to get home. Look at you, you're wrecked."

He reached her, and felt alarmed by his emotions. Her blue eyes seemed frightened as though he was a monster, and she seemed more terrified than he could ever before remember. Was he really that bad? Did his appearance cause her such distress because she knew his strength - or because he made her face her truth?

"Will you show us the book, Roz? It could change us all. We wouldn't have to be like this. We wouldn't have to kill each night. You'd be saving us from damnation."

Roz couldn't figure what he was talking about. Her mind raced, paranoid that the devil was coming for her soul because she had tapped into something that should be left well alone. Although she was so afraid, so alone and utterly sorry, neither her mind nor the drug would let up. Both tormenting her further, she supposed the cretin wasn't really there. The whole thing was an illusion; her worse nightmare coming to life.

Cursing beneath her breath, she blanked Jon and began staggering away. His temper was rising. He couldn't believe that even after pleading with her, she could ignore him and just walk away from his plight like the uncaring hussy she was. "You ignorant cow, why won't you help us?" he hollered.

"I'm not listening. You're not really here. You're not real," she sang, clutching her hands against her ears. Humming a tune, she knocked into a stack of cardboard boxes before lurching onwards to the alleyway.

Like a spark igniting doused petrol adrenaline exploded. Flaming rage grabbed him, and much as he knew he was loitering on dangerous ground, he couldn't walk away. He tried to calm down and ran after her. She refused to acknowledge him. He grabbed her bare arm roughly and swirled her round. "Give us the book."

"What? You want me to open the library now so you can get a book out, is that it?" Roz sensed the conversation was real, and he was really standing so close because the pain from his vice-like grip was excruciating.

"Quit playing games, Roz. I'm asking you nicely. Can we borrow the book? We can do a deal. We get to copy the book and Callum will give you back the two pages you staked Tom for."

"Let go of me, you're hurting."

"Didn't you hear me?" Jon seethed at her indifference. He grabbed her other arm, shaking her violently. "For fucksake, you little slapper, I'm not going to beg any more. If you don't help us willingly..." Pain!

He gasped, feeling the sharp and unpredictable agony in his groin and lower abdomen since Roz had kneed him hard between his legs. He was stunned. She pushed him from her and staggered away, leaving him doubled over. Anger mounted on top of agony. His senses were growing sensitive.

He tried ignoring the sudden awareness of his surroundings, the acidic smell of trash but he couldn't ignore his bodily warnings. He had to get back to the car. The pain throbbed like nothing else; weakening him, his knees threatened to buckle, and an unfamiliar nauseas feeling began churning his insides. Two minutes were too long coming for relief, and he wondered briefly how mortal men coped? - Bitch. He would get her back for this. One way or another she would pay the price.

He limped towards the car in a race against hunger. Mildly, he realised Roz was heading home. She was going home to Sophie, his sweet innocent angel. And the slapper was as angry as hell and raving like a loony. He saw Roz slump against the wall as she made it into the alley, and knew he couldn't let her reign her rage over Sophie. Sophie was in danger - mortal danger. But not from him, never from him: but from another Destiny. As the pain dissolved away, he realised he had to gain her friendship, grovel, be nice, calm her down and make her see sense and fast before his conscience faded and he would no longer care.

As Jon approached, Roz battled between reality and illusion. One part of her brain told her all the weirdness was drug-related and that she would wake in the morning with her feet on the ground and never touch the mind-bending stuff again. The other part of her brain could see the nightmare returning; the one man she couldn't abide was suddenly in front and droning words she couldn't care to make sense of. "I'm not listening to you. I'm not. I'm not. I couldn't care less. You're not real..." she chanted, cutting him dead.

Jon's temper surged higher. He had tried being sympathetic, yet she had shot him down using that motor mouth. Perhaps now he should just slap her? This thought had little effect on his conscience. The entire situation was now volatile as was his susceptible body. Persistently, she chanted some more. Her blue eyes, darting to either side of him, refused contact with his. He grabbed her face, crushing her mouth into an opened pout and forcing her to pay attention. He had to warn her. She just had to see sense. Time was of the essence now and every second that ticked past was one less to get away.

Roz fell silent. Her aggressor slightly loosened his grasp on her face. She watched his mouth moving and, by his eyes, realised something was wrong. They were angry, glaring with familiar contempt. He was going to break her neck. She had seen that look before. What if it was real and not an illusion? She had to concentrate, listen. Watching his mouth moving again, the volume of his voice came into focus.

"I'm changing, Roz, you know? My conscience is fading. Just let this drop and I'll see you tomorrow night; we'll discuss it then. And don't mention to Sophie that you're a vampire. It's not fair on her. She'll need to be told tactfully, okay?"

Vampire; surely she had misheard? "Fuck off, Jon. You're unreal." To her astonishment he let go of her face, grabbed her arms and pushed her hard against the wall. The hollow sound of skull against brick echoed in her ears. Pain shot to all areas and she couldn't locate the injury. Jon was still mouthing words and she became aware of the ringing in her ears and the pain in her arms. Her hands were tingling, free from blood. And he looked so serious. What was he saying?

"See? You're not so bloody strong when you're pissed out of your mind. I could break that neck, and I don't see what you would do about it, you worthless little tart. You might be a cured vampire but you could lose your soul again, where as mine is still gone. I'm a vampire with nothing to lose. So now who's got the upper hand, huh?"

Her hands were numb, her head banging, and as the word *vampire* cropped up yet again, Roz remembered Alex warning about paranoia being a bitch. That's it, she thought, paranoia. She laughed. She looked Jon in the eyes and thought what a clever and dangerous drug she had flowing through her veins. Vampires; yeah whatever...He let go of her blood-drained arms, but was still talking urgently, angrily. Saying something about her being real evil, sadistic... She laughed louder, drowning out the pleading words that he lisped, all the while watching his lips. And there was something erotic in his mouth. In his appearance something was different. Squinting, she noticed his teeth. Four fangs were slowly lengthening from his gums as he spoke. She thought he had used the word *vampire*, and now her eyes were seeing it. The wonders of the human mind! How exciting. How erotic.

She fell silent and, as Jon was about to finish his sentence, suddenly she leaned closer. He saw her face approaching, her blue alive eyes mellowing into something less fearful and not mocking. Trying to comprehend her manoeuvre, her lips suddenly met his, pressing hard, drowning all words. Her mouth was opening his, delivering a strong deep kiss and he found his mouth responding unhesitatingly as his diminishing brain searched about in the gloom for consequences. His insides leaped somersaults as she grasped the back of his head for more. His entire body responding to the kiss and his penis hardening, his thoughts turned to Sophie. Distantly she was there, her image beckoning him from this danger of kissing Roz.

And it felt good. Her lips were masterful in their manipulation. Her tongue sought his. That solid muscle full of hunger and lust was prodding in his mouth, darting in and back out then ran along his teeth in such eroticism his passion shook him with shock. But all this was wrong. As his tongue involuntarily danced in the dark with hers, he realised his true logic was fading. The vampire within was preparing to reign. He had to get away, get to the car urgently. He loved Sophie. She meant everything to him. He didn't need this harlot giving him grief.

The man inside did battle with his demons and was winning for all of a second. But then he tasted it - a mild sweetness.

A familiar sweetness, so subtle it was minuscule. That distant and delicate bouquet of human blood was engulfing his airways. Tiny amounts of energising cells coated his tongue, as her tongue ran over his. It grabbed all other attention. He was losing his conscience so fast he could easily ignore it, and his reasons for needing to leave her mouth and push her away were no longer manifesting. Sophie's image faded away.

His teeth were long, extending to full length, and they seemed to be sharper. Although Roz felt the cut on her tongue, she had come to the conclusion to go with the drug and not fight its effects. Illusion or not, she was having a good time. To her delight, Jon withdrew his tongue and caught hers between his front teeth. He held her tongue there in a strange, yet erotic act, and abandoning her lips, he took the full extent of her eager tongue in his mouth and began to suck. Her tongue was captured. To her, it was an extreme act of lust, different than she had ever encountered in her past. Vaguely she realised she was doing her most favourite pastime with possibly the most passionate and erotic lover she was ever likely to meet. The pain in her tongue was throbbing to each mighty pull as he sucked harder. Roz moved her lips again onto his and felt his hands on her silk black dress. In one sharp yank, he ripped her dress open down its full length.

The vampire shot his hands inside her dress, lifted her and moved sideways to a stack of plastic crates where he plonked her down all the while sucking the red nectar from her mouth. While the man in him pulled down his zip and freed his penis ready to have her, the vampire abruptly left her tongue and without looking at the victim's face, he flicked her blonde hair off her shoulder and fixated on her shimmering pale neck.

To Roz, every movement he did seemed extreme and direct with no messing, no hanging around. He knew precisely what he was doing and what he wanted. She realised he was going to have what he wanted whether she liked it or not. This thought drenched her pants. She'd allow him to do anything. She could think of nothing she'd try and prevent this sex god from doing. He tore her bra from her, chaffing her skin in the process. He tore her flimsy thongs from her in the same uncaring fashion, and her excitement grew so vigorously, her juices were coursing down her legs. Then, he grabbed her knees, and, as his mouth fell onto her shoulder and moved directly along to the nape of her neck, he yanked her legs so wide apart and so forcefully, her muscles went into spasms.

The pain in her neck was sharp, burning as he seemed to be pulling at her. The pain in her legs was excruciating because he was holding them too far apart and too tightly. But the shooting pain from the hot solid flesh that forced its way up inside her, was so severe, it stole her breath. Although she had never realised she liked pain, suddenly, she couldn't get enough. With her arms behind her, holding plastic, she supported herself. Moving her hips in time with his, she pushed for more pain, for all he had to offer. Although she hadn't had chance to glimpse his manhood in the pale light of the alleyway, she now knew he had more than enough to fill her.

Drinking her blood delighted the vampire beyond all boundaries. Because his whole body was eager for more blood, his sexual pleasures were being dwarfed by the taste so divine. Vaguely, Jon realised her name was Roz, but she could have been any one, any piece of meat. He pushed harder, wanting to feel the sexual stimulation as much as the vampire was enjoying her taste. He moved with deeper, sharper thrusts to appease his desires.

The woman gasped, convulsing to his movement in a frenzied and eager state. He couldn't care whether she was enjoying herself or not, but her movements were threatening to dislodge her neck from him. So, letting go of one leg, the vampire grabbed her hair and held her head still to keep her neck from escaping his teeth. Releasing her other leg, he held her rear to control her movements. Her legs remained open, not clamming up or entrapping him to restrict his movements. She allowed him the freedom as in her own delirium she squealed and gasped to each forceful thrust.

Her insides being prodded so violently, Roz could feel the end in sight. She gasped. Her orgasm demanded she gasp louder. Crying out in despair, scared she would loose it, scared he would stop, her failing mind began to swoon, her body began to tire and weaken. Energy erupted against him. Like a tidal wave it washed over her. She shook, shuddered then let out more gurgling cries. He muted her mouth with a hand that gagged her, which aroused her some more until star-like dust particles flooded her vision from all sides. Blackness blotted her view. Unconsciousness was coming to take her. Her arms failed to support her, her head swooned again, until his movements and the incredible pain and ecstasy died a death.

As the woman flopped, the vampire tightened his grip on her head by scrunching her hair more tightly, and, securing her neck to his sunken teeth, continued drawing her life force. Her beautiful, mind-blowing nectar streamed over his tongue to the back of his throat. He swallowed. He pulled in the next mouthful from her flesh. Although her legs had flopped and her back and arms had given way, he supported her without stopping and without thought, until he finished his main course.

His stomach filled, the vampire left the victim's blackened neck and released her head so it fell hitting the wall. More empty skull on brick. He continued moving, vacantly noticing her eyes were closed. He studied her grey face. Her red lips were now pale blue. Her exposed breasts jigging to each mighty thrust. His eyes travelled over her flat stomach. He watched himself enter her, then pull back to almost leave, before thrusting against her end again. Those bruised lips still seemed eager to take him whole, his eruption saturated those hungry lips further.

He withdrew and stood back. After tidying himself, the vampire took his packet of cigarettes from out of his jeans pocket and lit one. He scanned the scene; the flimsy bra torn in half, red pants lying on the ground alongside them. Indifferently, he blew out smoke, flicked the ash and was about to walk off when a nagging feeling told him not to leave the feed there to be discovered.

His cigarette drooping from his lips, he recovered her underwear and shoved them inside the waistband of his jeans. He grabbed her arm and hauled the dead weight into a fireman's lift and carried her to his car.

The high street was deserted, although he couldn't care less. He opened the back door and dropped the lifeless corpse onto the backseat. To fit her in, he crammed her head against the far door. He folded her eternally long legs, so her feet were resting on the floor, and slammed the door shut against her knees.

The vampire jumped into the driver's seat. Although logic hadn't yet returned, he sensed he would have to dump the body. His brain held no true reasoning as he drove off for the den. Everything was bliss. He could go fast, take the next bend skidding on his roof and so what? There were no consequences. All he could tell was that he was enjoying the acidic taste of his cigarette, the aftermath of great sex and the aftertaste of human blood. Death was grand.

The green car turned into the perimeter road of the southern forest. The headlights flicked on because it occurred to the driver he hadn't done so sooner. A foot rose high, slamming down to the brake pedal.

The car screeched, stopping in a dead halt. The body in the back hit the back of the front seats then fell to jam in the floor-well.

Jon turned slowly, raising his vision again. Too afraid to look, too scared to acknowledge... his eyes met the crumpled mess of his angel's best friend.

"Oh, shit."

He fumbled for the door handle and flung himself free of the gruesome car as though it was about to explode. "Fucking shit! - Oh, shit, no." He swirled around in horror to look back at the car.

After a moment's hesitation, Jon went to the rear door and flung it open, then grabbed the dead weight from the floor-well, and shoved it on the back seat. It was as though he was seeing it for the first time. Running both hands through his hair, he checked the deserted road. The crumpled body was a mess. The black bruised neck with its four holes mortified him. The exposed body with broken dress ashamedly began arousing him again.

He did his best to tidy her by pulling the material over her breasts to cover them, and covering her damaged neck with a handful of yellow hair before fanning some more over her deader than dead face.

He slammed the door shut in despair, and began hopping and dancing about in the dead of night like an Indian Brave. His emotions ran amok. He tried regaining his thoughts that were reeling out of control.

The abhorrence of his actions came flooding back. Jon turned to the car and kicked the door. Not dented enough, he kicked it harder, and then punched both fists down hard onto the roof before breathlessly resting his head there. He closed his eyes.

The last time he had cried, he'd been seven. Although he wasn't crying now, he sensed those tears returning.

He booted the car again, frowning back any such weakness. Vampires don't cry.

Shit. He had killed someone. Committed murder, necrophilia, had practically raped her. His mind rambled. No. She had wanted it; had begged for it. She had wound him up to it after he had warned her he was changing. Well one thing was for sure, his rambling mind concluded; she wasn't the cured vampire or the keeper of the remedies.

He rubbed his face and groaned. Now he was in the shit, up to his neck, drowning in it. And what was he going to do about it? He tried to think, tried not to remember how much he had enjoyed her: the blood, her tightness surrounding his penis.

"Shit," he cursed, stepping back from the car and peering cautiously in through the window at the lifeless body.

Sophie would be devastated. Absolutely no doubt about it. He wouldn't be hauled over the coals for this little number, oh no. He would be dumped on the spot. If Sophie were to shun him, hate him with all her heart, it would be the mildest of punishments, and he could expect nothing less. If she were to go public and tell all, he wouldn't blame her. People would no longer look to the skies for UFO's; they would take up their crucifixes and lock up their daughters. Sophie was so pure other angels would weep in envy.

Staring at the inanimate body of her best friend, Jon felt more and more like he was chained to a railroad track waiting for an express. With anxiety and paranoia flooding through his bloodstream, Jon leaned against the door. In despair, he considered his options. He could bury the body in the remotest parts of the woods, never to be found. Perhaps, burn it to a crisp and bury it. Or, burn it, dismember it, and bury each part over the radius of forestland. His thoughts were never ending. His options were confusing him, that it seemed his true logic hadn't yet returned, and if he didn't know better he would have presumed he had taken a substance that had stolen true reasoning. He would have to calm down. He needed time to think things through properly. His mind was erratic, and if he did anything in haste it would surely backfire.

Eventually, he got back into the driver's seat and pulled off, aware of death lying behind him and that he was the cause. No matter how much she had initiated it, he was the damned cause.

Eleven

Jon leaned into the car and grabbed the body, cradling it. "Shit, shit – shit." Her hair was a tumble of yellow and matted pink, her partially naked body pale grey. As he carried her across the dirt track to the mine, he could feel her growing cooler with each stride.

His thoughts slowing now, he wanted to look at her face. But death was in his arms, heavy and cold as marble. Although he faced death every night, this was different. Although he killed for his own selfish needs, countless creatures on countless nights this was so macabre it seemed unreal; and if it weren't for her deadweight and soft hair tickling his bare arm, he'd have thought it an illusion.

He went to the sleeping area, contemplating placing her on his bed; but he couldn't. He went through the adjacent curtain and laid her on Liam's bed.

Her eyes were closed. Her eye make-up was slightly smudged which enhanced the death-stricken look of black on pale grey. Her lips were together, tinged blue and purple and turned slightly at the edges as though she was finding pleasure in his despair, still mocking him even from the other side. Bitch. His conscience turned on him. Her neck was still blackened with four deep holes seeping blood. His heart plunging and his stomach jittery, he reached to her hair, which was fanned out, and again covered the wound so he didn't have to acknowledge his actions.

Jon stood back and lit a cigarette, wondering how he would dispose of the body so no person or animal would ever unearth it. Intuitively, he knew he had barely two hours before first light and deep sleep, so he had to think fast. Yet, he couldn't think. Death was in the flesh before him. Her soul had gone on over that she could even be watching over him as he watched over her.

Jon checked but could see no ghost, no faint image glaring daggers or mouth yap yapping at him. But still the thought was enough. He should show her some respect since he hadn't during her life.

As he moved towards the base of the bed, he allowed his eyes to glide over those long slender legs and, without realising it, his fingers ran their course; feeling their coolness, her skin - over the knee - on down the slender shin bone to her ankle and up to the tips of her toes. He drew hard on his cigarette, glancing back at her face then down at her foot then slowly up those legs again. She was lying on her back with her legs and arms straight; something wasn't right.

He went to her torso and tidied her broken dress to meet, although the buttons had popped off and some of the holes had torn. He lifted her arm, bent it and placed it gently down across her chest, then repeated the process with her other arm. He stepped back to admire the 'rest in peace' pose, cold fingers of reality prickled at his back, and instead of letting her be, he chucked her arms back to her sides.

"Shit."

Her eyes were still closed. And they would be. She was hardly likely to sit bolt upright, eyes glaring and mouth damning him, cursing, only to jump off the bed and chase him round the mine like a crazed zombie with a piece of wood in her dead hands to stake it through his cold evil heart, all the while screaming, 'pay back time you mother fucker.'

Conscious that he was staring at her neck, Jon instinctively leaned closer. The fear of her suddenly grabbing him by his neck, to shake him and throttle him with strength of a million dead faded as he waited for what he imagined he'd seen.

It came again; a subtle movement in her throat. Jon lunged for her neck, flicked her hair from the bruised wounds, and watched more blood quietly seep out through crusted congealing blood surrounding each hole. Concentrating on her throat, he heightened his sense of touch; with shaky fingers, felt her neck for the next pulse. It sprang against his sensitive fingers. She wasn't dead. Not yet anyway.

He had to get her to a hospital, get some blood into her and fast. How much had he taken: five, ten pints? He hadn't a clue. The stag had filled him enough. It was anger and desire, not pure hunger that had manipulated his transgression this time so perhaps she stood a chance. But blood transfusions drip in. The nearest hospital was fifteen miles away. And more crucially, what the hell could he say? 'Sorry nurse we had a little accident. Her neck might need a band-aid, and I'd better be going because the sun's coming up and then I'll need a burns unit?'

"Oh, shit." She was going to die regardless of his discovery.

Her pulse was fading beneath his fingers. Each moment she was slipping further from this world. There was no time, no excuses. Why hadn't he checked for any vital signs when he had realised she was lying in the back seat? Why hadn't he opened her eyes to see she still had her soul for her eyes would still have been gleaming at him? Because he was a jerk, his conscience shouted. A numbskull! Drivelling in self pity like a bloody great sissy, that's why.

"Roz, wake up!" he pleaded. Grabbing her shoulders and lifting her, he shook her violently so her head flopped and jerked to his vigour.

"Damn it, Roz. Please, you've got to wake up!"

There were no changes in her smiling expression. Her eyes remained ignoring him. After lowering her, his keen eye detected another pulse. She wasn't giving in easily. She had loved life and lived hers to the full. With a determined grasp she was clinging on to every last moment, relishing in its final throes of glory.

He slapped her face several times. She refused to retaliate. All he now wanted was for her to wake, call him a murderous bastard and hope he rots in hell. To hit him with both fists and even knee him again, three times as hard. But she just lay there so lifeless, on the brink, and wouldn't give him that satisfaction. Far as he knew, she had hated him and with good reason. Briefly wondering now where his loathing of her had started, he could only remember detesting her on sight the first time Sophie had introduced him to her. From that first instant, he hadn't let up, had shown no mercy in taunting her at every opportunity. He had always been nasty to her and contemptuous to her lovers. She had always retaliated, always voiced her opinion, until eventually, it seemed like a game - a dangerous game. In the battle of wills, they would bicker. Both equally defiant, insults would fly back and forth. But now she was winning; lying quiet and baring witness to his mind reeling in despair. Her lips turned in a smile proving she was revelling in it.

She was mocking him still. Jon felt the overwhelming temptation to leave her to die, turn his back, fly out the mine and return in two hours when it would all be over. What about Sophie? His conscience shook him; demanding he snap out of it, wake up! Sophie's best friend was dying, and what was he doing? - Nothing.

There was an option. A possibility that mortified him: tore him in two. If he wasn't able to get her to mortal help so they could transfuse her own particular brand of blood, perhaps he could administer his own?

But then, much as it was his blood it was Destiny's blood. She was the bare root who caused this disaster. Roz would become one of them by losing her soul to limbo. She would become part of Destiny's legacy. He couldn't do it. To imagine the scene of dripping his vampire blood into her mouth repulsed him. He turned away from her failing pulse, and all he could see was Sophie crying; her pretty eyes so full of life, so full of hate. He saw her lips whispering, 'Why, Jon? Why?'

"Shit, Soph. What am I going to do?" he asked. His voice brought him back to reality. Her image faded of her shaking her head, scorning him for being weak: weak for the temptation of heated sex and the taste of human blood and now weak because he had no courage to rectify his mistake.

He swirled round at Roz. Her neck still leaked her sweetness; her dying pulse still flitted once in a while. - And her soul? He opened her eyes to see them still glistening. - What of her soul? Her soul would be preparing to go to a better place than this hell.

If only he could think straight. Clear his head.

"Forgive me."

Guilt riddled, he put his wrist to his mouth and with normal blunt teeth pinched a blue vein with all his force. The skin broke and bled. He was mesmerised as the blood leaked a winding path down his arm and dripped off his elbow. This was his pain, his blood, his consequence.

Gently, Jon parted the blue, cool lips of his angel's best friend. His arm shaking, he moved the stream of blood across her face, dripping a red line that would be torturing his soul as it screamed, pleading with him from the bowels of the inferno.

He paused short of her open mouth. His blood, splattering on her face, ran down her cheek to her hair, which was already matted in her own blood from the wounds he had inflicted in greed and lust. The wounds he had tried to conceal and deny.

Jon moved his arm over Roz's mouth and his blood dripped in. It ran to the back of her throat. He gripped a tight fist and released, gripped and released, and pumped in some more.

The stream stopped. His two minutes were up; skin knitting together. His blood on his arm and her face and hair, dissolved and disappeared.

Had the quantity been enough? Panic gripped him. Time teetered on a pinnacle. He studied her neck still bruised and noticed her pulse had died. He opened her eyelids. Her blue eyes were dull as any he had ever seen. Her chest was still. With heightened hearing, he could detect no sounds of her heart kick starting.

She was dead.

He had been too late; her saving blood had been too late coming that she had died a mortal death in time for her soul to make it to higher ground. Considering this, he wasn't sure whether he felt relieved or devastated. His emotions were raw. He had scrambled about frantically in search of the right answers. And fate had done its bidding irrespectively.

Sudden gushing of air caused Jon to stagger backwards as Roz sucked in full lung capacity. Her chest fell as air exhaled from her gasping mouth. She pulled at the air above her, desperately sucking in more to gush into her hollow-sounding chest. The air rattled against her ribcage and, with sensitive hearing, Jon heard a solid thud spring to life. The irregular beats grew forceful, speeding faster before slowing to a rhythmic tune and then stabilising. Her raspy breathing quietened.

Jon expected her dead eyes to spring open and stare, gob smacked at his. Instead, her blood pumped flushed pinks over her. Her distasteful blue/purple lips returned in a flurry to brilliant red. The holes and black bruising on her neck healed to pink and disappeared. Her matted red hair returned to yellow. And, daring to touch her bare arm so slightly, her skin was again warm. Her eyes remained closed.

Jon retracted his hand from her and let out an agonising sigh. He rubbed his face to calm his adrenaline, through parted fingers, he eyed his creation.

Her long bare legs seemed to have grown in length, seemed to be more perfect. Her revealed tummy button seemed sunken in an even flatter tummy. Her perfect breasts, rising and falling to each healthy breath could be glimpsed as the material had fallen away somewhat, and he wondered how he had not cared to touch her there while he'd drunk from her earlier. Her lips were his favourite colour and he remembered their taste; that tongue so damned sweet, prodding, seeking out his.

He absorbed her entire length down and back up. It occurred to Jon she was a very sexy woman; a temptation for any man to succumb. She wasn't just attractive she was possibly beautiful; but then, the motor mouth was shut.

Face to face, he whispered, "Roz?"

She didn't stir. Perhaps she was in some form of rehabilitation after being starved of oxygen for so long? Although Jon feebly tried to arouse her, truthfully he didn't want her to wake.

Her lips were before his - so red, so tempting. Perhaps he could kiss them, wake her softly? But then all hell would break loose. She would fight him, scream at him, throw a real bender with vampire strength equal to his own; and he was enjoying the peace too much to tempt that.

Using the last hour before first sun, Jon took time to clean her free of him. He removed her dress and with the underwear he had retrieved in his waist band, had dropped them into the bin and then dressed her in a pair of black boxer shorts and red tee shirt which, as it reached her middle thighs was longer than most dresses he had seen her wear. He tidied her hair as best he could with his fingers, and all the while refused to imagine how she would react to her new existence.

Half an hour to spare, he stood back and smoked a well-deserved cigarette. He was pleased for the job hadn't proved easy. He had done everything without sexual connotation and he had done it for her.

He looked upon her body again, now decent, now dressed, and let his memory drift and eyes wander over the sexuality of it. Only then, did he touch her how he realised he'd wanted.

He placed his hand on her leg and it gently travelled down to her knee, then slowly back up, then more hesitantly on up. His hand paused, loitering short of the boxer shorts. As though her skin was ablaze and scorching him, he snatched his hand away and remembered Sophie.

"Fuck it!" he cursed under a gasping breath. He went to his own bed.

He lay there gazing at the crannies in the black ceiling; waiting for sleep to come take him from this madness, wanting to go to Roz again and feel her skin, kiss her legs, her breasts.

How could he even think it when his undying love was for Sophie? How much of a cad was he? How much did he want Roz to wake now and enter his sleeping area with those long legs; those bare legs that would approach him so seductively, then climb aboard and straddle him, as her sweet mouth reach down to devour his.

Shit. Come on sleep. Now would be a bloody good time. Come on!

But, it seemed the sun outside halted below the skyline.

It's no good. He sprang off the bed. He flicked the curtain from his way, went to his sleeping protégé and scooped up her resting body to take back to his bed. He lay beside her and watched her sleep.

Still the damned sun was hesitant to rise.

Would she be so livid she'd want to stake him how he and the others had sought to stake Destiny? The game was over. No more would he be detrimental to her. No more could he regard Roz without damning himself for his actions. She was his equal. She deserved respect. They shared the same blood so she was one of the gang; for better or worse. No more excuses. He rested his arm across her tummy in a need to protect. Was he betraying Sophie by this act? This need to feel close to some one, was it so terrible? He couldn't figure. His arm didn't want to move. The gentle rise and fall of her peaceful breathing soothed him and he found a certain comfort from the closeness that would stay beside him during daylight hours. Anyway compared to all he had done, this cuddle was nothing. As his heart slowed from all its havoc;

and dementia found solace, it crossed his fading mind that he could do this each and every day from here to...

The sun slid over the horizon to kiss the forests, spreading daylight over Sanctuary.

Twelve

CALLUM'S EYES SPRUNG OPEN WITH an adrenaline rush and searched the bleakness. Where was he; and why was he awake at this ungodly hour? He heightened his vision. The ceiling glared down. Sleep commandeered him. His eyes closed. He should sleep, could sleep...

Roz, Jon, the book, Tom, Sophie - the ceiling flicked from black to white like strobe lighting. He bolted upright. He had to stay alert.

He fell out of bed and began pacing the floor. He read the clock since his intuition for knowing time worked better with the journeying moon, than with the rising sun. He had woken earlier than planned, and couldn't leave for Roz's flat since they weren't due to start work for another half an hour. The bed was welcoming. He paced faster, working his legs.

He felt despair. He had made love with a friend's lover, a woman that wasn't his for the taking. Without hesitation, he had potentially caused so much hostility, he had betrayed a friend that was willing to help him and take him into his gang like one of the guys. He burned deeper with guilt; a small voice of the woman echoed in his memory, 'Passion is a powerful emotion, and desire a dangerous tool.'

"But love is the greatest of all killers," he answered aloud to the voice of Sophie. She was the jewel in the quagmire; this was love and it was killing him again, oh so slowly.

He hadn't been seeking the stuff; a new, deep and alive love with its dreaded curse weighing him down because since he had been twenty-mortal-years-old he had loved only one; his Sarah. She had been a lady of a higher calibre; a sophisticated genteel of the same age available to marry, but not to whom she could choose. She had arrived by carriage at her uncle's established estate and was to stay for a month with her cousins. Callum had been a stable-hand, tending horses; and Sarah loved horses. She spent many hours riding solitary, leaving her cousins practising music away from fresh air. Then, one day, she requested Callum's company, since she had grown weary of her own. They rode together, talking and laughing, soon after, meeting at secret rendezvous and kissing.

Now, Callum could picture her face so close to his, her delightful giggle and her plush, long skirts swishing to her elegant walk. And for the first time in one-hundred-and-thirty-years, he felt free from the burden; no heartbreak, no devastation for his love she ignored.

She had left a few weeks later to go home to the South where she soon after married a distinguished gentleman from her own class and breeding. Callum was mortified. He had loved her. He would have given anything to keep her. Yet he hadn't been good enough for her to marry. Not worthy enough to have truly known her, nor respectable or rich enough for her family.

With a heavy heart that never failed to cause him pain, he resigned his post and joined the Merchant Navy to take to the seas and ride out his sorrow. Within five years, he had been to all four corners of the earth, seen countless countries and taken many lovers. Their nationalities were irrelevant. The language barrier was no problem, and if she brought along a girl friend - the more the merrier. Yet still he grieved for his Sarah. All the lovers and whores in the world were no tonic for his dying heart.

At the age of twenty-five, whilst sailing the oceans to return to England an epidemic broke out on board ship: a fever that was to take many a sailor's life, as their bodies were buried at sea in increasing amounts. How those days of mayhem dragged, as each hypochondriac felt a prickle on the brow. Callum remained healthy, and couldn't have cared if he were to die. He was already dead. His heart held no yearning to live and he had abandoned all family in Ireland ten years previously to seek out his fortune. No one would miss him. Yet the fever took those alongside him: young fathers to the right, loved sons to the left. The good, the religiously faithful dropped like flies. Yet still the damned fever wouldn't shroud itself upon his begging.

Then most fatefully, three days away from England whilst lying in his bunk and listening to the whispered prayers and gentle sobs from the fellow crew that prickle broke on his brow. Fever bestowed itself, and at long last, rendered his brain disorientated and his body to drip with sweat.

He drifted from the subliminal to reality as the ship docked to port on a sunny afternoon, laden with goods. Only once the ship had been unloaded of its cargo, was Callum moved to top deck. In hushed tones, the remaining sailors proclaimed his death would occur before morning and left him lying on the boards, abandoning him and the cursed vessel.

Callum lay under the shimmering stars and silvery full moon with the boards creaking and the motion of the waves gently rocking. Still he drifted. He wasn't fighting death; it could have come to fetch him gladly. Through a haze of hallucination, he glimpsed the Grim Reaper fly over, wearing a swishing black cape.

Death flew onwards and Callum thought the Grim Reaper had missed him. But Death diverted course, circling around to make another flyby. He dropped to the upper deck, and Death, dressed in a black cape and black hat, stared down. His number was up. No more grieving for his Sarah, and thank God. Callum drifted fitfully coming back to consciousness, aware once more of Death loitering. Then Death shot into the air and dropped down beside him, and still Callum didn't care. He had grown up with images of the Grim Reaper with scythe held with skeletal fingers. Death lowered his face to study Callum more closely; he had long black hair and his face had skin, and in his hand was a long black cane with a silver knob. Not the Grim Reaper. Deliriously, Callum opted for the alternative, and uttered, 'Let the devil take me'. The devil threw back his head and laughed mightily to the moon.

The devil stopped laughing and smiled down with devious dark eyes and long white fangs, but no horns, and in a smooth deep voice said, 'Maybe, the devil shall take you, dear sir; but not this night.' Then the devil lowered his face to deliver a sharp burning pain in Callum's neck and as the fever took his mind back to the subconscious, or the devil took his soul to hell; still he didn't care.

Callum wiped the moisture from his eyes, cursing at his sentimentality; always he wore his heart on his sleeve for all to see and then again wondered if that had been the reason Tom had saved him? Could Tom have sensed his willingness to die and his aching heart? He didn't know, for Tom had given no reasons and Callum had never dared ask. Perhaps it had been because Callum had made him laugh by equating him to the devil? For also, as Callum woke all those years ago to find himself in some strange four poster bed with red rich covers and the devil smiling menacingly at him from the foot of the bed, Callum had asked him if this was hell? Again, Tom had laughed.

"Oh, my dear friend, why all this pain? These last six weeks since your demise have been hell! Why didn't you tell me so I could help? Between us, we could have defeated Roz, I'm sure. Why did you not speak of her? You could have warned me of her trickery. And now you are gone from me forever. And lo, in the midst of coming to this place, I find a love so true, I'm breathless, my friend. Breathless, do you hear?" Callum asked, desperately. He sank onto the bed, weakened. "Her name is Sophie. She is gentle as the softest breeze that kisses the face, and vulnerable as any a small babe in arms. She has been a tonic, so help me she has. No longer do I feel eternal mourning for Sarah. Yet, more grief upon more sorrow, not only do I find myself befriending her lover to such an extent that I can see him come to no harm, but I feel obligated to leave their love intact, finish the mission and leave with a dying heart yet again. Am I so awful that I must spend another century or so, grieving for another love lost? - And in a century from now, will I again find another lady so fair, lose my heart so gladly, only to then lose that love?" Callum shook his head to his misery. "I am in a perpetual nightmare where my conscience is my downfall, my friend, and I can't escape. So be it then. I'll find the book, find the cures, and leave my heart in Sanctuary never to return."

Callum began to dress ready for the blistering sun, scheming to ride to the outskirts of town and enter All Saints Road from the other end, so not to pass the girls on their way to the library. Being old and as wise, he would then use one of his many skills to break into the flat without anyone suspecting he had been there.

He could hardly contain his growing anxiety. Only after he had dressed in his leather and his crash helmet was secured, did the excitement of finishing his mission deliver him the energy to carry it out.

Fifteen minutes later, he was standing in Sophie's bedroom with the window open. Breaking in had been simpler than anticipated. He had parked discreetly in an alleyway. When he walked closer to the flat, he had noticed she had left her window open. Free from view of any eyewitnesses, he had sprung upwards, landing on the roof familiar to him. Assuming a position of a sniper, he had crawled along its apex, and jumped down to her window ledge, where, in a blink of an eye, he had flown in.

Keeping his tinted visor down for protection from partial daylight, Callum scanned his surroundings. He heightened his hearing and listened for any sounds in the nearby vicinity; a clock ticking, the fridge humming and, below foot, a music box chiming a lullaby to soothe. Callum opened the bedroom door and stepped into the hall. He peered into the kitchen then the living room. Passing the bathroom, he went to Roz's bedroom door and opened it to the disarray.

Magazines, shoes and clothes littered the floor. More clothes hung from the furnishings. Callum stood amongst the mess, wearing his protective armour because the air was contaminated with sun. Where to begin? He had to find the book. He craved normality.

⚜

The air was still. No breeze lightened the intense heat as the burning sun shone down from a blue cloudless sky. Sophie longed for a breeze, for clouds to smother the baking sun that prickled at her bare shoulders and face. Perhaps she wouldn't mind the discomfort so much if the blessed thing could change the colour of her skin from a dazzling white to a bronze warm brown. But then, she reminded herself, although she had no means to acquire a tan, at least the sun had no powers to burn.

She skipped the last of the steps to the library and as she expected, Mr Lucas had not turned up for work and neither for that matter had Roz.

Behind her sunglasses, Sophie scowled. She had woken with a hangover and still she had managed to make it to work on time. She had taken her herbal tea for medicinal purposes that would help her to become alert and focussed, and to stay awake for the entire day, yet still her head throbbed to the glare of the beating sun. Roz had no excuses, having stayed out for yet another night without so much as a phone call.

Sophie rummaged through the contents of her bag then shook it, hoping to hear the jangle of keys.

"Oh, bother," she groaned, propping her shades on top of her head. She tried to ignore the white glaring light and the shooting pain behind her eyes as she dragged through the contents.

"Damn!" She had forgotten the library keys and now she'd have to return home.

She placed her glasses down over her sensitive eyes, and descended the steps; deciding to pick up her order from the florist on her way home, save doing it later.

As she walked, her summer dress moved rhythmically to her grace. She thought of Jon. He had promised to visit her in the small hours and should have entered her room via the window; but most unusually, he had failed to show up. Realising this, her mood was indifferent, and swiftly her thoughts turned to Callum and his gentlemanly manner, his romantic words that were somehow comforting in a strangely familiar way. She recalled their fateful encounter and the way he had awoken her emotions, her body. Jon's failure to visit was a blessing because her body stirred to the memories of those loving moments in the library.

She needed time, some space to sort out her feelings and take stock of her priorities, put her love for Callum to some safe place never to be retrieved. This would prove difficult. To put aside such love and make do with the lesser love she had for Jon would be an act of great will and selflessness. For much as she wanted to go to Callum, tell him she wasn't a whore, that she loved him like no other and she did long to see him again, her need for Jon to love her was far greater. Jon loving her was all the more important to the whole scheme of things, than merely how she felt. A selfless act, indeed, that although would surely cause her romantic heart to break, it would undoubtedly benefit the many.

⁂

Callum stood in the hall, gazing distantly into each room. He had searched Roz's bedroom; in drawers, in the wardrobe, under the bed and beneath the pillows and found nothing. Perhaps he could have located the old parchment with a heightened sense of smell if it hadn't been for the magazines deluding him. He had searched the living room careful that everything was left as found, and the only books found there were historical novels and paperbacks of poetry. Desperately, he had raided the kitchen to a degree, yet could find only cookery books. No old dilapidated manuscript full of ancient remedies.

"What am I overlooking?" Callum asked. "You discovered the book, Tom. You knew its hiding place. What is it I fail to see?"

Was he too close to the answers? He took a step back, as though it would help. He began to focus on the answer. "That's it!"

Fate was watching as unbeknown to Callum, Sophie entered the building and began climbing the stairs to her flat. Callum took a step closer to the green leather chair next to the telephone table.

He ran his fingers over the light round indents near the front, obviously made by the pressure of heels. The chair had been used to stand on? He glanced up at the ceiling and saw a square loft hatch.

Callum failed to hear light footsteps approaching. Leaving the chair in place, he used his gift of flight, swooped up to the board, lifted it and flew on in. He landed silently on one side of the opening, and crouched down to lower the board over the gaping hole, when he heard the main door close.

Leaving an inch gap, he peered down at the hall. There was gentle humming below. The vision in a long, pink summer-dress strolled beneath. Sophie stopped beside the telephone table. Callum could see her face; her lips smiling slightly as she contentedly hummed her song while adoring the abundance of pink roses in her grasp. She breathed their aroma, and then, like an angel appreciating the wonders of Mother Nature, she gently felt the delicate texture of a few petals between thumb and forefinger.

Her sweet innocence shone through that Callum's heart was kicking like a bass drum. He longed to spring down to confess undying love. For her to confess hers, so he could take her in his arms and take her to her bed. But she was Jon's.

Sophie moved from his view and returned with a tall vase. She placed it beside the telephone and took time in arranging the pink splendour mixed with wild flowers. Finishing her display, she took a bunch of keys from beside the flowers and was about to leave when something caused her to falter. She turned to her bedroom, and Callum realised he had left her door open. Damn. She moved towards her room; feet disappearing from view. He heard the window being shut, then footsteps returning. She walked under him to the main door. Hearing this close, he let out his bated breath in a long-suffering sigh.

Callum fixed the board into place, and heightened his vision to scan his surroundings. There was a small hole amongst the tiles, letting in a thin shaft of light at the rear of the loft. Callum was able to remove his helmet and gloves without fear. He rubbed his hot face. The heat of the attic was so stifling; each breath was a battle. He dared to acknowledge the small ball like creatures hanging from the rafters. "Hello, little ones." The bats remained in deep sleep. Suddenly, Callum had a yearning to join them.

- Must stay awake.

He struggled to focus on the only object in the attic. To one side of the hatch was a cardboard box full to the brim of neatly placed books. A librarian's dream; and one he built all hopes on as he scanned the titled spines. Those of fiction were mainly romances of times gone by: villains and princes and damsels in distress. The non-fictional were mainly historical of past monarchs and England's struggles against the rise and fall of her enemies throughout the ages. Fascinated, Callum could have chosen any number of them and enjoyed reading each; shoot back to days of old.

Callum caught sight of the edging of a brown paper bag sandwiched between a book and the side of the box. Consumed by excitement, he opened the small bag and peered in. Inside was the familiar parchment he had anticipated. Fingers trembling, he lifted out the small book. He opened the yellowing cover to the front page. The inscription was written using a quill. It was written in black ink, scrolled lettering and

was in the same style as the pages he had found beneath Tom's pillow.
- Mission accomplished. -

It read,

DAWN

*For my undying Dawn, the only true light in my life. Because
I am eternally sorry, I endeavour to bestow this gift to you,
and you alone. Let no man take from you, that which I have
achieved; so you may walk out of the shadows and into the
light without fear in your heart in the knowledge that I will
always love you.*

*Let your conscience guide you, your heart not mislead you,
and your clever mind protect you from this day forth.*

*I entrust the remedies to you and only you, so help me God.
With all that I am, I love you.*

G.L.

Whoever G.L was, must have surely loved Dawn/Roz with a
passion, Callum deduced, turning the pages preciously as though each
word was gospel. Callum found all the answers to gain normality. He
learned of potions to bathe in, lotions for his skin that would protect
the entire body forever against the glare of the brightest sun. He read
of rare and exotic herbs to drink that would alter his sleep pattern and
enable him to wake by day and sleep restful by night. He read of a
remedy that repulsed him; a diet plan that would take six months of
gruelling hell, made up of evergreen leaves, berries and nettles amongst
other ingredients to wean eternally from the need to thrive off blood;
save having to kill.

Upon turning the next page, he found two torn edges next to the
binding. These two pages were missing and were safely hidden away in
his home in the North. They consisted of the antidote for a reflection

and would produce a fake soul to the eyes. This was the potion in which all glass could be treated. Reading the page facing him, it told of the missing ingredients for 'Stake Survival'. All this information was too complex to plant to memory.

Callum was full of elation; aware he was holding nothing short of pure genius. He could be normal; live as a mortal and cause no more suffering.

But alas, the remedy for regaining one's soul was not written. He wondered how Roz had apparently recaptured hers and more-overly, whether he would ever dare attempt to question her. He remembered her capabilities; the ruthless manner she had staked Tom and the brash display she had blasted his own queries. Callum decided not to take the book from her possession. Instead, he would meet with Jon and form a bullet proof plan.

Callum placed the book back in its bag and folded the edges how he had found it. He tried to remember the ingredients he had just read, but the lists were too confusing. He replaced the bag where he had found it then stumbled upon yellow-edged paper jutting from the covers of a hardback book. Intrigued, Callum lifted out the history book and found a piece of parchment with the similar wording as before, and it read;

I shall not be with you in the centuries which follow. Should the population of the equally ill-fated increase, there will inevitably be those who are pure evil, those who seek to harm, and those who breed destruction. Should my testament fall to any hands that aren't yours, be assured to use the clause that does follow...

Reading the clause, some of Callum's curiosity concerning Tom's demise was lessened. In understanding that once the stake survival had been set in place (an aura which surrounds and protects the heart from all types of wood, from any tree) this aura could not be broken. The clause was clever. Should a vampire wish to terminate another vampire who has the protective aura in place, a purposely-crafted stake should be carved with the victim in mind during the entire process, and then the stake should be engraved describing the reasons to justify such actions. Finally, the stake should be soaked in the executioner's blood for the entire two minutes before the blood disappeared.

Callum remembered the stake that had ultimately killed his beloved friend; he remembered the words inscribed in it, *'I have come to reclaim that which belongs not to you.'*

"Hussy," Callum exclaimed aloud, trying to focus again on the black words. They seemed to mingle and converge together. Each letter sprang from the page, danced and encircled one another in a blur before settling back down on yellow. He was so tired.

Had Tom protected his heart from wood, only for Roz to use the clause and make a special stake to drive through his heart, regardless of his efforts? How much of an evil, murderous harlot was she? How cold-hearted was she to take painstaking deliberation over such a fine piece of craftsmanship, bleed herself to prepare the wood and then travel the distance and stake a man lying asleep in his bed? Tom hadn't stood a chance. Callum was convinced Roz was modern. Maybe she had originated from a previous era, but she hadn't allowed herself to be trapped there. No, she had obviously moved with the times. And taking all the skills she had learnt throughout the centuries, she had become a clever and indestructible human being. No wonder she lived life so recklessly; so damn immorally, so immortally. Nothing could harm her. No disease, no matter how promiscuous. No man, no matter how she agitated him. Tom had surely met his match when he had stolen the pages from her. He had met more than his equal because she had the edge on him for Tom had seemed stuck in a previous century.

The modern times and advancement of technology scared him, Callum was sure, because for the last fifty years or more, Tom would hardly venture further than the realms of his property. The modern age; electricity, televisions and internet, seemed to cause him great distress, and any missing persons were reported as such across the globe that Tom must have felt insecure in his vices.

Callum's mood grew lighter, reminiscing of the evening he had ventured downstairs to find Tom waiting in the large hall. Tom, rarely showing emotion, beamed with excitement. He took Callum by the arm and led him through the heavy wooden doors to the gravel courtyard, and there, gleaming in the silvery moonlight, was Bess. On the seat were a new helmet and leather clothing and a motorcycle licence. Callum learnt to ride the machine. Having only rode horses before he soon discovered the temperament of the motorbike more appeasing.

Callum had tried to persuade his friend to ride pillion. Tom had sat bolt upright, clinging to the seat as though in fear, and although Callum rode slowly around the grounds of the house, Tom wouldn't relax. So long as Callum remained riding in a slow straight line, Tom would remain rigid behind. Any attempt to go faster or bank slightly to corner was met with the greatest of hilarity's because as soon as the bike throbbed faster or leaned slightly, Tom was off. - Gone. Leaving the seat, he would take to flight and land on the lawn, cursing the metal monster and telling Callum he was welcome to it because he wanted no part of it. Technology was beyond him, and he'd sooner ride a horse bareback and butt naked.

"I loved you, Tom," Callum whispered, still clinging to the parchment. "You were more than a friend. You were all I knew. Yet, all that remains are memories, my friend; countless memories of both good times and not such good times. Yet, I'm not strong enough to seek retribution for your downfall. Roz is wild, untamed and not sheltered from the world. Indeed, she is worldly wise. I can't match that. Forgive my weakness, but if I were to turn tail with the remedies copied, and leave her be, at least my survival would be the one good aspect to have derived from all this suffering."

Callum placed the parchment back in the book and returned it to the box. He was wise not to meddle. He had accomplished what he had set out to achieve, and merit should be paid for that alone.

He grabbed his gloves and helmet, and stood up to stretch his legs. The heat from the loft was sweltering, matching that beneath his leather. He pulled on his leather glove. It wasn't just the heat causing his eyes to waver.

His muscles were lethargic. The strength needed to pull on the glove was astronomical. He spared a glance at the fur balls hanging upside-down as they slept. They seemed to tremble awake then move. They began rotating, encircling each other clockwise. Slowly drawing to a halt, they then began turning anti-clockwise, multiplying in numbers, in disorientation. Callum tried to keep them still. They sped faster.

"Oh, no," he groaned.

The floorboards were dancing, lifting from their nails and tilting to greet him. Vaguely, he was thankful they seemed sturdy. His objectives turned to mush. He crashed headlong to the boards - his brain shutting down oblivious to the pain in his face, the crushed hand beneath his body, the jarring in his back, and the sound of his crash helmet rolling along the boards to the rear of the loft.

Only the onslaught of night could stir them now; the bats and the vampire in their tranquil dormancy.

Thirteen

THE TOP FLOOR FLAT WAS peaceful. The midday sun was shining through the windows to light the dancing dust particles in the air. In the hall, the telephone remained silent. The loft hatch remained in place, hiding all who were sleeping there.

Sophie entered having returned from work. "Roz?" she called. Dropping her bag onto the chair and keys onto the telephone table, she bent her head to smell her flowers. Their aroma was satisfactory and their quality almost perfect. But then they had a day or so to ripen before they'd be mature enough for her purposes.

Roz should have been at work. Sophie had rung Roz's mobile all day but got no answer. Sophie picked up the telephone and pressed the digits. The last incoming phone call had been made yesterday morning. Sophie realised the number given must be Alex's, since Roz had phoned her from his place. She tried his number, drumming fingertips, waiting impatiently and attempting to suppress her growing anger. No answer. Sophie slammed the phone onto its cradle.

Her morning had consisted of swinging between confusion towards Jon and Callum, and the mounting concern for her friend. The heat of the blazing hot day, and the aching still pounding at her head wasn't helping, for she felt a deeper degree of ill-temper than that felt in many weeks. She was uncomfortable with the discord. She'd have to calm down, take several deep breaths and be the Sophie she wanted to be; the New Age girl - kind and forgiving, gentle and at peace with her world.

She went to the bathroom. At the washbasin, she turned on the cold tap and studied her reflection in the mirror above. She didn't look tired. In fact, she looked full of life and soul as her deep blue eyes sparkled back. Some dark curls, which had escaped her loose knot, were hanging in coils about her face. She didn't wonder, although her face felt flushed with warmth why it appeared cool as ever with her pale complexion.

"You're not bad for two-hundred and fifty," she whispered. "Not bad at all."

She held one eye open between thumb and forefinger and teased the soft delicate lens from her eye. She placed the lens carefully on the shelf and looked up at the familiar sight of half a reflection. The ghostly apparition smiled back. "Hello, Dawn." She removed the second contact lens from her other eye. Her reflection disappeared.

She swilled her face in cool water, patting more on her forehead and pale, burning cheeks. She massaged her neck, her bare shoulders and the collar line of her dress, then dabbed dry.

Sophie recalled the first time she had seen Jon and his friends in the Bat Inn Hand. She had recognized them as vampires, yet couldn't help but stare. Initially she had liked Jon. His boyish mannerisms and cute grin was appealing. As time went by, his enchantment developed into an obsession and he had explained his affliction fully. He told her of his bodily changes, his soulless state of his empty shell. Of course, she had believed every word.

Sophie replaced the hand towel and caught sight of the lenses on the shelf, trying to remind herself that out of all the evil and persecutions from her distant past, some good had come. If her past had been any different, she would be nothing now but dust without having had the opportunity to protect the townsfolk this day, from the latter-day vampires in the vicinity.

She tried convincing herself she was good. Her insight floundered to the onslaught of blood-filled memories, and she was caught in a tempestuous whirlwind. She grasped the hand basin. Her eyes lifted again to the mirror and she saw the expanse of the white-tiled wall behind, the potted houseplant trailing its leaves from its hanging basket, the cupboard door. She focused on the glass itself.

The empty mirror was giving nothing away. Denying her existence, the looking glass mocked her face to face. It sneered that spiritually she was nothing: nothing good, nothing worth saving; gloating that no amount of being kind and selfless, no amounts of trying to be calm and at peace would make a shred of difference. She was lost, an empty, godless, soulless vampire. Much as she fooled all around her, it knew. The mirror could see through her. It wouldn't lie.

"Bastard!" she shrieked, slamming her hands against the mirror. "I'm trying to be responsible. I am good," she gasped, sobbing from frustration as pain twinged in her wrists.

Sinking down to the floor, Sophie leaned against the bath and wiped her tears. "I was the girl named Dawn. I am now the vampire named Sophie. – I am many things but I'm not lost," she whimpered. "I'm not."

From where she was sitting, she could see the loft hatch in the hall ceiling, and addressed it, "I'm not lost anymore. You know that, don't you Grandmother Lily? - I am good. You remember, don't you?"

Sophie had an impulse to go to the hidden manuscript, hold its bound pages delicately and feel her beloved Grandmother's immortalized words with her fingertips. Too weak to move, she retrieved the distant memory of the elderly lady she had loved so dearly.

Her Grandmother was standing in the sweet memory of their small shack in the North of England. A small, frail woman with long white hair that was always held in a bun, and piercing blue eyes which, genetically her son, David, and her granddaughter, Dawn, had also possessed. But, in appearance Dawn/Sophie resembled her mother. Dawn's features and hair colouring were from her mother, Rosa who had been an East-European gypsy with golden skin and who possessed a security in her femininity, proven by the manner in which she held herself. Or so her Grandmother had reputed for Sophie had never met her mother. As Dawn came into the world, Rosa frailly left it. The pains and difficulties of childbirth had taken their toll. The stem of bleeding was so profuse it couldn't be controlled. Rosa's dying wish upon glancing the new-born and then the new day rising from the horizon outside was that the child be named Dawn. Her dying prayer was that the child be like a breath of fresh air to the world and her smile as pleasing as the first warmth of summer.

David blamed the baby for his wife's death. For three weeks, he tried to love the child and forgive it, yet to no avail. He left the infant Dawn in his own mother's charge and left to again travel Europe, where he died some years later having never returned to England to that small shack near the edge of the forest.

It was there that Dawn grew. From an infant to a happy child with sun kissed golden skin like her mother's and wild untamed curls, and with eyes as blue as her father's. She grew as predicted, with a nature as pleasing as the freshest of air. Although she and her Grandmother lived away from the nearby village and could have been classed as outcasts, the villagers delighted at the growing child. They were warmed to pleasantries and greetings when met with her beaming smile full of deepest vulnerability and innocence.

When Dawn turned seven, her Grandmother explained about her remedies to cure the sick and drive out pain. The villagers considered her a healer, far less expensive than the local doctor. She showed Dawn the bottles lined along the high shelves, her medicines she would trade for household wares and sometimes money.

Soon after, her Grandmother took time to explain the properties of the wild flowers picked from the grass verges and nearby forest. Explaining further about herbs, tree bark, and rich leaves; the natural anaesthetics and poisons that grew in abundance, if one knew where to look. Within months, Dawn was crushing ingredients and preparing medicinal remedies to help all those in need. And the needy visited come day or night.

Dawn learnt fast. She was a natural healer, possessing a kind nature that could see no wrong in anyone; and any person needing help, no matter of payment, received it.

She grew with height that exceeded her Grandmother and healing capabilities nearly as equal until, by the age of twenty-five, her overprotective Grandmother swallowed all anxieties and allowed her the freedom to venture down to the village alone to tend to the sick. Dawn couldn't remain a spinster for all of her life. For several months all was well.

Sophie rested her head back against the bath. Admiration and love for her Grandmother Lily slipped away as memories conjured the vivid events of that most fateful night. A night, a million years later she could never forget. She never failed to recall the smells, the atmosphere, the every word spoken, and most traumatic of all - the deed.

As Dawn slept in the room shared with her Grandmother there came a sudden and frantic knocking on the door. She hastened to let in the panic-stricken stranger. He was a small lad of about twelve who bore a grubby face and ragged clothes. What the ladies found alarming was the look of fear and desperation in his wide eyes.

Breathlessly, he explained his visitation. A man in his early forties had been taken ill with excruciating pains in his chest and arm and was lying on his bed several miles away, begging for help to come swiftly. The lad was told to take the man's horse and come here to this place of the well-reputed healers. If a healer would be so gracious as to oblige the poor man in his hour of need, he would surely reward her most favourably and return her home.

To this, her Grandmother was adamant the man had suffered a heart attack and would go to him. Dawn wouldn't adhere to such nonsense. Lily was old, too frail by far to withstand the journey by horseback, and although her Grandmother remained dubious, Dawn was eventually allowed to go.

She took her place behind the lad on the black horse and, after promising to take care, blew a kiss and waved goodbye to her Grandmother.

The galloping journey took them through dense and dark forests, and although Dawn knew the side of the forest closest to the shack, the horse was travelling to the realms of new, unexplored territory. She held down her fear of the unknown and the blackness surrounding; a man needed her skills. A sick man lay dying; probably willing her to arrive, and she couldn't retreat now.

As the ride continued, she became aware that, although the lad seemed a competent horse rider, he didn't seem to be steering. Unhesitating, the horse rode fast at freewill as though it instinctively knew the better course to take, or as if it was being powered by a higher force.

Dawn considered the forests never-ending, when the horse reared to an abrupt halt, landing his front hooves and surprising both riders. Through the dark, she could see a tall, stone wall. But there were no gates. About to query the lad, he invited her to dismount without explanation or assistance, and as she turned again to view the wall then back to the lad; both he and the horse were gone to the distant rhythm of galloping hooves.

Fear from the lad's eyes manifested itself. The full moon broke free from its cloud and silvery light shone down as though the timing was of relevance; most perfect for the effect. Dawn noticed although the wall seemed to extend infinitely either side of her, there was a break in its entirety a little way along. Cautiously, she made her way to it and found a pair of huge iron gates, and as she pressed her hand lightly to them, they opened most graciously with ease.

Moonlight flooded the grounds, the well-kept lawns with pruned rose bushes and hedges, and the wide pebbled path that wound towards the stone steps of the magnificent mansion. The mansion itself was flooded in silver. The abundant windows, reflecting white light added to an already mysterious air. The only signs of life were the yellow flickering lights coming from a window and the double French doors beside it that lay behind a stone veranda.

Dawn felt apprehension warning her to leave and find her own way home yet the mansion was strangely beckoning, drawing her in, tempting her to move closer; come see. Entranced, she walked the path, climbed the steps and, using the brass knocker, knocked three times on the looming wooden doors.

One door opened to a tall gentleman dressed in black. He had long dark hair. His intense dark eyes seemed to read her soul. He smiled, and in a smooth deep voice, drew out, 'Dawn.'

Although taken aback by his statement of her name and his authority, Dawn accepted his invitation to enter as he beckoned her in with a low swooping hand. She walked past. He leaned gently to her as though taking in her aroma and then continued his bow. The door closed.

She was in a fine hall. She looked up to the top of the lavish, red-carpeted stairs and asked after the sick man in need of her assistance. The voice, startlingly close from behind, replied, 'It is I.' Then, unnaturally swiftly, before she realised it, he had taken her shawl from her shoulders and hung it on a hook and she was being led into the room flickering yellow where he said he would surely explain.

Dawn realised everything needed further explanations, because the dining hall was a sight beyond her wildest imagination. Countless candelabras containing seven candles apiece stood surrounding the nearside of the room. Lighting its expanse in haunting flickers, each flame glinted on the plush rich wood furnishings and silver ornamentation. Amongst the wealth of it all, stood a long faultless table surrounded by twelve chairs. At the farthest end, away from the candles, was one solitary silver goblet and at the nearest end, facing it, was a lavish meal set on silverware and enough food to feed an army with fruits of all descriptions.

The gentleman watched her take in the view, and asked if she was hungry from her journey. Without waiting for a reply, he had taken the back of the chair and gestured for her to be seated. He strode the length of the table and sat down to his goblet. Only when he had beckoned for Dawn to begin eating, did he begin to explain, watching her every move in some form of appreciation.

He introduced himself as Thomas Montford, master of the house, and that he had summoned her here under false pretences. To her astonishment, he explained how his heart had desired to meet the fair lady of his dreams; the child he had watched from a distance; the mysterious, honey-coloured child he had seen grow; the young teenager, picking her wild flowers; the young woman who had developed into an enchanting beauty had blossomed before his eyes. How his heart had melted at the visions until he could no sooner abstain from meeting her, than stop breathing.

Dawn sat gawping in surprise. He asked after her Grandmother's good health and casually proceeded in seeking her approval of his fine home. Dawn complimented his house to the utmost she had ever imagined, all the while unaware of her childlike innocence shining, illuminating in her eyes from her very soul. She was ignorant of her purity filling his mind and senses, as her own mind, being most gullible and naive of men, absorbed his romantic words and read his unusual smile as being pleased.

Then he seemed thoughtful, staring at the contents of his goblet before taking a deep drink. He set it down again, lifting his attention back to her. What he then suggested caused her such a degree of confusion and embarrassment, she could only giggle. He repeated himself; wishing to take her hand in marriage, for her to become one with him and run his home like lady of the manor as only one as beautiful could befit.

Sceptically, she was about to inform she was merely a peasant, and therefore couldn't possibly fulfil such a role when, as though reading her mind, he answered her thoughts. Explaining the class difference was of no relevance, and if it were, perhaps she could explain it to his suffering heart. He assured her he had never in all his years, looked upon a creature so beautiful with a kindness that radiated from her very essence, and an innocence so rare, he longed to capture it, bottle it and keep it safe from all harm. He seemed surprised when Dawn contradicted his compliments, informing she didn't regard herself beautiful or worthy of his attention. To which he shook his head, as if realising she was even more innocent. He studied her intensely then demanded she drink from her goblet. She thought it was red wine. He told her she was indeed beautiful to the eye, beautiful by nature and so would indeed compliment the beauty of his house and please him greatly.

Thomas Montford then rose and walked towards her, asking how much would she like to be dressed in the finest of fashions, the smoothest of all silks, the clusters of diamonds? How much would she like to wake in a fine bed surrounded in more finery than she could ever envisage? He stood behind her, and promised all would be hers at her consent.

Dawn's deliberations turned to her Grandmother. With enough money she could live out her remaining life in comfort. Perhaps even be allowed to move into this luxurious home. The hushed, strained voice from close to her shoulder startled her. Thomas Montford informed her that he would have no objection to her beloved Grandmother taking up residence in the east wing. Was he able to read her mind? His breath whispered over her bare shoulder, his hands gripping the rear of the chair. She remained fixed on her empty plate. Scared rigid by his closeness, scared he would want to kiss, and then he would know her inexperience, be disappointed by her clumsy attempts at doing something she had never practised.

Then, as though somehow knowing this, Thomas Montford gasped. He tensed. His grip seemed to tighten on the chair as though he demanded his hands to stay there. He seemed hesitant to speak. Dawn sensed something within the situation was growing fraught.

With the weight of his gaze on her shoulder, her cleavage, then her neck, the pendulum of time seemed to stop swinging as though her world had shifted.

She felt his lips on her shoulder. Feather light, they moved the journey of her bronzed flesh to her neck, where they whispered, informing her all she could see would be hers, and begged her to consent. Dizzy with confusion and fear, she couldn't decide. She didn't know this man and should be courted and wooed for a lengthier time. Yet, his mouth was opening against her neck; drawing her skin in and sucking lightly, his hands remained gripping the chair, threatening to snap it.

He told her she was his torturer and that both of them needed some air. He suggested they look upon the moon from the veranda, in the hope that it would somehow clear their minds. She stood under the midnight moon, clutching the stone banister whilst looking out at the lawns.

Swiftly, Thomas Montford was behind, leaning closer until she was trapped. There was something odd about his manner: hesitation, an inner battle or conflict was taking form. She failed to understand. With a gravel voice, he beseeched her to face him, and as she did he held her face and told her she had never been kissed.

Dawn didn't protest to his mouth covering hers, to his lips manipulating hers to open and move in time with his. Nor did she protest when his lips seemed to harden. They became more forceful, more desperate. His hold on her cheeks seemed to crush her bones. Only after he began pushing against her, so that the stone behind seemed to embed itself, and something hard about his personage seemed to stick rigid through her corset at her abdomen, did she then mildly protest with hands against his chest. He refused to leave her until her hands turned to fists and began beating against his chest, and her muffled protests caused him to break the kiss. She presumed all was well, as he released her face from his mighty grip. Politely, she informed him that this should all wait until they were married, to which he had snapped, 'Too little, too late.'

He grabbed her and hauled up her skirts in a second. She fought hard, but was soon lying on the cold stone slabs with him on top, forcing her legs apart with the strength in his. She felt the pain in her neck; unaware of him savouring the purity of her blood, as yet untainted, and taking as much as he could before tarnishing its flavour.

The pendulum began swinging from the opposite side of time. Her world began rotating in the opposite direction.

He gripped her wrists together tightly. She struggled and pleaded with him not to do such things, then felt the sharp burning pain tear up inside her. Her blood was now tarnished. She screamed in fear, and the only witness to her cries shone gloriously down from above.

"Evil bastard," Sophie hissed, wiping her tears from her cheeks. She got from the floor and went to the basin. She swilled her face, dried it vigorously, took each lens and placed them in her eyes. In the mirror, her face was pure misery.

"You caused me to bleed, Thomas Montford. And then from my neck, loads more. And then I caused you to bleed. It may have taken all these years, and more courage than you'll ever know, you evil brute, but I caused the black blood to flow from your cold, twisted heart like never before seen. And now, my rapist, my murderer, I hope you're rotting in hell." Seething, she marched into the hall.

Passing the telephone, she remembered Roz; the inconsiderate friend she had brought from the gutter to share her home; and whose job she had saved on countless occasions; the same one whose concept of sex was merely a game, a laugh; manipulating men to lavish gifts and clothes on her without pride or shame as she opened her legs to anything. But then Roz hadn't known rape. She hadn't been abused physically or then mentally. Shame, guilt and degradation weren't in Roz's vocabulary.

Sophie went to the stereo to play a classical CD then went to the kitchen to prepare salad.

All her ingredients chucked onto the side; she began slicing a plump tomato. Thomas Montford had taken everything from her within one hour: her virtue, her innocence: her soul. She had past out and could remember nothing of the events that followed except that she had woken the next night in her own bed with her Grandmother watching over in concern.

She sliced faster, more furiously and remembered how many years it had taken her to trust men. How much more pain she had felt upon taking several lovers. Although time was meant to be a good healer still the memories hurt. Still Thomas Montford wounded her.

The sharp pain brought her back to the present and she focused on her thumb leaking red. She noticed she had sliced through her skin. She raised her thumb to her mouth to console. She stopped.

Blood!

Red blood was oozing through the slit and dripping onto her plate, splattering, tip-tap. Mesmerised, she watched. She was supposed to be cured from this yearning to suck it, taste it, yet instinctively she wanted to. If she were to raise her wound to her mouth, would she then be on a slippery slope of addiction and back to being an active vampire again? Would it then take another six months of gruelling hell to wean back off the stuff?

Not wanting to find out, she went to the sink and held her thumb beneath the blast of cold water. The water, tinted pink, gurgled round the plughole and disappeared downwards as more pink water fell from her thumb. She remembered that first night back at the shack when she had stared at her Grandmother's neck. She had wanted to gnaw on it. In turmoil, she had kicked a chair from her way and ran out into the night, to flee to the forest where she had tasted first blood.

The water now running clear, she retracted her cold hand and healed thumb. The skin was perfect. The dilemma had past. She turned to her plate and found all traces of blood had gone. To be sure, she hunted in a cupboard, hurling bottles and containers aside and found what she desperately needed.

- A bottle of bleach.

She poured a capful onto her plate and scrubbed. She was frantic. Not focusing on the task so much as the tempo from the stereo, she raised her hearing save raising the volume on the stereo, and began humming loudly to the music. She had to be rid of the blood. Not so much as a cell should remain. She didn't care if the food chemically burned her throat and stomach because it was better to be clean. She scrubbed faster. To choose another plate was no option for she would be playing Russian Roulette that this plate would eventually find its way to the top and be used by her one day - one day when she least expected it. She hummed louder. To throw it away would be inconceivable because it was one of a set.

Fingers tingling to the burning neat bleach, Sophie threw lettuce and tomato onto her plate. She grabbed the block of cheese and erratically began grating pieces off which bounced onto whole lettuce leaves. She sat down at the kitchen table to eat. Then she stopped humming.

She had been cured. From three years after the event until this day, she had been able to function normally. Sophie ate clean salad whilst giving thanks to her Grandmother.

Her mother, having come from Europe and being well travelled had heard tales of strange happenings in particular countries such as Romania and Bulgaria. She had heard of the undead roaming the earth, drinking live blood and sleeping in comatose states, and whilst in the days of her pregnancy, staying with her mother-in-law Lily, Rosa had reported as much.

So, when Dawn showed signs of these symptoms, Lily understood her fate. Her granddaughter: her kindly, sweet Dawn was a vampire. Wrapped in guilt and encouraged by Dawn's self-loathing, Lily set about finding remedies for a cure.

Using the knowledge of the dangers the legendary European vampires faced, and any written text she could research on the subject, Lily's door became closed to all outsiders. She worked hard, day and night, searching for cures to each of the problems her vampire encountered.

Within three years all the cures had been found. Dawn had undergone six months of stomach cramps from a torturous diet, and many more pains both physical and psychological. The highlight of that dark era came the morning her Grandmother handed her a single glass monocle. Dawn stood before a small looking-glass and, holding the monocle to her eye, witnessed the ghostly figure of herself appear. Although Thomas Montford had created a monster, she didn't appear to be a monster. Soon after, her Grandmother purchased a pair of spectacles to prepare, and a level of normality returned to the shack. But by then it was all too late.

The villagers were in uproar. The women suffered agonizing labours. Other women were suddenly pregnant for failing to acquire their contraceptive herbal drinks. The men suffered aching backs and gout-ridden limbs. The mortality rate of children increased. All these were sent fleeing from the shack, turned away with the vicious tongue from their local healer, Lily.

They became incensed because none of the villagers had seen Dawn in three years. Rumours began spreading about the wicked and crazy witch that lived in the shack at the edge of the forest. So cruel and uncaring was she, the old hag had locked up her granddaughter and allowed her to see no one. The rumours worsened: hearing tales of sobs and screams coming from inside the shack; that the witch had turned on her own flesh and blood and was torturing the poor child!

Then the next ill-fated night came.

The villagers took it upon themselves to play judge and jury. They gathered outside the shack with fire torches blazing and demanded Lily come out and show her granddaughter to them. Lily explained Dawn wasn't there; she had gone to the forests to be alone for a while. The villagers jibed, taunting her that she would never let Dawn out in the dark on her own. Their feelings escalated. The accusations grew more hostile, and caught on a wave of emotions and the need for a trial, the village women pushed past Lily, checked the shack to be empty as reported, and then grabbed her, pulled at her hair and spat at her, calling her their cold hearted witch, crazed by the devil and she should burn for their suffering. They demanded she would be wise to tell them the truth. But what could she say?

By her silence, seen as obstinacy, the whispers amongst the hordes began to climax. The hissing words began to echo, "Burn the witch. See if she's evil. See if the devil protects her now. See if she drowns or floats." The men-folk, driven on by their women, grabbed Lily, held her kicking and screaming in protest high above their heads and began the marching procession away from her shack and the forest, away from their village to the wide still expanse of the deep blue testing water of the nearby lake.

Dawn heard the commotion five miles away and flew back. She then ran in the direction of the voices taunting, "Witch, witch. Crazy hag..." and there, atop of a steep grass bank, she fell to her knees and hopelessly watched the scenes before her.

Down at the water's edge, the villagers held their torches towards the water. Waiting in a deadly, hushed silence as the circular ripples in the water grew less in circumference and the bubbles less frequent.

Dawn was angry and desperate. Her grandmother had left this world; leaving her behind. She could have flown down and knocked half of the villagers into the water for none of them could swim either. She could rip the remainder to shreds in one mighty swipe, declare herself servant of the devil and give countless more heart failure. But she couldn't. Not any of it. The vampire within had not stolen her kind nature. The villagers thought they were justified in their actions. Besides, if she were captured, everything her Grandmother had accomplished would have been for nothing, and her own destruction that Thomas Montford had set out so deliberately to accomplish, would have been achieved.

Although she had drowned and should have been vindicated, her Grandmother was pronounced a witch by the multitudes.

Every year on the anniversary of that night, Sophie would return to the lake, with one single white lily and one red rose, and throw both to the water in remembrance of both her Grandmother Lily and mother Rosa.

She had never ventured to the other side of the forest, and had never dared go near that high wall. Not even during the three years as an active vampire, before she had been cured. She never saw Thomas Montford again, nor hadn't wanted to.

But then, this year, everything had changed. Fate had allowed her to avenge herself. She had used her fine stake and sent evil back to evil; sent Thomas Montford back to the devil; and purged the earth of such vile a monster.

Thomas Montford had been the devil's own advocate. Sophie knew he was black hearted and destructive without a shred of good in him because he had sent for her with a premeditated plan of killing her and banishing her soul. He had enjoyed raping her. He probably got ecstatic on the realisation that he was creating evil, making her abandon her kindness; wake her from naivety. She assumed he delighted in making her the devil's tool whereby she would have to join him in the evil cause of misery to the world.

Thomas Montford hadn't won. She wouldn't be ruled by evil. Deep in her essence she was good. She knew time could change no man, not really, not when it counts. Because, seven weeks ago, as she had taken courage and gone to retrieve her pages from his evil clutches, he had again tried tricking her with words of cunning. Perverse as he was, again he tried to molest her; dragging her down to his deathbed to attempt once more to rape her.

Thankfully, this time she was not some helpless virgin. She was a cured vampire, but of equal strength and ability; and his ultimate death had come swiftly with both hands. She was also cleverer. Not being so gullible, she saw through his riddles and scheming and sent him down so-merrily-on-his-way, everyone should thank her.

Sophie finished her meal with the mild taste of bleach burning her tongue, knowing the world was a much safer place with Thomas Montford not in it. She would keep her solemn promise to her heroic Grandmother; any other vampire seeking her book would meet the same fate. So help her, they would.

Fourteen

WITH AN HOUR TO GO before sundown, Sophie had finally reached Alex on the telephone. He had explained he'd left Roz the previous night to find her own way home. Sophie was not amused. She had given him a piece of her mind for his indifference; swearing that if anything had happened to Roz, karma would find him.

Night had settled over Sanctuary. Sophie had waited with a growing anxiety for Jon to visit. Yet he had failed to arrive. Although logically, there could be no connection between Roz's disappearance and Jon's inconsistency, she couldn't help but jumble the two together; she was being ridiculous.

Flying low to the trees of the southern forests, she sped onwards, watching the ground and skyline with daylight vision and keeping vigilant. She knew where the den was because she had visited it twice in two years at Jon's request. If he wasn't going to pay her a visit, she would have to pay him one.

Sophie landed to the forest floor. She tidied her hair and tucked her flimsy, white blouse into her jeans and still she felt hot. The heat of the day had not relented by the disappearance of the sun; the air was heavy, clammy and, to her sensitivity was thick with static.

In case of witnesses, she climbed the embankment, using her hands for support and scrambled out onto the pitted dirt track. Jon's car was parked discretely amongst bushes.

He had overslept the previous evening, so possibly he hadn't woken yet. After all, he was inferior: a mere babe. He was nowhere near her on any gauge. So it wasn't his fault if he was still in a juvenile slumber, reluctant to wake. She would forgive, as she always did.

Sophie leaned in the mouth of the tunnel.

"Jon, are you there?"

Her words echoed back. No other voice followed. Sight raised, she began walking through the tunnel to the cavern, feeling along the walls as though she needed them to guide her.

Jon wasn't in the living area. There were no sounds other than the trickling spring-water.

"Jon, are you there?" she called. No one ventured from the sleeping area and no one called back. Enough of the farce; Sophie marched in regardless of all consequences. She flicked the curtains aside and checked his bed.

Empty.

"Damn and curses! Where are you?"

Something was out of place. Though she couldn't figure what, and was too highly strung to contemplate. She went back to the living area.

Three chairs, the sofa, the coffee table with cigarette butts scattered on the floor, the crates of drink stacked high; she scanned the layout then back at the coffee table.

Two cans of lager placed opposite each other?

Sophie went and lifted the first. It was half full. She checked the top and sniffed the bitter contents, then repeated the process with the other can but could find no clues as to the consumers; no lipstick smudges, no personal smells above stale alcohol. What had been her misgivings regarding his bed?

The covers were crumpled, the pillows indented. There was nothing unusual in that. Just because he wasn't meticulous in tidying up, it didn't make him a criminal. After all, there was only so much she could do to help him with his personality. Manipulating him to be a neat little housewife wasn't relevant enough to be on her agenda.

Taking her time, Sophie wandered curiously around the back of the furniture, checking the cans on the table from each angle. Observing the trickling stream and the towels lying crumpled on the floor beside it, she wandered on round, passing the crates, mainly clean from dust, since, she supposed, they were renewed fairly regularly knowing the gang and their thirst for alcohol. She skirted round a box lying in her wake.

She stopped.

She turned slowly as though a monster had materialized, and felt foreboding she could hardly contain. Frozen, her brain scrambled messages to move closer.

Closer to what: the box that constituted a bin? The blackened depths inside which had triggered something in her mind, her memory?

"No!" Sophie choked. Franticly, she lunged at the contents. The blackness inside wasn't some gaping chasm or bottomless pit. It was black silky-smooth material. - Familiar material.

She lifted it out, grasping the straps. The remaining material fell to its entirety. And there to her horror were the shreds of what had been her friend's dress. The buttonholes were torn. Some buttons were missing, broken from their cotton threads as others, like weeds, dangled with bent heads.

Inside the box, she noticed the skimpy pieces of material now lying on a pile of cans. It was Roz's underwear. From what she could tell, they were Roz's *torn* underwear; thongs broken at the hips and a bra savagely torn apart at the middle.

"Oh, God, Jon, - what have you done?" she gagged, staggering backwards. The backs of her legs hit the arm of the sofa. She slumped down. "This isn't possible. This can't be happening." Consequences raced, not focusing on any one thing. Shock lodged her joints, and her lethargic body moved to automatic.

Dazed, she threw the material with vampire aim; it drifted down into the box. Determination drove Sophie to wade back to the sleeping area.

Jon could not have been disloyal to her. His love for her was too great. He adored her. She was his guardian angel, his conscience. Surely it was not in his capabilities to commit any misdemeanour, let alone something as cruel as rape? His enchantment for her was so profound, he would rather stake his own heart and perish than cause her any upset.

Staring at the crumpled covers once more, Sophie fought to concentrate; focus on what had plagued her regarding the bed. By the state of the covers, he hadn't slept in it and then had attempted to make it. He had most definitely slept *on* it.

She rounded it, studying it from every aspect. Crumpled sheets... and what?

Crumpled pillows: crumpled pillows, side by side.

Sophie was a vampire. She knew they slept soundly. They would slip into the deepest levels of unconsciousness and not return until ready. And they always remained in one position, usually on their backs to save trapping limbs. Yet there were two indents in the pillows.

She had to clear her mind from rambling in a state of inertia, and think logically. She heightened her sense of smell and lowered her face to the closest pillow. Taking in a deep breath, the aroma of a familiar shampoo and hairspray was overwhelming. Shocked further, she staggered back in revulsion. She gagged, spluttered and held her neck to help prevent vomiting. And still, the smell of Roz taunted her senses.

Sophie regarded the bed; too scared to touch it as though it was diseased, her eyes darting back and forth along its length. She pictured the two of them sleeping together. Abhorrence coursed her every bone, trembling every curl of her hair as frenzy took its grip and she realised the only explanation why the two would sleep side by side during daylight hours was because Roz was now one of them. A vampire!

Sophie was mad, and from the depths of her mind she could see Jon revelling in his cruelty. His dark hair was wild from lust; a smile of pleasure on his lips, mocking her that he had enjoyed her friend so much, and her blood had quenched his true thirst. The salacious Roz appeared beside him. Gloating in another successful conquest and that he had been a formidable sexual animal.

In a quivering voice as anger raged, to the figments of her imagination, Sophie spoke, "So this is what you've done? Very well then, so be it."

She marched to the foot of the bed and turned to them lying there, smiling their fangs. "You are mocking me? Then you are truly ignorant. You have no idea of my capabilities as you act so complacent. Do you think you know the situation? You know nothing, my friends; absolutely nothing. Who do you turn to in times of trouble? Answer me!"

- Silence.

Sophie stamped her foot, hands on her hips, and leaned closer to the empty bed.

"What's the matter? Lost your tongues suddenly? Feeling confused, ah? Well let me enlighten you. I have a little secret. I am a vampire. The villagers called my beloved Grandmother a fruitcake, a witch, but they were so wrong. She was kind and caring and bloody hardworking. She worried about their health well into the night, endlessly slogging. And how did they treat her after she had spent three years of her life curing me? They drowned her. Shit, Jon, they drowned my Gran."

Still, she saw him smiling.

"You don't care. Deep down, beneath what you think you are, you don't love me. What am I doing? Why do I waste my time trying to make you good, when really you are innately evil; every negative aspect known to the universe?"

Sophie marched to his side of the bed. She leaned down to the empty pillow only stopping when her face was close to his.

She said cruelly, "You don't love me, Jon. How do you like that? It's all a con, a spell of enchantment. You think you're besotted with me. You presume you would wither and die if you were to ever lose me. Ha! My Grandmother wasn't a witch. She was a healer. I'm a healer. I have given you a conscience. You should thank me; you no longer conspire with your friends to take human life. You nag them to take responsibility for their actions. You do this because you can't handle my tears. You would sooner stake your own heart than let me suffer. The thought of sinking your teeth into me repulses you. You think I don't know? It's because of me you get the others safely away from human blood. It's because of your supposed deep love that keeps this town safe; the little children sleeping safely in their beds."

Sophie straightened up, regarding Jon then Roz, then Jon again. The empty bed refused to respond.

"How did you bypass me, Jon? How did you escape me; your fake conscience, and make this slapper into a vampire? Did you think it would be a good idea to discard another soul so recklessly to the realms of damnation? Did you get a great kick out of it? Or did she beg you to do it? - Oh, so that's it. Roz would find something erotic in becoming undead. So what did she do? Flash her panties at you and beg you to make her bleed? Shit. Are you so weak to fall for her seductions? Well, I hope you're happy. I have now wasted two years of my time protecting this town from you and your evil, when really, upon meeting you and your pathetic clan, I should have staked the lot of you and put you out of your misery. But I found good within you. A small ounce of hope that you weren't all evil, that you were worth being spared. Within me, I found good enough reason to love you, Jon. With that cute boyish grin and your cheeky little ways, I felt protective. I wanted to protect *you* from yourself as well as the vulnerable townsfolk."

Pacing the length of the bed, back and forth, Sophie rubbed her hot forehead. Her entire face was hot, but not from the heat of the night because within the cavern there was a dank coolness that should have brought relief. Her face was hot from raging temper; the rising realisation of her stupidity and wasted years of caring.

Reeling round to face the empty bed, she narrowed her eyes, regarded Jon and smiled cruelly. "I too have been unfaithful, you little upstart! I have found a man, a mortal with whom I could be completely happy; a romance far greater than what we share. A love that is so rife when I think of him, my heart melts and my knees go weak with rapture. But I was willing to sacrifice that love; to let it go because of you. I was willing to let Callum walk out of my life so I could carry on being your fake conscience because unlike you, Jon, I'm not selfish. I care about all life. I respect the thin veil of life and death. And this is how you repay me. You make my friend a vampire: a bloody vampire without so much as thinking whether or not you should; without one single consequence."

She walked to the base of the bed to leave them mulling over what she had said, but added, "You think you want each other? You think you're safe? Well, Jon, how many times has Roz angered you? How many times has she provoked you to lash out and shut her up permanently? Think! - What prevented you breaking her neck to stifle her contempt? Me. You thought of me. I must have practically appeared before your eyes; my enchantment spell is that strong. I am the reason Roz has survived these two years. Your evil is the reason she is now a vampire. - Well I resign, I really do. You think you're happy, and want each other so much? Wait. Nemesis is coming through the night. By daybreak, ultimate death shall be yours."

Sophie marched through the living area to the tunnel. She remembered to lower her sense of smell as thoughts of Callum came to mind. Her memory was so strong she could almost smell him as if he was there. The leather aroma of his jacket seemed to fill her as powerfully as when she had rested her head against his shoulder and wept tears of celebration and longing. His gorgeous hair, more yellow and pleasing than seeing the sun for the first time in three years, shimmered again before her eyes. She could smell its aroma as though he was holding her close. Her tormenting memories were not greeted by annoyance. She no longer had to resist him. She openly welcomed memories of tender moments. She no longer felt ashamed of her desires and the pining to be with him. She could be with him in rapture again; let him worship her with love requited.

Sophie entered the stifling hot air of the night and, using daylight vision, noticed thick storm clouds folding to smother the sky.

"Well, just great. How ironic. How absolutely perfect!" she snapped. "Now, where are you my little underlings?"

She made her way across the track. A smile broke on her lips that refused to touch her eyes. Dementedly, it stayed fixed as she bent to retrieve all that she needed to finish this.

The sturdy young branch was too large to be called a stick. She pulled off the protruding twigs from its length, and decided the jagged end was too kind. She turned the stake over, grasping it from the other side; this end was far more pleasing. It was blunt. It would take more force to push it through the lovers' hearts. She was capable. Thomas Montford's chest had greeted her stake with little resistance; she may as well have been pushing a pin through a piece of paper. It would be the same for the others; for Jon and Roz, then Liam, Daniel and Greg because all the vampires were now begging for it. She had been naïve, stupid in believing any vampire could be safe. They were all driven by selfish desires of the flesh. If Thomas Montford had ever caused her pain, Jon had added insult to her eternal burden.

She scanned the sea of green: the southern forests. "Come on, lover boy. Come to mummy," she whispered, hatefully. Flying, she smirked. "I've got a present for you."

She flew over the southern forests, knowing the gang used these as their hunting ground. She used sensitive hearing to detect any voices or animal squealing. She scanned the forest floor below, hoping Jon would look up at the skies, see her fly and be dumbstruck, whilst she landed and staked his murderous heart.

Without warning it came. Not the odd droplet to tickle the skin but a deluge. The skies opened and Sophie was drenched.

To see through the slanting veil of pelting rain was proving more difficult. She searched, regardless. Blinking the water from her eyes and flicking her saturated hair from her face while listening for any signs of vampire activity.

The forest hissed relief for each droplet splattered. The leaves crackling and ground sighing, creatures scurried excitably in the knowledge that the air was electric. In the distance, amongst the rise and fall of the land, mists began to form. Lying low, the vapour drifted like smoke, spreading further and growing denser as though the forests were on fire.

The smells of wood and fresh leaves would have drawn Sophie's attention if her sense of smell had not been filled with the aroma of wild flowers. Her hair was saturated. She could smell her wild flower shampoo. The same fragrance was lifting from her bare arms of her pink bubble bath concoction. The fragrance was the potion that kept Jon humble; the enchantment spell that would infect him and engulf his senses when with her, and then duly reign over him in her absence. Her spell would seem even greater to him now. By now, he would be feeling a deeper degree of love for her that his heart would be intoxicated and he would feel as if it was bursting with ecstasy.

"Tough shit," Sophie snapped, spitting raindrops. "You love me so much right now, it's stifling you, throttling you. Well tough. Gag you bastard. You want me to come; say I forgive you? To put my arms around you and be the sweet adorable angel that would forgive your lust? Well maybe. But I won't forgive you taking another soul and throwing it to infinity."

The cruel laugh of her maddened hysteria was drowned, washed away by the rain so that no one could have heard her approach.

⁂

Jon sat back on his haunches, watching the new vampire finish her first feed. Her tongue was softly lapping at the blooded flesh of yet another fallen deer. Her eyes were closed as she concentrated on the sweetness in her mouth. Although his conscience had faded and not yet returned and his logic was failing him; he sensed her pleasure.

They were feeding early. After explaining vampirism to Roz, back at the mine, and convincing her of her undead state, she had been eager to learn more. As he explained about their capabilities to heighten their five senses, Roz had gone on and done just that. Manipulating him in the process, their hunger for blood moved them forth to a swift transgression. They had abandoned the mine, took to the air and found blood to appease their craving. After the initial shock of her undead status, Roz had proven to be a natural: a natural at flying and at killing. Most alarming of all, she seemed naturally glad to be a vampire.

Through the rain, Roz raised her eyes at Jon, and although she remained feeding, Jon knew she was smiling and those red lips were again covered in blood. He remembered the taste of her blood when her tongue had quickened in his mouth, coated in her bittersweet nectar. He stood up and walked away from the scene. Far enough away from the temptress kneeling and suggestively licking, he pulled out a cigarette. The rain wilted it. He scrunched it up and threw it away in annoyance.

From behind came the distinct sound of a body falling to the forest floor. It thudded then sighed. He turned and noticed Roz was on her back, the rain splattering on her face, a smile of delight on her lips. Her hair was soaking wet. Her tee shirt was as saturated and clinging to her body; those firm round breasts, the fall of her flat tummy.

Jon turned away to fix his gaze on a tree; any tree, any trunk. Through the thunderous noise of the pelting rain, he heard her lips smacking together in deep satisfaction. Behind him, her bare legs were outstretched; gleaming saturated. Those endlessly long legs that would wrap around him.

In one manoeuvre, he turned and strode the distance back. Towering over her, he stared at her breasts.

Roz couldn't fathom what was going on behind those dark, dead eyes, yet knew although he was frowning, he was about to launch himself onto her, to which, although she had no means to reason she could feel no objection. The vampire fell to his knees alongside her. She was vaguely fascinated as he reached down to one of her legs. She felt his cool yet strong hand on her wet flesh. His grip tightening, he moved it up over her thigh, circling round with pressing fingers between her legs. She felt the urgency in his strong fingers as they slipped inside her loose boxer shorts and then, more determinedly inside her.

She raised her knees and let his fingers move, her insides clamming tightly around them. Feeling the power in his hand, the motion of his wrist, he rocked her whole body to his rhythm and, as she writhed, spitting raindrops in sudden rapture, his other hand went to her face.

The vampire moved his fingers to her mouth. Her face was wet. Her lips were soaking. He slid two fingers inside her mouth, mimicking his other hand. Her lips closed around them and she began sucking. He slid her four fingers; both hands. Slowly, suggestively, she moved her head, her lips back and forth over his fingers. She gasped and licked their ends, then sucked deeply again. Suddenly, her hand was on his crotch, pulling down the zipper and subtly he realised, she was about to take his penis into her mouth. But then devastatingly, he realised his fingers were inside her stirring her juices, and inside her mouth. Suddenly, she was throbbing in an orgasmic flurry, clamping his fingers.

Jon was dazed as though he'd been hit with a sledgehammer as Roz squirmed and gasped in ecstasy against his now motionless fingers. She was freeing him from his jeans. He retracted his hand from her mouth and slithering tongue, and grabbed a firm hold of her searching hand at his crotch.

"No; stop!" He fought, wanting her to overrule him and take responsibility for the actions that would follow so she could then take him in past those red lips and use that hungry mouth on him. Sucking hard, she would move those lips along his penis, how she had done with his fingers; give a blow job Sophie would never dream of doing. Sophie!

He left her, gasped for air through a constricted throat. He remembered the deep love he had for his angel. Regret throttled him with mighty hands. Yet, as though he enjoyed torture, he remained staring at Roz. Digesting the way she clutched her lower abdomen in desperation, whilst her orgasm ended solitarily. Satisfied, she gasped and lay back, blinking away rain. Her pupils were black and dull, not glistening alive how he had always seen them. Her irises were still a pretty blue, although they were dull. He had done that. He had stolen their sparkle. He fastened his zip.

"That was excellent."

"Shut up," he retorted. "*That* shouldn't have happened."

"You've got your conscience back?"

"Shit, Roz. How am I going to do this? How am I supposed to take care of you and let you stay with us when you keep on doing what you do?"

Roz sat up. "I didn't do anything. You started it."

"Yes. But you're breathing. You're walking about dressed to kill with your legs and all on display and your tee shirt stuck to your chest."

"And whose fault's that?" Roz smiled, as he squirmed.

"Mine," Jon answered weakly. "Guilty, guilty, and frigging guilty, alright? Happy now are we?"

"Yes," Roz said, standing up beside him. She leaned closer, aware of his hardened lips, his dull dark eyes that searched hers in a mild hysteria. "I've never been happier."

Waiting for a retort that failed to come, Roz looked through the rain towards the trees, hoping that Jon had really changed towards her. His attitude had seemed to mellow now, but more especially back at the mine. He had been devastated by his actions. Apologetic and almost hysterical with panic, he explained to her that she was now a vampire. She had thought the conversation was a joke as they sat opposite each other, drinking lager. His frustration had put pay to that. His dull eyes, that he made her study were a bit of a shock. But only when he explained about the five senses heightening, and she had tried it was she totally convinced. That was the only time he had ranted and cussed. And that was only because she had moved them too swiftly to the active vampire before he had had chance to explain more.

If he had insults to throw at her now, he was guarding them well. Yet, she wanted to be sure. "Sophie's going to be pissed."

Horrified, Jon saw Sophie in his mind's eye, crying at the death of her friend, at his infidelity. As though his heart was tearing open, he felt this agony.

"Aren't you going to call me a bitch?" Roz leaned in. Pain flashed across his handsome features. "Sorry," she added lamely. "I'm a bitch. There, I've said it for you."

"No." Jon focussed. "No you're not."

For a moment, neither spoke. Jon fought not to wonder what those lips would have felt like had she sucked him. He wanted Roz so badly, grief ripped him to shreds.

Sensing his torment and the sexually tense atmosphere, Roz spoke through the pelting rain, "Perhaps we ought to get back to the mine and dry off? I'm soaked."

"No," Jon shot. "We'll stay here for a bit longer."

"Why? In case it's escaped your notice, it's raining."

Shrugging, Jon felt like telling her his fears: that the others would probably be returning and his fear that he and Roz would be alone - with four beds. - Four comfortable beds. And he was scared. He, a vampire, felt fear warming his face and turning his back to ice as panic swept over. He was turning schizophrenic, he was sure. He feared insanity. He no longer knew who he was. Could this be as insane as it gets? In all his years, the one thing he had been certain of, the one thing that was consistent and reliable amid the madness of the world was himself. He had always known who he was and what he wanted. Yet, now he was confused, felt abstract, functioning separately from his love for Sophie. He had separate sensations. Yes, he was going mad. Two women were driving him insane, and sooner or later something would give. Something inside would snap.

He felt safer here than anywhere. Safer in the forests, north side of the town that Roz had flown to in her flying practice. The same forest that he had tried to protest against her heading towards, saying it was more usual for him to use the southern forests.

"Come on, we're going home," Roz announced. She took a gentle hold of his hand to persuade him to follow.

Jon was breaking inside with love for Sophie, his guardian angel. He was engulfed with abject fear. He let Roz guide him.

Fifteen

"DAMN THEM! DAMN THEM ALL to hell!" Sophie shrieked, wiping away bitter tears of frustration and lashing out at the main door of her flat. It slammed shut, splitting the frame. Gasping at her explosive temperament at not finding the vampires, she glanced about the hall, listening for signs of movement in the other rooms. "Who's there?"

No one replied. She flung open Roz's bedroom door then marched the length of the hall and checked the remaining rooms.

All was peaceful. All remained how she had left it, yet she sensed foreboding; something had intruded.

"Is that you, Grandmother?" she asked, crazed. Her clothes and hair were dripping wet from the storm. She scanned the living room then her bedroom. She looked at the loft hatch. - Closed. She looked at the vase of wild flowers and pink roses that she had on regular order.

She would purchase some each week from the local florists as though she had a fetish. Though the assistants never paid such a remark directly at her, she had heard their sneering whilst walking a distance away. She had put up with their insults and their ignorance for Jon's sake, and for their own safety's sake: for the sakes of their young virgin sisters, their aunts, their mothers.

"Ungrateful little bitches," Sophie hissed. "Well, no more. I shan't be patronising your little business any longer. Everything has changed."

She went to the kitchen and threw the wooden stake onto the work surface. She grabbed a pair of large scissors; she returned to the vase and smiled hatefully at the wild flower heads and pink rose petals. She hacked; the long blades sliced together in a wild frenzy at the pretty bunch. She beheaded in a haphazard fashion until they lay surrounding the vase on the table and floor. She admired the display left standing in the vase. The green mutilated stalks stood in attendance, stripped of their pride, of their glory. Shamed, they stood rigid in defiance, with only their thorns to boast.

"For you, Jon," Sophie smiled perversely, bunching them together proudly then letting them drop back into position, "because I loathe you."

Returning to the kitchen, she called to the vase, "You know, in the beginning it wasn't easy sleeping with you, Jon. Every time I looked into your dark dead eyes I could see death staring at me; could see Thomas Montford's eyes glaring at me as he did his evil act. It took a lot of courage to run my hands through your dark hair in those early days, trying desperately to separate both of you vampires from my mind, my emotions. And to tell you the truth, I thought I was doing remarkably well."

Rummaging in a cupboard and sending bottles and containers sprawling again, she called, "I suppose I shall put this little caper down to experience. Regard you in a hundred years from now, as nothing more than therapy. What do you think?"

She found the large wooden scrubbing brush, and ran her hand over the course bristles. Perfect.

"You know, try as I might, I honestly can't find forgiveness for you. I would like to greet Roz with open arms and let bygones be just that. But you've created a vampire who'll wreak havoc in Sanctuary as she bonks and chews her way through all the men. Much as you don't seem to care, I can't let that happen. You understand, don't you?"

She slammed the cupboard door and, making her way past the vase to the bathroom, she regarded the blunted stems. "I'm doing this for your sake, honey, honestly I am. I'm doing this for all their sakes," she told him, nodding to the world outside the nearest window. "You can't expect me to sit back and let Roz run loose now? She was bad enough with her lusting when alive. But now she is a vampire?"

One hand on the wet hip of her jeans, she regarded the stems. "I'm sorry. I know this seems extreme, but really I am being kind: kinder to the majority, the general public. Surely, you can see that?"

Remembering the one other ingredient she should now discard from her enchantment spell, she bent her legs, not using the chair for Roz's benefit; she flew upwards, lifting the loft hatch. She landed soundlessly in the attic.

Her babies were gone. They had obviously flown free into the night. Loyally, they would return by sunrise to hang in the bows and guard her secret.

The contents of her box were all in place. She lifted it and slid a small plastic bag out from beneath.

Back in the hall, she took the vase and bag to the bathroom. Inside the bag was a lock of Jon's short dark hair. She used strands at a time to burn to dust with a candle over her pink bubble bath made with the scents and juices of the wild flowers, nettles and bark. This would make the enchantment spell personal to Jon.

"Shan't need this any more," she said to the vase. She dropped the bag into the toilet and pulled the flush. The water gurgled. The bag fought desperately against the force spinning it round and round then disappeared from sight. She hissed, "Take it personally."

From outside, the first low rumble of thunder erupted from a distance.

Sophie turned the bath taps on full. The water level slowly rose. She caught a glimpse of herself in the mirror. It was a shock. She appeared incensed; crazed. How could these people make her so angry? None of this was her fault. Yet the mirror showed a mad woman glaring daggers. She screamed out bitterly and threw the vase at the mirror with all the vampire force in her. The mirror shattered into a million pieces, spraying the bathroom. The vase shattered, water and dead head stems flying in every direction.

Now there was no reflection; just cardboard backing.

An inner calm crept over her. She was doing the right thing. She would wash her skin free of the love potion that entrapped Jon. She would take Jon's conscience away from him, take away his love for her and set him free.

"You think you wanted each other in a moment of passion? You thought you could tolerate Roz and hold down your aggression towards her when she tells you you're a cretin and a loser? Well no more, my friends. If you want each other so very badly then you can have each other."

Sophie dropped the scrubbing brush into the steaming depths. It sank with a thud and rocked slightly. She remembered the relentless scenarios in which she had eavesdropped on Jon and Roz bickering. How often she had lain in her bath full of potion, listening with heightened hearing to Jon and Roz arguing in the living room; him whispering to break Roz's neck. Roz retaliating to his sarcasm that would have killed her two years ago had Jon no conscience. They detested each other. Their hate, they made apparent. And that same hate would be their demise. She was counting on it.

They would fight, soon as Sophie freed her body of the potion. She would open her pores to the heat of the fresh clear water and scrub herself until she bled. In two minutes, her skin would heal, free of abrasions, free of his love; free of the torment of constantly caring.

They would argue. Their innate evil would rule their black hearts and vile tongues until one of them would lash out, physically wounding the other. And then all hell would break loose; Sophie was convinced. Roz would stake Jon, or Jon would stake Roz, she didn't mind in which order the events would take place. Then this town would be safe. She would be liberated of this madness, the burden of it all. She'd be free to go in search of love; real, true love that she had glimpsed in sparkling light blue eyes.

Once bathed, Sophie would dress fit for a gentleman. She would go to him and confess her love. She knew his address. Callum would surely be pleased to see her if he hadn't already left Sanctuary. He would take her in his arms. Kiss her hands, her shoulders, her neck, and speak with an open heart so endearing, and again seduce her with untamed passion.

Be gone of his haunting her from a distance, the smell of him following her about, tormenting her mind, torturing her emotions. She had even imagined the smell of leather from the bound books in the attic to be his jacket. The smell of leather was here in the bathroom, his soul alongside her, haunting and pestering as his psyche beckoned her from afar to love him; begging her to always remember.

"I remember you, Callum. With all that I am I could never forget. Have no fear, my love. I am journeying to you. But first I must purge this town of evil. Then I shall be beside you, my sweet. And the rest of the world can melt away."

⁂

"This is no good. I've got to go and see Sophie," Jon stated. Hearing the first rumble of thunder from outside the mine, he thought for a moment that it was a motorbike drawing up. He remembered Callum. Jon had planned to meet him in the pub earlier this evening. But he had completely forgotten about the biker vampire with his crazy notions about some magic book here in Sanctuary. He had more serious things on his mind: the new vampire, Roz.

Jon was ready to escape, and staring at her with tense nervousness like a child hardly able to stand still in a sweet shop. She sensed desperation; regret too deep for words to describe. Compassion filled her. She hoped it was compassion. Something was stirring her heart; must be pity?

"Don't you think you should get out of those wet clothes and wait for the rain to stop before you go and see her?" she asked. Swapping legs, she placed her other foot on the arm of the sofa and continued to dry the wet limb with a towel.

No, Jon wanted to say. He should leave the mine right now. Go to his love. The word stuck in his throat. That long wet leg raised and bent. She slowly lowered her frame over the gorgeous long limb and reached down to her foot with the towel, with deliberation; a work of art. Slowly, she pulled the towel back up the leg. The towel glided over her soft skin, so suggestively, so damn provocatively.

Roz knew he was a time bomb. Tick-tock. - A bottle of pop. He was having some major internal conflict. She carried on massaging her now dry leg.

He could go and help her with this task. Horny vixen. He remained rooted while he wanted nothing more than to loose the towel and rub her dry with his hands. He would lean over her, no problem. He would run his fingers over her flesh and push her in the back so she was leaning over the sofa enough to pull her boxers from his way. His penis was a scud missile. The target would be begging for it; a lopsided smile. He was going to hit the target: shag the new vampire. The very one he had frigging murdered.

"Shit," Jon croaked. "I've got to go."

"If you must…" Roz straightened up. "Do me a favour; fetch my clothes from my room. The night's still young and I might just take a trip to the Crypt."

"You're winding me up?"

"I don't know. Am I?" Roz asked, rounding the sofa to confront his predictable irritation. He no longer intimidated her because she now knew what was odd about him and she no longer considered him a weirdo. He was a horny devil of the night, lusting for blood and virgins. His swagger was not arrogance, but a confident prowess.

"You can't go," Jon stated adamantly. "If you think I'm letting you loose in this town now, you've got another thing coming."

"Who's here to stop me? – You want to try?"

"Yeah," Jon shot. "Why? You think that I can't?"

"Damn right! You think because you created me, you now own me? Well you're wrong. I never asked for this. You gave me no choice. Just because you feel guilty as hell, doesn't give you the right to tell me what to do. Nobody owns me, and no one ever will. I'm going to come and go as I please, and see who the hell I like. You can like it or tough shit. Got that?"

"No," Jon seethed. Annoyed at the game recommencing, her defiant smirk was riling him more. "Run that by me again. The town slapper is now a frigging vampire who thinks she can and do what she likes, and sod everyone else. Is that it?"

"Slapper?" Roz said, leaning closer with narrowing eyes full of apparent contempt that swiftly matched his. "Well, I didn't hear you object, last night. You've got double values. You're in love with a sweet little angel. But really you want a sexy devil to screw. Someone who'll do all those things to you that veggie Sophie would never do. After all; she doesn't eat meat. You screwed me last night ruled by lust, and you want to again; twice as hard."

"Bullshit!" Jon spat. "I wouldn't touch you with Liam's. I'd have to be completely out of my right mind to go anywhere near you, so don't flatter yourself. You're probably only a last resort for most men at the end of a night. They turn to you when there's nothing else available. Straightaway you're on your back whoring it. Women like you cause so many problems in the world. It was a woman like you that killed me the first time round. And with your laughable notions, you're killing me again," he leered. But suddenly her hand was on his crotch, massaging him.

"You're wrong." Roz grinned, feeling his want harden so dramatically, she felt sure his head would spin with the drained blood supply from his brain.

"Fuck you," Jon hissed, pushing her away more forcefully than intended. She hit the wall.

Pain jarred her back. Pride dented, she saw him hesitate to approach and console her, then turn to the tunnel to go to Sophie. Jealousy burned hotter. She wanted him to stay. She didn't want to be left alone. She yearned for him to manhandle her until he realised his physical needs, his true subconscious desires. She launched herself at him; rugby tackled him to the ground with strength that was now hers. They fought; tumbling over each other in the skirmish and dust. Roz came out on top, mad as hell. She pinned his wrists with all her might. "Give Sophie my love and tell her it was good."

"What?" Jon was repulsed.

"Tell her I think you're a good screw and I thoroughly enjoyed it," Roz deliberately added to his misery. Jon wrenched her backwards and landed on his feet as Roz went sprawling to hit the rear of the sofa. Jon lunged in front of her; face against face.

"Say that again, and I'll break your fucking neck."

"And in two minutes I'll be back. Or have you forgotten what you've done to me? You gave me your blood. You made me immortal. How do you think your angel's going to cope with that? You took my blood during sex, and you enjoyed it as much as I did. So what are you going to tell her? That it was my entire fault, even though I'm the victim? Are you going to tell her I seduced you, when really, if the truth be known, you've been dying to have me for these last two years?"

"In your fucked-up dreams."

"No. In yours," Roz retorted, shoving him hard and springing to her feet. "I've seen the way you look at me. I've seen that look a hundred times in loads of men. All the contempt you showed for my lovers was jealousy. The love you reckon you have for Sophie is a fallacy. You don't want me to go with anyone else. You're dying to have me again. Forget Sophie!" Roz smiled cruelly and added slowly, "You want me. So take me."

"No!" Jon snapped. "I love her with all my heart. For fucksake, what are you trying to do to me?"

"I'm just telling it how it is. After she's dumped you, you can come to me for comfort because I'll be right here waiting."

Jon nodded; a slow thoughtful nod that told her compassion wouldn't follow. She had no misgivings about his anger.

"I wasn't jealous. You're jealous." Jon held his temper by a thread. "You're jealous of the love me and Sophie share because no one in their right minds has ever loved you. And that makes you mad. So now you're doing your damnedest to break us up. Well then, I was wrong. You are an evil little cow. I should have let you die when I had the chance."

Roz was confounded. He had voiced unknown feelings. He had pulled out a brand new weapon and was fighting below the belt, and it stung like pain only her father could inflict. The pain twinged deeper. The contempt in his dead eyes threw her over the edge, and she lashed out with all the hurt and hate from her past that was lodged deep within her psyche. For all the love she had yearned for as a child that her parents failed to deliver. For all the hurt her selfish, money-grabbing parents had given her, instead. For all the low self-esteem she had suffered when all she had wanted was their affection, or at least some attention, or at least a smidgen of a smile being paid in her direction. And, more prominently, for all the shame and degradation she had felt for the many lovers she had taken to compensate. Jon had touched a nerve. A nerve so raw she had spontaneously sprung at him with the agony. Hitting him with fist flying, and anger and frustration behind each mighty swing, all the while shrieking, "Bastard…"

Somehow Jon managed to grab her fists, and with all the energy left in him, he fought back. Pinning her wrists against the wall, he did his utmost to hold her there, and remembered the sudden danger from her merciless knee, yet he couldn't take his attention from the tears streaking her face. With his own emotions raw, he couldn't move away. She was gagging in despair with pain so visible. He couldn't move away. Pinning her there, their bodies so close, was right where he longed to be. She had been right. Love or not, he wanted her. As Sophie's image gently surfaced before his mind's eye, he lowered his lips to her and forcefully kissed her.

His kiss was met with equal hunger and identical despair. Both were hurting in their own private hells, yet lust surged through them. Letting go of her wrists and grabbing her face, Jon broke the kiss. He hesitated in confusion. His heart was screaming at him to get away; go to Sophie for her enchantment still beckoned him. His desires were screaming to take this woman, go with his instincts. And his mind, caught in the crossfire of mixed messages, was just plain screaming in a tormented hell of its own. Battling internally between love and lust, neither would budge.

Roz realised she was in danger of losing him. Regardless of witnessing her tears brought on by genuine misery, by his vicious tongue, he would leave her and go to his precious Sophie. His manly strides would take him away and leave her insides aching, her body craving his. Sensing his sudden vulnerability, Roz drew strength to dominate. She had to win. Adamantly, she took a hold of Jon and forced him around until he was the one with his back against the wall. His arms were firm. His upper body was solid. She could have felt protected if his attitude was that of the same. How she had always longed to be loved and protected, yet only now had he forced her to realise it.

Jon could do nothing but lean back against the wall, feeling helpless at what was happening. He needed support; hoping his knees wouldn't give out, his legs wouldn't buckle as Roz undone the zip on his jeans. Her golden matted head lowered as she sank to her knees. She took his hard penis from his jeans; fingers coiled around it. Masterfully, she took him into her mouth; that sweet mouth had been the death of her was the death of him. She swallowed in the full extent of him, and suctioned her vampire lips around it.

"Oh shit," he uttered, wanting to cry, to blab like a baby as Sophie's image refused to leave. He despaired for strength as Roz worked slowly with hand and mouth, tongue slithering hungrily; all was his insanity.

"Don't stop," he urged, watching her devour him back and forth. His mind was jelly, his legs wobbly. All he knew was that she mustn't stop. He grabbed Roz's head. He gasped, cussing and convulsing. She felt cool liquid squirt and coat her throat and mouth and swallowed.

"I love you," she thought she heard him whisper. But then, she had heard that one before; right at the same time of celebration. He convulsed again, seemingly weakened further. "Shit, Roz. I really do love you."

"Yeah." She smiled up at him, wiping her mouth. "That's what they say. That's what they all tell me."

He slid down the wall. He sat gawping at her in a strange daze as though he had just woken from a two-year sleep.

Sixteen

CALLUM WATCHED THE RAIN PELT against the window of his bed-sit room. Tapping ferociously, beads rolled downwards, merging on a jagged course in a race to the bottom. Were their destinies set, the winner predetermined even before a single drop had landed?

Past the mystical beads, the darkened houses were shimmering wet. Out to the horizon thunder was brewing. Forked splendour; most sinister, most powerful was capable of sheer devastation in one crazed and unpredictable strike. Then it came.

The zigzag line in all its magnitude cut the black velvet in two with haphazard glory. Callum marvelled at it. - Indeed, awesome and deadly, yet always beautiful.

Crackling thunder rolled toward him, he raised the towel and carried on drying the damp ends of his hair. He wanted the rain to stop so he could visit Jon at the mine without seeming as if he had just survived falling overboard. He had gone to the Bat Inn Hand after waking in the girls' attic, and waited for Jon, as planned. But he had failed to turn up. Callum almost felt tempted not to share his discovery of the book, yet he couldn't be that devious. He couldn't just ride out of Sanctuary without sharing the cures with the one true friend he now had. He would wait for the storm to pass, go to the mine and tell of his discovery. Then the two vampires could scheme to take a copy of the book without the cured vampire ever knowing.

There came a gentle tap at the door. Would Jon call at an hour before midnight? Callum dropped the towel onto the old chair beside the television, and went to the door. "Who's there?"

"Callum, it's me, Sophie. I need to speak with you. It's urgent."

The object of his desires was inches from him, separated by wood; separated by Jon, loyalty and friendship. He'd do best to send her away. Callum lowered his daylight vision, and switched on the light. He opened the door.

The light of the room flooded the saturated woman in a yellow haze. Lank hair weighed down in streams of dark wet waves, her dripping scarlet summer-dress shining colour up at her pale complexion. Despair at losing her multiplied ten fold. She was as beautiful as his memory could carve. Her lightly smudged make-up surrounding her eyes would have brought to mind someone of an unstable state, but to him they were endearing. Her eyes were made larger, wider, like a child's full of innocent wonder that his heart melted.

Subtly, something changed. Her lips began quivering; there was a desperation that grabbed him and pulled him to his senses.

"Forgive me. Do come in." Standing aside, he gestured with a swooping bow. "I'm so surprised and honoured you're here, I forgot my manners."

Awkwardly, she stepped into the room. She stared at him, wanting to speak, to reply. Her words were lost to her gasping of air, and she was now shaking so violently, she might have caught pneumonia.

"I'll fetch you a towel. You'll need to dry or you'll catch your death."

He went to the en-suite, missing her cold glare for his haunting words. Missing the way her frightened eyes darted about the room like an animal caught in a trap. Missing the way she rubbed her arm as though to consol.

Inside the en-suite, Callum grabbed a dry towel. He knew what a fever was. He remembered how it had felt to shiver uncontrollably with extremes of temperature. What had possessed her to come to him in the rain wearing only a flimsy dress? His eyes wandered over the tiles, the washbasin, the shelf and then his glasses. – He wasn't wearing his glasses!

Although he hadn't heard her move, she was there. Sophie was in the doorway, staring oddly. Quivering lips opening and closing to unspoken words.

The mirror was out of her sight. She couldn't see his lost reflection from where she was standing, could she? Yet she was trembling in horror; somehow she knew. This was ridiculous. He was being paranoid. He felt defenceless, vulnerable without his glasses. So why was she so threatening, as though she was reading his soulless body? It was his imagination. She was nothing more than freezing cold and waiting for him to wrap the towel lovingly about her shoulders.

Quietly, she began to stammer. Her words growing more intelligible, he took a step closer. She took a small determined step back.

"You knew Thomas Montford?"

"Excuse me?"

"Thomas Montford; you knew him?" Sophie repeated.

Callum dropped the towel. His mind racing, scrambling for safety as shock punched him hard in the stomach.

"Tom? Yes, we were friends," he said breathlessly.

"Tom?" Sophie asked, revolted by the kind reference to her rapist and murderer, her mind scrambled over the junk there.

"How do you know? Are you the keeper of the book? Are you… were you a vampire?" Callum was perplexed.

"You know damn well that I am. That's why you're here, isn't it; to get my book?"

"Yes. No." He faltered. He took a step closer into the room. She took another step back and held out her hand, demanding him to stop.

"That's far enough."

"Sophie, please. I wish you no harm. In a million years, I could never harm you. Not one hair on that pretty head."

"Damn right, you can't!" she shrieked. No longer shaking, she glared at him with maddened intense eyes. "What's the matter? Am I scaring you, Sir Vampire? You seem baffled."

"I wonder how it's possible for you to have regained your soul. That your eyes twinkle even in anger; I too, long to beckon mine back."

"My soul?" Sophie asked, so stunned, she laughed insidiously. She leaned towards him and spitefully sneered, "You should know, sir, that once the soul is lost it is gone forever – and then some more. You want to see my soul?" Raising her hands to one eye, she removed the soft lens and held it up, balancing it on the tip of her finger. "There's my soul. - And here is the real undying, dead me," she said, pointing at her dull eye with her free hand.

Overwhelmed, Callum watched her remove the second lens, stumbling in the murk for consequences to this disclosure. Astounded by her blue vampire eyes, he tried desperately to listen.

"Contact lenses," she stated, plunging them into her pocket. "I have no inclination which century you're from, but you have adjusted in accordance with your motorbike; I would've presumed you clever enough to have thought of contact lenses."

Weakly, Callum said, "The glasses aren't mine."

"So whose are they, pray tell: Thomas Montford's?"

Callum faltered again. What could he say? She wasn't acting like the kind and genteel creature he had fallen in love with. Right now, she seemed possibly mad and possessed; incensed enough to stake his powerful friend.

"Yes, I am right. You've answered me with your silence. You should guard yourself better if you're to survive this."

"Please, Sophie. I have no quarrel with you," he pleaded, wanting to move closer and calm her. Wisely, he stayed put. "I love you."

"Poppycock!" Sophie shrieked. "Don't insult my intelligence further. I see through your games. How you must have laughed at my naivety! How easy you must have found it to romance the book from me. Did Thomas Montford tell you I'm a sucker for romance? Did he tell you I'm gullible to men who pour out their hearts and confess their undying love? And was this before or after he described my appearance? - Did he tell you I'm a good lay?"

"Sorry?" Callum felt sickened.

"You heard me, lover boy. I bet he told you all the sordid details. Did he tell you, I was easy picking?"

"You and he were lovers?" Callum asked. Devastated, he sidled past her and slumped down onto the bed where he tried to get a grip.

He seemed to be dazed, staring to the Earth's core. He was good. A fine actor fit for any Oscar; but she was having none of it. She could see through his games, through his show of vulnerability. He was Thomas Montford's accomplice after all.

"He raped me," she stated. Ignoring Callum's show of physical flinching, she added, "He took my virginity. And he enjoyed it. I have suffered this for two and a quarter centuries. I have roamed this planet reliving this charade. Your friend, Thomas Montford, enticed me under false pretences to his mansion..."

"Please, Sophie, I wish to hear no more," Callum shot, unsure now of any of Tom's vices. Tom had been more inclined to use the pleasures of whores; they were less complicated. All this was in the past; Sophie was before his time. He hadn't even been born.

"He wined me with his blood and dined me with a banquet, all the while gloating at what he would do. He took me out onto the balcony and under a silvery full moon..."

"Oh, Sophie, please stop. You torture me enough!"

"Shut up. I haven't finished. Your friend, Tom, as you so nicely say it, forced himself upon me. He hurt me, Callum. He pinned me to the ground and took my virginity without compassion and with all the evil he could summon. - And he bit me."

"Dear God," Callum uttered, feeling her pain.

"God had nothing to do with it." She turned and went to the window. The storm had past. She added thoughtfully, "The evil within man is the cause of so much misery; don't you agree?"

"I swear to you, Sophie, I had no inclination of these events; of any of it."

Sophie turned. "I swear, if you insult my intelligence again, I'll end these shenanigans once and for all. Are we clear?" He nodded slightly. She turned back to the window, intent for the horizon to produce flickering lightning. To herself, she added, "My Grandmother warned me not to let my heart misguide me, and I failed her." She turned back. "You took me in. As wise as I am, I fell for it. I thought I loved you, Callum. I came to confess my love and all the while I was nothing but a mere game: a means to an end. So tell me, at which point were you going to deliver retribution for Thomas Montford's demise? Was it to be after you melted my heart? After you bedded me? No, of course it would be once you had the book in your clutches. Tell me, because I really want to know." She drew closer. "How well am I doing?"

She was mistaken, but she needed to hear the right answer. He had to pacify her.

"I need the love which you confess. In my bewilderment, I'm pleased you too have experienced the same centuries, endured the same events. I crave to be beside you during the centuries which follow. All I sought was to be normal. I envy you, dear sweet Sophie. You can walk in the hottest sun. Eat food. Sleep by night, and wake to the birds singing. And most of all, I love you with a heart that wishes to no longer beat, should you deny me your love."

Sophie leaned back, regarding him more thoughtfully for he seemed sincere. "You may continue. I'm still listening."

"The truth is, as improbable as it now seems, I knew nothing concerning the keeper of the book when I arrived here. I dwelled with Tom, and that is so. He gave me his blood to save my mortal bones from fever. He did this out of compassion, gave me eternal life and a home. But you must believe me when I tell you; I never really knew the real Thomas Montford. I respected him, and I never dared question his authority, or his reason for coming to this town. He explained nothing. You must trust me, Sophie. So imagine my horror at finding him gone from me forever, and all I had to show of his whereabouts was a stake lying in his bed. It was only upon discovering the two pages and the spectacles beneath his pillow, in the early hours of Wednesday morning, that I understood such a book to exist, and the motive for committing such a severe act to the vampire sleeping."

"Are you saying I had no right to stake him?" Sophie asked poignantly. "Sir, you are much mistaken. He raped and murdered me and turned me into a blood craving, evil freak. He also tried to molest me again that very day."

"Excuse me?"

"He wasn't asleep. - When I staked him, he was very much awake with his hands wrestling to get inside my skirt. How do you like that? He saw what was coming. He saw the stake being driven through his vile heart. Do you know how he reacted? He lay back and smiled. The evil bastard smiled!"

"No!" Callum sprang to his feet. He now knew even less of his friend than he had presumed.

"Sit down," Sophie demanded. To which he did, shakily, as still his mind buzzed. "That's better. Your vampire eyes seem less threatening when you lower them in shame."

"Yes, I feel shame. I don't condone the actions of my friend, nor do I seek retribution for his demise."

"Then, my dear sir, you are most wise. - And fortunate for you, I believe you're telling the truth." Relief swamped his light blue eyes then held intensity as they questioned her intentions, though his soft lips dared not speak his curiosity. His blond hair glistened healthily in the yellow light, and memories returned of the time she had studied every golden strand. He had elevated her hands to his kisses. He had kissed her arms, her shoulders, her neck, and lips. Softly, she said, "In retrospect, I should have recognised you from another era. The gentleman within so outshone the vampire; that I suspected nothing. It would be my wish to put aside my animosity and allow myself to know you better. To see if truly, the man you appear to be is the gentleman from times gone by, and not the blood lusting vampire you have within you."

"I am a gentleman," Callum beseeched modestly. "The vampire is the shackles, the tormentor that raises its ugly head each night as I grow hungry. That is why I seek the remedies: to become vegetarian with no killing."

"Honestly?" Sophie implored. "You mean that? You wouldn't use the book for mass powers of destruction?"

"My heart longs to be free. I desire peace. It is the rattling of my hunger that drives me to the brink of damnation, as I refrain from taking human life."

"Oh, Callum, how wrong I've been! How insufferable I've acted. We are the same, for I too was repulsed by vampirism all those years ago. My Grandmother found the cures to heal the vampire within and to take away my self-loathing. I killed each night in a blood bath of hunger, greed and sin, until I was in despair, insane with no self-worth that I wanted to die again. But, tell me - don't you hate Thomas Montford?"

"Tom had best intentions for me. I was a son to him. There was no malice. In our long-lasting friendship, he showed me compassion and generosity. But I can understand he was no saint."

"Damn right." Sophie rested on her haunches and gazed at the man she couldn't help but love. "Do you think we stand a chance, my love? As you said, we could live out the centuries together. Be as one?"

"I would like that. All things are possible. Would you see it in you heart to relinquish the remedies to me and aid my return to normality?"

Sophie bit down on her lip. "I'm unsure. I promised my Grandmother to share the remedies with no one. You'll understand what restrictions such a promise brings." She added hopefully, "Maybe in time?"

"Sophie, my love - you are choosing me over Jon?"

"Jon?" Sophie stood up. "Jon's gone."

"Sorry?"

"Jon's dead." She wore a disconcerting smile. "He was evil. He was scum. I wasted two years trying my utmost to nurture him into some fit human being. But ultimately, the devil in him shone through. I saw his true colours for what they are; black."

"You've killed him?" Callum was aghast. "You've staked him?"

"I should like to have been the one to drive my stake through his murderous heart. But alas, I couldn't find him, or Roz."

"Roz?" Callum was more alarmed by her twisted expression than her hate-felt words.

"Jon killed her. He made her into a vampire, in lust and greed. Thought they could run circles around me, they did. Thought I was a numbskull, a half-wit; but I showed them. Have no fear of that account, dearest. Jon is obsolete. - Obliterated. Jon and Roz are merely the air about us," Sophie sang smugly. "The villagers proclaimed my Grandmother a witch but she was just a kind-hearted healer. And that's what I am; a healer, a curer. But Thomas Montford had a lot to answer to when he made me into a vampire; and gave this healer you see before you, time to roam this planet. I had time to learn and experiment. I protected Jon. I was his fake conscience. He thought he loved me, ha!" She threw her hands to the air and announced, "It was a spell of enchantment I held over him. One whiff of my wild flower aroma would keep him on his toes for nights. And he nagged his gang to stay controlled. He loved me with all his might. Bless him. Yet still the evil out did the good I had given him. - And so, he is no more. I washed the spell away, and left him with the meagre conscience he really has. So, by now, the hate that ruled both Jon and Roz will have undoubtedly finished them."

"You're mad," Callum stated, in bewilderment. "What have you done?"

"I'm not mad!" Sophie hissed. "The villagers said my Grandmother was crazy, but they were ignorant. - All she did was care; care too much by all accounts. Just like me. So never question my sanity."

"No. You are," Callum clarified, standing up and quelling her demented earnestness. "Jon was a good friend. He too longed to be normal, but you never gave him that chance. Judgementally, you kept the cures while the tormented lad chased after you, as though you're some great ambassador on a mission to purge the world. - And then, when alas he fails your holy worshipfulness, you kill him as you did Tom. It would appear we have all been enjoying a ride on your 'merry-go-round' - and this vampire's getting off."

"What?" Sophie spat.

"I no longer wish to know your acquaintance. Not for fear that I too shall fail your expectations; but because I'm not accustomed to mingling with the insane." Going to the door, he added, "Goodnight."

"You can't be serious? You're joking?"

"My dear, you are warped of evil. It has taken this to make me realise I'll do well to escape you. I bid you goodnight and farewell."

"How dare you!" Sophie growled. "I am not evil!"

"You are tarnished by your ignorance. You are a control freak who couldn't contain your anger at other's misfortunes."

"That's not so. What Jon did was malevolent. He stole Roz's soul. And she... with her lustful cravings would be set loose to screw and chew her way through all the men. I was doing Sanctuary a favour! I am good!"

"If you are so good, why didn't you put a spell on Roz to suppress her yearnings? I shall tell you; because rage and jealousy ruled your head, and you could see no further than instant revenge in that darkened heart." Callum took a hold of the door handle.

"That's not true!" Sophie yelled. "My powers are limited. It took all my energy to keep Jon at bay and to function normally. Have you any idea how hard it is to keep up the charade of being normal amongst vampires? - Oh, of course you would. Two years, and no one suspected a thing about me. I was even clever enough to change my name every so often and stay untraceable. But you've been here five minutes, and you forget to wear your glasses when opening the door."

"Goodnight, Sophie," Callum said calmly.

"Ah, I see through your scheming. You've twisted all this to make me out to be wild." Narrowing eyes, hands on hips, she nodded a slow nod that sent Callum's bones to ice. "And so it was your intentions. You are devious. - As was your friend. But I saw through his cunning as I see through yours now. It's a clever game you've played. That I wonder briefly, who taught who because yet again I was fooled. I came here trapping you like an animal. All along you have wanted me to leave. Well sir, I am going nowhere." Sophie walked towards the window, listening intently for him to open the door and try to escape. Just let him try. As she felt the smooth plastic of the television, her attention darted about. She noticed the black window, and saw the emptiness of the room reflecting. Their reflections were lost to their souls. How Thomas Montford would be laughing if he weren't screaming from the bowels of hell, knowing his bloodline had met for it to come to this.

"My dear, Sophie, you see everyone as inferior. You're obsessed that I realise no amounts of explaining will convince you of my innocence. I no longer care what you think. Think as you like because I know that you will." Callum pulled down on the handle. He heard her shriek, "No!"

She was flying at him, carrying something large and familiar. He heard tearing of flesh. Pain shot through him as he fell back against the door with the impact.

Sliding down the door, he sat with knees raised, and stared at the object framing him. It seemed attached. It seemed to be protruding. Dazed, he noticed the blood; so much blood; the deep red stuff, almost black, streaming from somewhere, covering his sweatshirt; seeping downwards to saturate his jeans; gallons of nectar was pumping from somewhere: but from where? - From him? - From his heart!

Sophie towered over holding the back of the old wooden chair; the large framework of wood pinning him there. The leg of the chair was embedded in him; lost in his chest. Then he felt real pain; the agony of his shattered existence. So much blood, his brain registered; more than he'd ever seen spilt. And it was *his* blood.

So this was it? Love had always wanted to kill him. It had been the root cause of his first death as he had tried to escape its curse, and now it was adamant on killing him again. Gasping for air as his chest burned hotter, Callum felt the familiar onslaught of sleep - a deeper level of sleep that would carry him away from this madness. He needed more oxygen. He needed his brain to function, to focus so he could see his lost love again. She was still clutching the chair. Her image was fading yet he could see her trembling. He thought he could see her lips screaming his name in some form of desperation, though his hearing was failing to the sounds of gushing liquid inside his skull. Swooning, gasping for more air, he uttered, "You are like the lightning, my dear; powerful, unpredictable." He gasped again, tasting his rising blood in his mouth.

Sophie stopped screaming, "Callum." Her mind jolted. What had he said?

"And even whilst crazed you are beautiful."

"No. Callum, don't go!" she shrieked. His eyes began to roll. He was slipping away. She fell to her knees. "Callum, I'm so sorry! I didn't mean it. Any of it! I love you. Stay with me," she pleaded, feeling his warm sticky chest as she tried to think of a cure. "Callum, don't leave me here!"

Using all his strength, he gazed at her beauty; and through bloodied lips, uttered, "I loved you, Sophie." He smiled weakly, and, as a lone tear fell from his eye, he added, "I love you." His head fell.

Sophie spluttered, through bitter tears of her own, "Oh God. No, Callum. Please don't go!"

He was going to disappear. The gentleman she truly loved was leaving her; killed by her own hand, by her own making: like Thomas Montford. She had slain all the vampires she knew except three. Was it because she was good? Was it because she was insane? Callum had been right. She was manipulative, a control freak, and when things weren't going according to plan, anger would burn, and evil would take possession.

"Oh, Callum, you are innocent. I know that now," she implored, lifting his face in her bloodstained hands. His eyes were closed; a slight smile frozen on his lips. "Callum, I was so wrong. It should be me lying here. It should be me."

Her sobs broke free again. Uncontrollable tears scorched her face as grief stabbed through her heart as if it was her heart staked. With trembling blood-drenched hands, she tried desperately to massage life back into his handsome face; vaguely realising she was smearing more of his blood over his perfect lips, his painfully pale cheeks. He looked grotesque. Her tears fell onto his cheeks, streaking some red back to white. Hopelessly, she whispered, "I love you."

Sophie let his head rest forward. She staggered to her feet. She couldn't bear for him to disappear forever. She couldn't have the memory of his body dissolving back to air haunting her for centuries. She had enough to contend with knowing she would never find love so deep. Never have the warm and trusting gentleman kiss her with such tenderness, and romance her with an honest heart so earnest like that from centuries past.

Gripped by her own dying heart, Sophie scanned for an exit. Despair. Callum was propped against the door. His golden head was bent low over his chest, his long hair falling forwards with the ends stuck matted in blood that still streamed from him.

So much spilt blood - too much death.

She staggered backwards, knocking into the bed. Sidling round it, she was repelled by the crumpled body of her vampire lover, the pool of black blood creeping along the floor to follow and torment; plague her forever.

She lunged for the window and grappled with the fastener in desperation, she shoved it open with her palm - her clean, white hand. Its bloodstains were reverting back to unblemished skin. His blood was dissolving, disappearing. What of his body behind her?

Too afraid to watch his body disappear, Sophie made a last attempt to escape the horror. She leapt onto the window ledge and into the night.

She didn't care if the town saw her fly. She didn't care if tongues started wagging of the undead roaming the land. - Callum was gone. Thomas Montford had taken his soul and discarded it. And she had done likewise to his body. Callum was eradicated. Of every essence completely snubbed out.

Seventeen

THE NIGHT WAS FRESH NOW the storm had died. Three vampires flew low on course for the mine entrance. They noticed Jon's car had gone. They banked right; in single formation, glided in through the tunnel and landed in the cavern.

Liam said, "Remember not a word to Jon. Got that?"

"Yeah," Greg clarified, looking at Daniel for affirmation. "Daniel, are you with us? Got that? Don't mention to Jon what we've done. As far as he's concerned we had a lovely time, and no one got hurt," Greg informed slowly to permeate Daniel's brain.

They peeled off their wet tee shirts, and went to the rear of the mine to fetch dry clothes. Greg and Liam stripped off to their boxer shorts.

Daniel said, "So we don't mention the virgin then?"

"No," both said simultaneously.

"Shit, Daniel," Liam said, exasperated. "Put her out of your head. Don't even think about it or you'll slip up. You know what Jon's like; we'll never hear the last of it."

"I can't," Daniel stated. "I can't stop thinking about her. It was so good; really, really good."

"Oh, fuck..." Liam said.

Although Daniel wasn't the best to judge insight, he realised that both Liam and Greg were no longer glaring at him but looking in a weird sense of horror at the curtains behind. He turned slowly, nervous of what had caused their inertia, as both were frozen ridged. Behind him, standing enigmatically and wrapped in nothing but a sheet, was Sophie's blonde and leggy friend, Roz.

"Hello boys," Roz beamed flirtatiously, brow raised; eyeing Liam and Greg up and down wearing boxer shorts. "You're eager to see me, then?"

"Your eyes," Daniel stammered and staggered closer to Liam. "Your, your eyes..."

"Are dead," Roz finished for him, echoing the thoughts of all three as she walked into the living area. She plonked down on the sofa, and tidied her sheet about her, amused at their awkwardness.

"How the hell..." Liam gushed. "What the fuck happened?"

"Umm - I was bitten." Roz leered sarcastically.

"You don't say?" Greg retorted. "Where's Jon?"

"He's gone to see Sophie. He's been gone ages so he should be back soon. What have you boys been up to then?"

"Nothing," Daniel blurted. "And I don't know a thing about no virgin."

"Shut up," Liam told Daniel. To Roz, he asked, "More to the point, what the hell has Jon been doing?"

"Me mostly."

"No shit?" Liam nodded. "What about Sophie? I thought he was supposed to worship the air she breathed, the frigging ground she walked on?"

"Not anymore," Roz sang, relaxing back to the memory of Jon rambling on about how Roz had always ignited his fire. How he had always felt the urge to guard her from other men as though he had a sense of belonging; all this before taking her in his arms and confessing his eternal love. He had led her to his bed where they had partaken in more blood-lust; biting and torturing with sexual activities that would leave other sadomasochists weeping in envy.

Greg unwrapped a new pair of jeans. "It goes to show. You can't trust anyone these days."

"I'm glad you can feel so relaxed," Liam told him, not taking his eyes off Roz. "But the point is we've got a female bloodsucker in our midst. And Jon's a hypocrite, laying down the law. - What does he go and do? - He kills a bitch and makes her into one of us."

"She's not a bitch." Jon entered the cavern, carrying a large box which he dropped to the ground.

"Clothes!" Roz announced, springing to her feet. She went to the opened box full of familiar crumpled garments. "How did it go, Jon? Did you tell her?"

"No," he said, taking a gentle hold of her shoulders and falling into her dull, blue eyes that he could no longer remember not adoring. "She wasn't there."

"What do you mean, she wasn't there? It's half-four in the morning?"

"I know." Jon shrugged. "Nothing of hers is there. Her clothes have gone. So has her books and stuff from the living room. It's all gone. It's as though she's disappeared. "

"Weird. Where would she go? Why? – you don't think she knows about us somehow?"

"I don't care."

Jon wasn't hiding his bemusement, but still Roz needed convincing. "It is me you love, isn't it?"

"You better believe it." Jon planted a soft kiss on her lips.

"I'm sorry to break up this happy moment," Liam said, approaching them now dressed. "But what do you think you're playing at? I mean, putting it another way; what the fuck are you doing?" He glared at Jon with rising irritation.

"I'm moving Roz in." Jon shrugged coolly. He turned and headed back out of the tunnel, leaving Roz choosing something to wear.

Jon walked out into the night. Liam and Greg followed. They waited in disbelief as Jon leaned into the car and pulled out another box.

"You are a complete bastard," Liam stated.

Greg slapped him in the chest, warning him to use tact. To Jon, he asked, "So you love Roz now?"

"Yeah."

"And you don't love Sophie?" Greg prompted.

Jon nodded. Smiling deliriously, it was as though he was bewitched. "She's good. She's real good. You know?"

Liam wondered how the hell Jon had managed to have two gorgeous women fall for him.

"She gets me right here." Jon punched his chest. "And well, as for everywhere else..."

"What about Sophie?" Liam asked.

"I don't know, mate. Perhaps a vampire's heart is a fickle one?"

"Mary, mother of God," Liam uttered. "He said the 'v' word."

Daniel flew out of the mine entrance. Landing amongst them, shaken, he said, "You guys had to go and do it. You had to leave me alone with her. Well, thanks a bunch." He looked back towards the entrance.

"What happened?" Liam demanded.

"Nothing," he muttered. "But she's female. A goddamned female... and the last one we met..." he broke off, staring at the car; the car loaded with Roz's belongings. "She's moving in? She really is?"

"Yeah, so get used to it," Jon said. "Lighten up. It's Roz. You know Roz. And anyway, Daniel, you're already a vampire so there's nothing she can do to you, that hasn't been done."

"He said the 'v' word!" Daniel gawped at Jon.

"Yeah," Liam agreed. "It keeps tripping off his tongue."

Daniel said, "This is too creepy. I don't like it. And I don't want any goddamn female living with us. No way. Absolutely, no frigging way, man!"

"Get real," Jon said. "The only other female vampire we knew was Destiny; and so what? She may have been crazy but she's gone. They wouldn't all be the same even if there were loads of them. I mean, us men aren't all the same."

Liam said, "You've got that right. We don't go round killing then donate our blood."

Daniel chirped up, "We just suck them dry then let them die."

Liam and Greg realised it wasn't worth commenting.

Jon said, suppressing a grin, "So you guys have been having your own fun? Well, I'm glad. After all, we're vampires and it comes with the job description. Though keep your antics at a distance, we're not through with dwelling here yet."

"I don't believe I'm hearing this," Greg managed to say. "You don't mind? Suddenly, after all the lectures, you have no opinion?"

Liam said to Greg, "How can he mind after what he's done. To take a mortal's soul has got to be the ultimate sin."

Jon said, "That's not an issue. The truth is I feel great. It's as though I've been away for two years, lost in a foggy wilderness. Now I'm back; cured from giving a toss."

"Bullshit!" Liam stated. "You don't just change like that. What did you do, drop a Relaxative? You don't just stop loving someone then instantly love someone else."

Jon said, "I know it's crazy, and I can't begin to understand it. One minute I was in love with Sophie and wrapped in guilt, and then Roz saves me with the most amazing blow job. I thought I had lost it. I thought I'd lost my mind. What she can't do with her mouth. Now I'm here. I'm sane again."

Liam said, "You jammy bastard. I need to be saved."

"Save yourself; now, grab a box and help us get sorted." Jon walked towards the tunnel.

Greg and Liam reluctantly helped carry Roz's belongings into the mine. Daniel held back. What of sanity? He fixed his attention on the trees. Droplets of water fell from the rich green leaves. Solitarily, he wouldn't be able to convince Jon of his mistake. He wasn't a strong enough voice to object to a female vampire dwelling amongst them, but he would watch his back.

Females were strong, irrational head-cases. Destiny had taken his soul in exchange for eternal misery. He had made up his mind a long time ago to trust none of them. Happy as Jon seemed, Daniel would trust no female vampire because they were neurotic. Women were a complete mystery - a law unto themselves.

Disconcerted, he followed after the others. Hands in pockets, he kicked stones into puddles, and from inside the mine, he could hear raised voices of a celebration. A 'welcome back' party; but not for those who had arrived from a fun -filled trip. It was a party for Jon: for the return of the real him, the return of his lapsed morals and vague conscience.

How suddenly everything had changed, and just when Daniel had grown used to Jon's griping. And it was all because of Roz...

"Bloody women," Daniel cursed. "Bloody female vamp… vampires."

Eighteen

THE EARLY OCTOBER EVENING WAS awash with orange from the fading sun, sprinkling warmth onto the autumn leaves of the nearby forest. Over the high wall, the trees guarded stories they could tell.

Sophie returned her gaze to the veranda. The memory of that cold, stone floor again caused her back to burn cold. It was four weeks after the atrocities at Sanctuary when she had staked Callum. Still Sophie couldn't come to terms with the carnage she had inflicted.

She was in the mansion in the North. This had been Thomas Montford's home. The very same house he had sat at the table and promised her she would be lady. Time had travelled full circle because here she was lady of the manor. She tried convincing herself, on many occasions over the last four weeks that she had earned it; justifying she had endured two and a quarter centuries of hell, and she absolutely deserved this house. Yet, still she couldn't feel dignified. She didn't feel a lady of nobility even though her plush surroundings demanded it. There was only one person noble enough to fit its finery; the true master of the house - the late Callum O'Donnell.

Having spent most of the day in tears, Sophie turned shakily, cautiously eyeing the furnishings within the dining hall. The long table with all its chairs was still as perfect as she had remembered, still shining as if polished but a moment ago, yet she hadn't touched it. In four weeks she hadn't dared touch it. Not so much as a little finger to the highly glazed surface. Not so much as a whispered breath over the candelabras surrounding it. Yet all remained clean. Just as bizarrely, outside, within the perimeter of that dreaded wall, nothing seemed to overgrow and nothing born of nature seemed to die.

The house, as with all the people who had ever dwelled in it, seemed lost in a time warp that she could be twenty-five mortal years again. The house was overbearing as ever. The expanse of each room was intimidating enough, but Sophie felt a presence. The entire house was alive, breathing; with all seeing walls that would remember her in a long gown and shawl, now dressed in a long white nightgown, ready for bed. If the humiliation of them witnessing the rape wasn't bad enough, now it seemed the walls could read her heart. They knew she had snatched their rightful master from them. They seemed to be doing their damnedest to punish her because each night since her arrival, she dreamed twisted nightmares full of turmoil that left her drenched in sweat. Yet before taking up residence, she could hardly remember having dreamt during the nights of being cured. The house was doing it. The house conspired by placing images in her subconscious which mirrored her conscience. The presence gloated at her fitful sleep as she fretted and woke in tears, each night without fail. Her nights were bad. Her days were bad. By day, the house tormented. She couldn't touch the furniture. She was apprehensive to walk through doorways in case she touched their frames, awakening the heavy wooden doors to spring to life and slam into her.

Perhaps she was being irrational? The eerie sense of the judgemental house was her guilt. If she were honest she relished it. She longed to be punished. She shouldn't know peace.

She had staked Callum, the true gentleman of her surroundings so she deserved the nightmares. She deserved all the pain this mystical house had to offer. If, as planned, she lived out her eternity within these walls and cried every day and night to their scorn, it would be punishment enough. Yes, she was worthy of this house. Also, because Thomas Montford had been one of its masters, she decided that perhaps, after all, the house deserved her. The walls were accustomed to housing killers of innocence.

Grief not torturing enough, Sophie walked through the dining hall, sidling past the furnishings. The long red-carpeted stairs was beckoning her to climb, threatening to trip her.

She reached the second floor landing without surrendering by taking to flight. Let the stairs break her. To the right, the landing merged into a corridor that led to the east wing. There Sophie had found Callum's personal smells to be most profound. The corridor was dense with the aroma of his hair and leather clothing. In one particular bedroom, she had discovered his smell to belong to that bed. It was a large four-poster with fine covers of red and gold embroidery and heavy curtains with internal wooden shutters to block out all light. She had taken this as her room. She had chosen it to be close to him, so with each breath she could never forget what she had done. She would rest her head against the flavours of his hair. With heightened sense of smell she could imagine his head resting against that pillow. That same pillow had now absorbed a million regretful tears.

Sophie turned left and proceeded along the landing to the one door she dreaded most; Thomas Montford's master bedroom. She grasped the brass handle, expecting the door to fling open and drag her into the room then slam shut to imprison her. Sophie was met with darkness. This was the only room that she hadn't dared venture into to pull back the drapes, fling open the windows and try to air the place free from the smells of the vampires who haunted her.

Suddenly, it seemed Thomas Montford was there. His presence was greater here than anywhere. Heavy was the depressive, tangible atmosphere.

It had been eleven weeks since she had last ventured in. Her attitude back then had been an entirely different one, though her anxiety remained the same. This was the bed in which Thomas Montford had lain. Sophie remembered the events more vividly. Weakened by the intensity, she sat down in a bedroom chair facing the bed.

The atmosphere seemed to thicken to such a degree, if she weren't to believe Thomas Montford's soul was burning in hell, he would be here close by her. Could his soul live on to haunt her? No. It was the house of memories; too many negative energies in need of exorcism; these blessed walls with eyes dotted in the wooded knots within the panels. Sophie needed to confront the ghosts of her past. The walls had ears that longed to listen.

Let the exorcism commence.

On the anniversary of her Grandmother's death, Sophie had returned to the lake as she had every year since her murder. But this year had been different. Each year at the same time of night, she would throw her flowers to the waters; one white lily and one red rose, where they would float just how her Grandmother couldn't. They would drift to the furthest untouchable place of the distant embankment. She would grieve for her Grandmother and say a prayer for her mother. But this year had been different. - As she knelt near the harrowing water, she had heard a swish of material and her blood turned to ice. Thomas Montford was standing behind wearing a black cape, with a cane in his gloved hands. He peered at her with dead eyes beneath the brim of his hat. The form of him dwarfed her as ever the man had. He didn't attempt to speak. He stared at her soul-filled eyes without shock, without emotion. He didn't ask how it was possible her eyes now glistened. He didn't utter an explanation for his visit. Sophie's pulse raced with awoken fear. He smiled knowingly. Then, he was gone. Taking to flight, he left her trembling; wishing she had stayed at home in the safety of sanity.

A week later, after returning home to Sanctuary, she had gone with Roz to the Crypt, and after leaving Jon had returned home as usual, alone. The flapping wings from the bats in her attic told her all was not well. She investigated; checking her book still remained intact only to discover the remedy to bring the eyes alive had been torn out. Thomas Montford was the culprit. He had seen her eyes. He was the only one to know her eyes should be dull vampire eyes. Angered by his invasion, raging from his audacity, Sophie promised her Grandmother she would take vengeance.

Sophie waited a week, acting normally at work and in the company of others. When alone, she set about making a deadly stake fit for a lord as sinister, all the while chanting a mantra; she was strong and capable enough to stake the devil's heart. She wore protective crystals then smudged the room of negativity with incense while hoping peace would return to her failing mind.

The following Saturday, she travelled to the house of Thomas Montford. In the security of the midday summer sun, with the stake strapped against her upper leg and hidden beneath her long summer dress, she entered the foreboding gardens again.

The loathsome doors intimidated her again. Sophie climbed the steps. Unsure how to enter since she had concocted no such plans, she was surprised at trying them that they were unlocked. Indeed, they opened easily, too easily, as though they were being pulled from the inside; yet no one was there. The house was silent. Sophie gathered courage and made her way up stairs soon discovering the master's bedroom.

Her murderer, her creator was asleep on his bed; lying on his back, facing the ceiling, and wearing black. His boots were still on, though his cape and hat were on the bedroom chair. With hands folded across his chest, he appeared to be revelling in death, whilst a disturbing slight smile remained frozen on his cruel mouth.

Sophie crept towards the window and pulled open the curtains and shutters slightly, drawing a thin beam of light across the foot of his bed, missing his feet by inches. The spray of sunlight was a force field separating her from her killer.

Her rapist was sleeping peacefully. It sickened her. This man should know no peace. This man had been her aggressor. He had sent her to hell and back and endeavoured to turn her kind nature to evil. This man didn't deserve to be staked whilst sleeping. Sophie wanted him to experience the stake tear through his twisted heart. She wanted him to acknowledge the hate in her eyes and feel her contempt. Most of all, she wanted her Grandmother's immortalized pages back.

Taking his cane from beside the bedroom chair, Sophie prodded the sole of his boot, and called, "Sir, I wish you to wake."

Undisturbed, he slept on. Sophie prodded harder. His eyes remained closed but a low voice said, "I hear you."

Startled, Sophie retracted the cane back through the midday beam.

Thomas Montford drew in a deep contented breath, and rested his gaze on her. "At last, you have come."

Rattled by his calmness, she replied, "I've come for my pages you so casually stole."

"Ah yes; the pages indeed," he pondered. "And you shall have them, child, be patient. But first, indulge this poor man some grace. Tell me of yourself. Are you happy, Dawn? Are you now at one with your existence?"

"I'm not here for the chat. I've come for my pages. Nothing else is of consequence."

"Put aside your scorn, little one. You'll have all you desire in due course. Even that which your heart, at present, is ignorant of," he informed, glancing at the bedroom door as though perhaps he could see along all the east wing passages. "You shall fulfil all you come here to achieve and more, I assure you. But first I wish us to talk."

"Sir, there is nothing I wish to discuss with you; I have nothing to say."

"You are facing the past which you despise. You are facing the pain which stabs you to the core. The vampire who stole your pages, your virginity, your very sweet soul without regret; yet your tongue wishes to be still?"

Sophie thought, *he was scum; the absolute epitome of her worst memories.*

"So I am scum? I'm the epitome of your worse memories. Well maybe that is so."

"You're reading my mind?"

"It is my curse." He twisted his smile. "Now you are frantic not to think of your weapon you have concealed about your person. But, my dear, I've already glimpsed it. I saw it in your eyes when I first looked upon you. And, my dearest Dawn, I wouldn't think highly of you if you hadn't sought protection. You are, as always, most wise. - I am most flattered."

Sophie was dumbfounded. Did she possess the courage to accomplish her mission? Thomas Montford had insight of her intentions, before she had the inclination to act.

His soft chuckle broke the silence. "You feel defenceless, helpless in my company, as again, I power over you? I am a poor man: five centuries old. I am the one lying with the midday sun at my toes, little one. You have the power. You have the inner strength to avenge yourself; for now, you are a vampire of equal strength. You're not the virgin as was when we last exchanged pleasantries. You are clever, a healer of good gypsy blood. Your mother, Rosa, should have used her gift of insight that I glimpsed within her. It is hereditary so open that clever mind to me, I beseech you. Read mine. Feel astounded at what you'd discover."

"Go to hell! - I wouldn't want to know what goes on in that warped mind, even if I could!" Sophie retorted, leaning at him angrily. The light of day touched her face.

"Ah," Thomas Montford gasped in pain, in pleasure. "Your beauty is all the more radiant in the light of the cursed day." He glanced at the window. "But the sunlight burns at my eyes. Close out the light and let me look upon you without bother."

"No chance. - I'm not that stupid. You're trying to trick me. With such cunning schemes; trying to weaken me. But I can assure you, it won't work."

"You think so ill of me," he said distantly. "Yet you don't know me, child. You know nothing of my suffering. It is imperative you understand. You have a need to know me."

"I don't wish to know you, sir," Sophie blurted, suddenly wanting to be home in Sanctuary, in Jon's shielding arms.

"Does your vampire lover please you?"

"How dare you even ask! You're sick. You rape me, and then you want to know if my lover is good in bed?"

"I merely asked if he pleases you. Are you content?" Smiling deviously, he added, "I'm aware he gratifies you with pleasure. But I would like to hear it from your lips that you love him." He lifted his head off the pillow and studied her. "Ah, to a degree. Then more to my point; does he love you?"

Sophie lowered her eyes to conceal her thoughts.

"I prove my point, my dear. You are a clever small thing! A healer you are and a good one at that: so kind and caring. You protect your vampire lover and all the itsy-bitsy townsfolk. How amusing! Sanctuary would be honoured, if the folk only knew." He glanced at the door. "It's good that you surround yourself with other undead."

"Shut up!" Sophie snapped. "I've come here to finish what you started a long time ago, and take back my pages from your venomous clutches. I've heard enough of this mockery, this claptrap. Do you hear? - Enough!"

"No, my dear, you're not entirely correct. You came here because I sent for you: as though I had sent a messenger boy with horse - you came. I choose you to be here. Your pages are of no relevance to me."

"This is a trap?"

"Of sorts: though be still that swift hand and sharpened tongue; for you are no trapped creature awaiting your doom. You're merely conforming to my request."

"And that is?"

"To search out your feelings; put all that is past behind you, look to your future without prejudice. I can't survive any longer feeling your hate. I can take no more of the pain you cut me with, sweet Dawn. Further more, I can't allow your self-righteous heart to rule your actions and ruin all that could otherwise be your happiness. We both need freeing from hurt and sorrow. You harbour such anger."

"You tainted my innocence!"

"You need to realise; I'm not your enemy. I've called you here to help you, child."

"Why now? Why wait all this time? You didn't care about me back then." Thomas Montford winced. She continued, "You raped me, you bastard. You made me into a hideous vampire; the ultimate freak-show. You left me for dead, for my Grandmother to discover your actions against Universal Law. I craved her blood. I was a killer. You didn't care about my devastation then, so why now?"

"Because I love you." Thomas Montford seemed defeated. "I've always loved you. It is how I explained on that fateful night. I watched you. I saw you grow from the child of the forest into a woman of such beauty you surpassed all others. How I delighted at your inner qualities, that your radiance outshone the silvery moon, your eyes sparkled beyond the beauty of the stars. You were everything that I'm not."

"You've got that right." Sophie was shocked.

"Listen with your heart. It is of the greatest importance that you know I speak the truth. Even if upon leaving this room, you doubt my every word."

"You're talking in riddles. Explain yourself."

"I wish I could. I may have said too much already." He glanced at the door as though in deep thought. "Perhaps, I have not said enough?"

He turned again to her. "Upon first seeing my house, you liked it, did you not?"

"You know I did," Sophie said, humouring him to keep up with his riddles.

"By your eagerness, you would have married me to obtain it. How my heart has grieved since. I was a fool. I sought two things upon this earth that could potentially fulfil me; the first was to find love. I moved here in search of you many moons before; searching for a woman who hadn't even been born; commanded by a witch, centuries ago; I fell in love with the promise of you. I bided my time. Secondly, I longed to be cured of this curse. My desire was to seek remedies so I could walk in the sun again, and again sleep by night. But alas, I was no healer. The locals proclaimed your Grandmother was a healer; and her growing fledgling, as fine! So I protected you in your childhood as I watched you grow. I did this from afar. When you grew to womanhood, I fell in love with you; the essence of you humming in the forest as you collected your stock. I sought your help. I enticed you here to confide of my vampirism without scaring you, in the hope that you would find the cures. But as opposite you sat, your youth and beauty filled my eyes and your kindness stole my heart. I wanted you so much; the vampire overthrew the gentleman. It is with sheer sorrow I confess this. This vampire was weak. I suffer constantly for my lacking."

"Oh, God!" Sophie exclaimed at his conviction, his despair. She was repulsed by the memory but could she heal him now? Could she dare heal herself?

"I was selfish, Dawn. I took everything from you in one moment, and that is true. But when you believe I have no remorse and no compassion, you are wrong, so wrong. This gentleman wanted to court you steadily. I would have showered gifts upon you beyond your wildest dreams. I could have shown you the world and dressed you in fine silks, draped you with gems. - And you would have grown to love me. You would have relinquished your heart to me. I am sure, Dawn, eventually you would have loved me in return. And then, you would have sought your Grandmother's great wisdom on my behalf through the greatest of motives; love for your vampire."

"You went through all this knowing my Grandmother would find the remedies?"

"It was never my intention to take your soul."

"So if it wasn't premeditated, why did you make me drink from the goblet?"

"The goblet was of wine; rich, red wine you could never have afforded to taste."

"I've always believed it was tainted with your blood."

"My dear, it was only after the instance of taking you, when you had swooned and fainted that I gave you my blood to save you."

Sophie slumped down on the bed, ensuring the sun line remained between them. "This changes everything."

"Indeed. Remember this. For his sake, remember this. All that you perceive as evil may not be. All that may happen is because it is intended for your future happiness. It is intended because I love you. You look upon me now in a new light, no longer full of darkness. You must remember my impatience is my failings, not my evil. Your qualities were so appealing, your virgin blood so tempting that this impulsive vampire failed you miserably."

Not understanding all his riddles that he chose not to break away from, Sophie asked, "Why wait until now to tell me all this?"

Thomas drew breath. "I tell you now because it is high time. Your hate for me was damning, and my love for you, too strong. One vicious thought tore my heart to shreds. I have mourned you. I was devastated to know I had hurt you, yet there was no turning back. No escaping what injuries my selfish lust and greed had inflicted in your kind heart. I was not deluded that I had taken your Heaven bound soul, and discarded it to nowhere in particular. And moreover, for the following three years I witnessed your Grandmother's success as she discovered the cures one by one. For three years, I watched you from a distance, witnessing your hatred, reading your thoughts of self-loathing. I was shamed. But alas, when I was endeavouring to grow courage to approach you, the villagers changed that fate. They took your Grandmother and condemned her to her watery grave. By then, I realised any compassion you could have developed for me was truly lost."

"Sir, you watched me?" Sophie asked, horrified.

"Always: and with grief. I had lost you. When you fled from this place to return each year to that water's edge, again I watched you. For the hours you would kneel in silent tears for the women's passing,

I would bare witness with a heart as heavy. I would listen to your thoughts and feel your raw emotions as though we were one."

"I had no idea!"

"My curse has been to love you. I am telepathically linked to those I love. And I can't take this pain any longer. I have loved you for two and a quarter centuries. There are younger stars in the sky. I have journeyed along all your emotions with you. Every mirror you break in my memory, cuts me to the core. Every scream you unleash in the forests, resonates through my heart and tears me to pieces. Every damning thought you have of me kills me again. I want it over. No matter of distance or time; constantly you are near me – hating me."

"So much pain," Sophie weakened.

"It is tragic," Thomas agreed. "I sense your compassion mounting?"

"You could've confessed all this to me then. I'm sure I would have found understanding, had I known."

"Ah, you are too kind indeed. And that was my problem. For you to have pity on me would have been as harrowing. I didn't deserve your help. I didn't deserve you. I have never deserved you. You were too gentle and caring; and still you are. Time has been gracious to you, whereas, for me it has brought only misery of burden. I've influenced many events and many people. I've taken lives and souls for which I should repent. I have bedded many lovers, trampled over many hearts. No-one from my past compares to you. Those ladies weren't you; they failed to compensate." Looking at the window, he said, "Now, Dawn, block out the sun and the pain from my eyes so I can see you more clearly."

The vampire healer obeyed. Thomas Montford seemed defenceless, no longer sinister, no longer a threat. Where was the harm? She drew the curtains and shutters together and heightened her sight further.

"And now," Thomas sighed. "If I were to swear on my honour that I have no intention of raising my head from my pillow, would you sit beside me?"

"No, sir; I'm quite fine where I am."

"If your weapon were in your grasp, would you then attempt to move closer? I long for your kindness. Grace me with your charm so my heart can find solace. - Then, I shall willingly return your pages."

"Do you swear to it?"

"Take your weapon in your hands, child. Don't turn your back to do so."

"I have no intentions of turning my back on you, sir. " Awkwardly, she hauled up the skirt of her summer dress and pulled the stake free from its strapping, knowing her rapist was watching her, tentatively.

Thomas Montford gasped as he relaxed back against his pillow and, for a moment, Sophie presumed he was responding to her show of flesh, her bare leg. But then, eyeing her stake, he said weakly, "It's a fine work of art, my lady. You have armed yourself well."

"Thank you, sir. I felt you deserved it."

"Still you hurt me with cruel scorn. Such a fine stake is unnecessary. For although I read your book and discovered the clause, I have no desire to protect my heart. My existence has come to an end, that indeed, any wood would suffice."

"I'm taking no chances."

"Come sit beside me; let me look upon you with these tired eyes."

Sophie sat on the bed, gripping the stake firmly in both hands.

"You wear glass against the eye?" Thomas asked, his dead eyes burning with admiration.

"They're called contact lenses. I buy them and prepare them, although I used to wear glasses. But since you've watched me each year, you'd know that."

Thomas Montford smiled wryly. "I regard wearing glass so close to the eye as absurd. How can you wear such sharp material without discomfort?"

"Easily," Sophie remarked.

"Would you share your remedies if your vampire lover were your equal? If his heart ruled him with patience and endurance, and his conscience were to guide him naturally?"

"I admit there is good within Jon otherwise I wouldn't waste my time. He's reformed, yet I fear when he is hungry his conscience is lost far greater than mine ever was."

"Yes," Thomas said, a little impatiently. "If the vampire was worthy, would you then share your secret formulas? Would you cure him, my dear?"

"I have yet to find one that is as honest as the day is long. Besides, I promised my Grandmother faithfully that I wouldn't share them."

Thomas sighed. "You must listen to your heart, my dear. One's head can obscure the truth. - But your heart is good. Listen to it."

"Fine," Sophie stated. "Now, I'm a little pushed for time; my pages? - I *am* sitting beside you, after all?"

"One more favour is all I ask," he said sullenly. "I ask you find it in your charitable nature to release this man of his suffering. You must understand that this is not my England: my dwelling is of yesteryear. My England is dead. My heart remains in the past that I have suffered greatly with the cruel hands of time. So now I ask for one small gesture; a gentle forgiving kiss from those lips so yielding."

"You take too many liberties, sir. I don't wish for a kiss. You are still my rapist."

"Ah, but you do. - And if you want your pages, then you will."

"I could stake you and hunt this house high and low until I find them."

Urgently, he said, "You won't find them. So vast is my house, and my hiding place too clever. And all this fuss over one small kiss for a weak and dying man. Yet I sense the thought doesn't repulse you." He gazed at her hard. "You fear such a kiss would render your weapon useless should you need to use it. Take heed, child, you'll be given the strength."

"Still you ask too much," Sophie hesitated.

"I ask that your lips take away my guilt. I ask for an act of forgiveness for this repentant heart. Now, place your lips to mine. End this grief. Release me of my conscience, I beseech you. Take a hold of your kindness and heal my suffering. Witch of Ages, do it."

His thin lips no longer appeared so mean. His eyes seemed gentle. Holding her stake more firmly, she closed her eyes and lowered her lips to softly kiss his. They were warm, strangely soft to the touch and not cruel as her memory dictated. He pressed firmly, emotions ignited. She broke the kiss. His eyes remaining closed with a deep furrowed frown spread across his brow to ward off sorrow. The vampire seemed human.

"Thank you," he whispered. He opened his eyes and they appeared moistened.

"Now, my pages?"

"They are but ashes on my fire."

"You lie!"

"And you hesitate," Thomas whispered.

"I don't understand. I thought we had made an agreement? You said..."

"I lied. Though I thank you for the kiss, you are generous to a fault." Sophie stood up, he asked, "Where are you going?"

"To check your fire, you bastard!"

The master of all vampires bolted upright, grabbed her waist, and yanked her down on top of him.

"No!" Sophie cried. His strength seemed mighty enough. He was a liar; a fraud to the end. He pinned her to him, his other hand grappling to get into her skirt. Sophie shrieked, "No! Not again!"

"I do this for you..." he said, struggling with her, and Sophie thought she heard him add, 'both', but she was too distraught to question it. He was feeling the flesh of her leg with vice-like grip, wrestling to go higher. She was too determined for him not to take advantage of her again. She was a white witch, a healer; a god-damn cured vampire. There was nothing on this earth she hadn't been through and survived. She would finish this evil once and for all. She pushed away from him, she raised the stake high above her head and plunged it down; down through his black soulless heart.

Air gushing, Thomas Montford stared at the stake impaled in his chest, saturated deep red. Sophie flew off him.

The blood was streaming from around the stake. He stared at it triumphantly and sighed deeply that Sophie could have presumed it was one of relief because she had hit the target well, that his quest, so far, had been accomplished. But she didn't. Instead, she supposed it was his dying sigh. He closed his eyes, relaxed his head against the pillow and smiled.

Everything he had said had been a lie. He had been cunning and dangerous as ever the man could be. He had enticed her here with one intention only, to rape her again. Sophie vowed she would never again fall for such cunning. She would never be so gullible, nor trust romantic words with twisted motives. She was growing cleverer and wiser, and would never again be so naive.

Sophie had run out of that house without waiting for him to disappear, without searching for her missing pages. Her nerves were too raw that to stay another second would encourage the evil within the place to take possession of her. She would return home to Sanctuary, pretending she had gone to visit her family as usual, and Jon would be none the wiser. No one would ever know. Her double life, her alter ego was safe. The entire world was now safe – a better place.

Now, eleven weeks on, and after all that had past, Sophie remained dazed, wiping the tears from her eyes. Now she knew differently. She stared at the bed, made so perfect without a crease, and uttered, "You sent Callum to seek me out. And on his Black Bess, he dutifully arrived. Why?" Taking in a deep breath, she questioned louder, "It was your wish that your son fell in love with me. Why didn't you just introduce us? You knew we were compatible, that we would lose our hearts gladly and would discover sweet ecstasy. You knew our hearts better than we knew ourselves, so why play this game? Did you presume he'd enjoy the adventure? He did everything as you supposed he would, and look where it got him! You failed, Thomas Montford; we both failed. Well I hope you're satisfied, because I've killed him! I presumed he was playing tricks, like you. I thought every word he spoke he was twisting around, thinking I was a stupid. Yet I was wrong. I have misinterpreted you, and him; and I staked him. Oh, what have I done? - I staked him and you, and I've committed Jon and Roz to death. Because I listened to my fucked-up head! I should have listened to my heart as you instructed. I thought I was good and kind. I believed that one day if I could just prove myself worthy enough, my soul would be returned to me. But again, I am wrong. - So that's it then, I am truly lost."

Now, she knew sheer devastation. Now, there was no hope. No future. In front of her was gloom; behind her had been gloom with Callum shining through it. She had snuffed out that light. Without hope there could only be despair. She wanted to die. She could easily die again.

Did she have the courage to make a stake and gouge out the words, 'For his death, here is mine', and then stake her own heart? It was an option.

Springing to her feet in a crazed fit, Sophie bolted out of the room. Running the length of the landing and corridor towards Callum's room, she shouted at the house. Her voice echoed off the all-seeing walls, "I loved Callum! Truly I did! Yet, everyone who has ever loved me dies. They die because of me! My good intentions are an illusion. To this end what good am I? I am evil! - So hear this, house, because I know you're listening. If you want to avenge the callous staking of your two masters who loved me, so be it. Do your damnedest! Drive me insane! I'm there already. - Give me the incredible nights of hell. Make my mind wither eternal meltdown. Do as you will; I deserve it. When you have driven me to the brink, I'll craft my stake and use it!"

She fell, face down onto Callum's bed and, breathing in his adorable aroma, she cried. She wreathed in agony. She wanted Callum's arms around her. She sobbed. She craved the security of his love. She needed him to dry her tears and mend her broken existence. She sobbed louder. She wanted to rewind time with the gift of hindsight, and treasure her blessings. She cried until she fell to sleep.

Nineteen

SOPHIE LAY IN A FITFUL sleep sensing a presence speeding towards her through the night sky. Tossing and turning, she buzzed with images of the entity on course for the house - on course for her. Soundlessly it arrived. The soulless creature swooped up to the windows on the second level and peered in before swooping down to the ground level windows. It checked each room as it rounded the house in search of her. It was going to get her. It was hell bent on that. Yet, she couldn't wake. She had no means to escape the oddity, which contained death and a determination to reach her at all costs. It would crash through her window, showering glass over the bed and would lash out at her with all the hate and madness of the underworld until she was twisted, bleeding and begging for forgiveness and it would merely laugh as it hacked her to pieces and she would invite it gladly save this nightmare.

Window by window, Nemesis drew closer. The house invited it. The house was pleased. The face was at her window, peering in...

Sophie opened her eyes, gasping, and shot her attention to the window to face her tormentor. Nothing was there. She ran to the window, heightening her sight, and peered down. The cobbled path was empty of predators. The neatly cut lawns with its rose bush borders hid no mysterious spectre. Nothing was lurking. Sophie pushed her loose curls from her face, held her fringe high on her head and tried to get a grip of her mind. She needed more herbal tea remedy to assist sleep so made her way out of the bedroom, along the corridor to the landing.

From the top of the stairs, she scanned the hall; all the doors were open to the rooms. Everything was quiet. She grasped the banister, held her long white nightgown and descended cautiously. The house watched. The presence was all around. The atmosphere was heavy, crushing her body, her breathing.

In the hall, the eeriness was more profound. Sophie made her way to the kitchen.

This house had a hold over her, as she now realised it had from day one. But this time she couldn't escape its clutches. She was its prisoner. The enchantment of it was her undoing. The presence was real. Perhaps Thomas Montford lived on as his undying soul monitored her every move? He was very much alive and here because in truth, he had never left. He was angry. He had failed. He had wanted the two vampires he loved to come together as one. She had failed. She had deluded everyone. She had eluded destiny and now the ghost of Thomas Montford was dwelling with her.

In his dining hall, hidden against a backdrop of shadows, a figure in black was sitting at the far end of his table. Wearing leather boots, he had his feet elevated to the table and crossed for comfort. He lazed in his chair, waiting for the lady to return. She had descended the stairs and made her way to the kitchen. Silently, he leaned to the table and lit a solitary candle. He relaxed back as the flame flickered, danced and dazed him; such a beautiful yellow.

He detected Sophie's return; bare feet padding along polished floor, carrying a tall glass of brown liquid. He stayed in hiding amongst the shadows. She was obviously wearing her lenses; he was watching her reflection in the glass cabinet in the room and opposite the doorway. Her white gown was moving as always to her elegance. Although he read her unease, she was as ever graceful. And through the veil of dark sweeping curls, her face was divine.

She turned to the stairs and took a hold of the banister. Time had slowed. He digested her every reflection, as slowly she turned seeming to seek something. She looked into the room opposite his, then into the next and the next. She turned to the main double doors before turning some more. Her eyes fell to the candle. She seemed confused. Her gaze was deep; intense. It reached out, wrenched his chest open and grabbed the stuffing from within. The moment seemed endless as she questioned the flame; flickering alone – alive despite her wishes.

He sat forward. He came into view. Her gaze shifted from the flame to merge with his eyes. Her expression remained unchanging, blank, paralysed by shock. Her fingers must have moved for the glass slid through them, falling ever so gradually down past her white skirts, past her bare ankles where it hit the floor, crumbling to the impact and spontaneously exploding as millions of splinters sprayed in every direction and landed dancing, bouncing and tinkling about her feet. The liquid hit the deck as one solid object and fanned sideways, reaching in a wider circumference and splattering her feet and the hem of her gown. She didn't notice.

Her voice crackled, "Callum!"

"Sophie," he said flatly.

"Oh, Callum - you're alive!" She grasped her hands together in wonder. "I can't believe it; you're alive!"

"No, my dear; I am very much dead, as always. Though not as dead as you had intended."

"That's not so..." Sophie absorbed his pale yet gorgeous face. He wasn't wearing his glasses; his eyes were dead. Thankfully, his hands were in view and empty of any prepared stake. Did he have one hidden away? Regardless, he was a sight to behold. "Sir, you'll never know how much I've regretted..."

"You are in my house," Callum interrupted bluntly. "And, my dear - you are in my bed."

"I can explain if you would just let me finish..."

"In my opinion, enough has been said already. Now you may go," Callum announced, encouraging her to pack.

"Wait a minute. You've read my book? You protected your heart?"

"Lucky for me, I had the good sense."

"Oh, Callum, that's brilliant! I've spent four weeks in hell, my love."

"You may collect your belongings, and close the doors gently on the way out. This house is old and should be treated with respect."

Sophie shook her head in disbelief. "But I love you, Callum."

"Then I don't wish to meet those you hate, for what carnage should befall those poor souls!"

"I can understand how you must feel. Everything you say is true. Everything you said on that dreadful night was me summed up. I know that now. These four weeks have felt like an eternity. I have had time to reflect. I have weighed up my weaknesses, and have analysed the atrocities I have caused."

Sophie made to rush to him so he could see her truth. Pain shot in her foot, scrunching fragmented glass, and hobbled backwards to sit on the bottom stair. She crossed her leg, studied her injuries, and began picking out splinters. She winced and gushed, "You hate me. That's the least I deserve; I'm not worthy of your forgiveness. I can't undo the past. I have no cure for my dying heart this time. Just allow me two minutes for my foot to heal and I'll go; leave you forever, never to return."

"Fine," Callum agreed. Abruptly, he kicked his legs off the table and stood up. He turned his back on the wounded goddess for her not to witness his grief. His emotions were torn; grating. He attempted denial by looking across the grounds towards the high wall – the grounds were immaculate as ever - then back at the veranda. His blood ran cold as he pictured his friend, Tom, on top of Sophie, chewing at her neck, breaking her inside. Callum drew in a deep, steady breath. Not a welcome distraction. He tore himself away from that cursed veranda. - The scene of the rape. He gazed up at the full moon and star spangled sky, and remembered his own gruesome agony. The chair leg had torn through his heart so that he had eventually past out; though not before he had caught Sophie's sorrow. He had still been conscious enough to hear of her undying love, of her bitter regret and anguish. The stake burned deeper with her despair, yet Sophie cried tears which fell onto his face and ran down his blood-smeared cheek; and this had burned with anguish more excruciating than any wood could deliver. He had felt her truth then and he had done for four weeks since. Her suffering was his. They were united by the blood of Thomas Montford; they were as one. If only Callum could break this curse? He needed his sanity back. She had taken this from him on first sight. He needed his home back; after all he was the rightful master.

Her foot mended, Sophie stood up. "Sir, I would like you to know that I did enjoy the good times we shared. Sitting behind you on Black Bess was a dream. That kiss haunted me then, and to this night..."

Callum held up his hand to cease her words. Let sanity come swiftly.

"I'd like you to know also that, as you once said; I shall relive our loving moments in the library a hundred fold in my mind. Your absent kisses will torture me forever as they have done these weeks."

"Enough!" Callum swirled round to the window again to avoid her gaze yet caught her reflection in candlelight as a diamond tear fell from her eye and exploded on the sodden floor.

Sophie said, "I've cried rivers; oceans even. But I can tell you're not interested; so goodbye, Callum."

"Wait!" Callum hesitated. "I made you cry often."

"Yes. Oh, yes, I have cried." Sophie implored hopefully. "Love hurts."

He turned. "So too does wood. You may go now and gather your belongings." He ushered her away. Complying, she held her gown high and began climbing the stairs. When she disappeared from his view, Callum moved into the doorway and watched her some more. She was elegant. Even in distress, she was engaging. In her flowing gown she looked apt in the plush surroundings of his house. In his opinion, the lady fitted the place well. But she was neurotic, a control freak; there was no cure for these foibles.

Reaching the last stair, Sophie heard the vampire's approach as he flew through the air; and realised he was about to fly over her head and land in front. He would be brandishing a carved stake that he had retrieved from his hiding place. Engraved would be the words, 'I have come to reclaim my house.' With a vengeance, he would stake her and send her plummeting backwards, hitting each stair to her ultimate death. She was no longer invincible. Her heart would be vulnerable to such a weapon.

Sophie shut her eyes, and waited for karma. She waited, cringing in anticipation to take a nonexistent form. Callum had landed. He was so close she felt his warm breath on her flesh.

Callum towered majestically, triumphant as he leaned closer to her face; drawn like tides to the moon. How easily he could touch her lips, kiss her tenderly. How difficult it was now to send her away. He was more than torn; he was in shreds; emotions bleeding. Her fragility shone from her wincing expression. She wasn't just a cured vampire who chose to stake him; she was a woman; a victim of assault; robbed of soul. She was lost on a sea of misery, being swept along by universal forces beyond her control. She needed sails, a rudder and a compass. She needed stability. As Callum admired the lady he couldn't help but love, he knew the definition of forgiveness, for this was it; he understood her journey.

"Sophie?" Callum whispered. She opened her eyes and noted his empty hands. "I wish to ask one favour from you, before you go."

"And that is?"

"To break this bewitchment, the spell you've placed over me? I long for you to set me free. This love overwhelms me. I can suffer no more; it's unbearable."

"But, Callum, there is no spell." She was shocked by his admission. "I have never placed a spell of enchantment on you. It's your own freewill that's brought us to this point."

"Damn! It's as I first presumed!" Teasingly, Callum threw his hands to the air. "It is as I've dreaded. The torture I have been subjected to, and my love - is real? Damn it!"

Back and forth, he paced the landing, acting out despair; he ranted, "Am I to spend all eternity like this? Am I to go insane with such ardent feelings that can't be contained? Oh, how I wish it were a spell. To be freed from this dreaded curse; for this love restricts me." He turned to her and pleaded, "Please, Sophie, you are a healer, find a cure to take away my love for you. My heart longs to beat freely, yet it is restricted by a force mightier than the desire to exist. It is gripped more tightly by a restraint so powerful that if it crushes me further I will surely perish, relentless of my struggle. Cure me, Sophie! I have been wounded enough; subjected to enough cruelty. - I searched your vanity case for the remedies soon after you left the flat that Saturday night. I discovered the bottled aura to protect my heart from wood. Yet that was the only remedy I found. Alas, I found no evidence of a love spell binding us together. More sorrow upon more devastation, I found no antidote. Please, Sophie, if you wish to make amends, if you truly repent then take this love from my strangulated heart. Heal my pain. - Release me!"

"Your love is natural, I tell you! This one's not my doing. - It's not my fault!" Sophie was adamant, but to her astonishment, she noticed his amusement. "You are mocking me, sir?"

Callum leaned back as though astounded then chuckled. "Yes, I'm mocking you."

Bemused, Sophie studied him further. "You're no longer angry with me?"

"How could I be? My anger has subsided as my love grows more fervent with every heart beat in your company. - As I lay bleeding with wood embedded in my chest, I heard your words. I felt your bitter tears of regret. Since I know what heartbreak is, I know your remorse. If you had lingered instead of exiting the window, you would have seen my chest heal. As it was, you had flown safely away before I had managed to tear the powerless wood from my wound."

"You knew I was here in your house; and in great turmoil all this time?"

"It has taken this long to gather strength enough to confront you and reclaim my home. I needed space for rehabilitation."

"That's so mean. I thought you were dead. I've been consumed in self-pity, died slowly with misery. Misery enough, I was slowly going out of my mind. Paranoid even this damned house is conspiring."

"Hush," Callum urged. Placing a stern finger to her lips, he glanced about. "The walls have ears. Don't offend them."

"Sir, I don't find that amusing in the slightest."

"I speak the truth."

"So there is a presence? I was hoping it was my imagination. I get the feeling we're being watched right now. - Can you feel it?"

Callum shrugged, though his dead blue eyes were intense. "Stranger things happen in the space between heaven and hell than I care to dwell on, my dear." His finger was still against her perfect lips, and he became very aware of it.

Sophie swam about in his amorous expression, wanting to feel his kiss again; knowing he wanted the same. She gazed into his crystal blue eyes that although were dull, would otherwise be glistening with emotion and vibrancy how they had in the library. She imagined if he were to wear contact lenses, how alive they would seem, how they would sparkle with a soul again; as they had the times he had worn his glasses. Contact lenses were a cleverer mask. She might have suggested as much, but Callum moved his finger from her lips and ran it along her cheek, tracing her bone structure, feeling the softness of skin that sent shockwaves around her body. He placed his hand on her throat and felt her pulse flutter ever wanton to his command. He glided his hand to her bosom and rested there to detect her heart quicken to his persuasive touch. Then he held the nape of her neck; fingers lost in her hair. He brushed his lips to hers and delivered a kiss so soft.

This was sacred. They clung to the kiss preciously. Healing all trauma with a kiss so divine. They were no longer torn, raw and broken. She was no longer lost. Love was their cure. Happiness knew no boundaries until Sophie broke away abruptly.

"We can't do this! I've caused so much anguish. I've put Jon and Roz to sure death - and you want to kiss me?" Sophie spun her back to him to hide her shame and clung to the banister. The hall below was as vast as the hellish chasm she was in.

Callum clasped her shoulders, lips against her ear, "We have all been victims of your conscience, of your delicate disposition. A conscience so great and good, we failed to rise to your expectations. It is as I presumed when I first glimpsed you walking towards me; you are pure, kind and vulnerable; a saint amongst devils."

"You don't think I'm mad? You don't think I'm evil?"

"You are ruled by goodness; you're not evil."

"Oh, Callum; do you mean that, honestly?" Sophie implored, turning in his arms to check his honesty.

"Never have I lied to you, Sophie. As I have said before, my integrity where you are concerned will always remain intact, and my word is my oath. I don't break promises."

"Too late though for Roz and Jon," Sophie remarked sullenly.

Callum took her hands in his. "Cheer up; Jon and Roz are well and safe. I stayed on at the room for the past four weeks. While visiting the forests, I heard their laughter ring out, and other sounds of lovemaking. I never approached them, but they are happy."

"Then all is well."

"It would seem their destinies were meant to be as one. You would do best not to meddle in future. You are a very impassioned lady. You could cause the planets to collide, and wouldn't know it."

"Perhaps you should have told that to Tom?"

"Tom – you refer to him as a friend?"

"I've come to realise he loved me. And he loved you. He sent you on a mission to search me out, to find a love so deep – a true cure of all woes. His meddling nearly cost you your existence and my sanity."

"Everything has turned out for the best." Callum raised her hands and kissed them. "All is forgiven, my love." He turned one hand over and planted smaller kisses along the blue veins of her wrist. "We're both here; we survived." He kissed her arm past her elbow. His lips travelled up to her shoulder, tracing kisses up to her neck. He nestled, savouring her sweet aroma, and whispered, "Now I shall take you to my bed."

"No, you won't," Sophie giggled in rapture. "I may well be a lady from centuries past, and you may well be stuck in a time warp alongside this house, but I'm also a modern girl; so I'll say when we go."

"How forthright of you, my dear: you like to dominate?" Callum teased.

"Welcome to the new millennium." Sophie began walking backwards, paying Callum devilish enticement and slowly undoing the top two buttons of her nightgown. "Now, sir, - I think I shall take you to *my* bed."

⁂

"Dawn is coming," Sophie announced to Callum who was lying beside her.

Callum stroked her soft shoulder. "Dawn is here already. She is in my arms."

Sophie propped herself on her elbow. "I would very much like to stay here. You're not going to send me packing now you've had your wicked way, are you?"

He laughed, wrestling her onto her back. Her face was radiant with joy, her soft lips smiling, and her eyes twinkling with false life. She was beautiful, so captivating, he thought he'd never be able to let go. He kissed her deeply, tenderly.

Sophie knew that soon they would be lost, out of control in a passion equal to the lovemaking that had just gone before; when he had caused her to grasp the bedposts to contain her brain, and again made her cry tears of relief and joy. "Stop," she urged as his mouth moved onto her cleavage. "Callum, there is something I want you to have."

"I have all I require right here," he teased, but Sophie scrambled free. She wrapped a sheet around her and left the room.

Lying back against his pillow, Callum pulled the covers up over his chest and gazed at the ceiling. "Thank you, Tom. I know you're listening. Sophie senses you too. Now, I understand what you meant when you told me all those months ago, that your best gift was yet to be delivered. She is a gem, and one worth the trek to hell and back for. I shall treasure her, I promise. I will bring happiness to her heart; I will love and protect her. From here on in, she will fear nothing."

Sophie returned carrying a glass of brown liquid. She urged, "Drink this."

"This is your herbal remedy?" Callum asked, putting the glass to his lips and screwing up his nose at the repugnant smell.

"Drink it and you won't fall to sleep. Hurry; the first light of day is coming, my love, and we have much to do."

He knocked the drink back and forced himself to swallow then gasped. "We do?"

"Yes. If you are to be completely cured you have other processes to achieve; the next step is simply to protect your skin. For that I have memorised the lotions. They're basic enough it'll take me ten minutes to rustle them up."

"Ten minutes…" Callum uttered. Ten minutes against one and a quarter centuries of not feeling the sun on his skin. He should have planted the remedies to his memory when he had read her book in the attic, but to learn them all would have been too extensive. Several of the cures consisted of barks and herbs too rare to rustle up so quickly. He should have copied the entire book out by pen, but had been too eager to escape her flat that he didn't dare dally. After all, perhaps it was for the best? Sophie was offering him the cures freely because she cared.

Fifteen minutes later, Sophie was standing in front of the French windows in the dining hall, awaiting Callum. The sun had not yet shown its orange crest to the skyline. If Callum didn't hurry to prepare his skin in the bath full of potion and then massage lotions into his skin in a one-off procedure; he was going to miss it.

The stone veranda didn't seem so damning or so ice-cold this morning, although the house remained ever watchful. She supposed she could learn to deal with it in time, and, like Callum, eventually not even acknowledge the presence.

As Callum descended the stairs, Sophie was unable to contain her excitement, and called, "Hurry, my love." Callum entered the dining room, the majority of his body wrapped in a sheet, limbs glistening from her remedies. The candle he had lit earlier was guttering in an attempt to stay alive. Sophie said, "Did you completely submerge yourself in the potion? Tell me you applied the lotions well; even in your hair?"

"I have been thorough. Do you presume I wish to fry until I am charred to a frazzle?" Suddenly Callum's sense of humour escaped him. His happiness diminished, and as he approached Sophie, a cold chill shifted his senses. He hesitated. She was holding out her hand beckoning him toward the window. Although he had prepared himself physically, mentally he was doubtful, emotionally he was terrified. He didn't feel protected from the light. He felt naked, vulnerable and defenceless. Could she be tricking him? - If her potions and lotions were fakes; he *would* go up in a puff of smoke. Then his murderess would be victorious once more. He looked at the veranda where she had claimed his friend had raped her. What was her game?

"Come here," Sophie pleaded gasping breathlessly, "Don't be afraid. I know it's daunting, - I was there once, remember? About four miles east of here in my little shack; I went through the same torture of trust. That's why I can't wait! This is so exciting! I'm dying to see your face when the sun hits you!"

"Is that so?" Callum was more dubious, trying hard to ignore her eccentricity while suddenly rooted since his legs refused to budge.

"It's coming, light-speed at us. We should celebrate as though it's the first dawn of all time. Mother Nature is beautiful, isn't she?"

"Indeed," Callum agreed. "She is also thunder, the lightning and the shifting elements with unstoppable force. - She is unpredictable, deadly and beautiful."

"All the more for seeing it: come here, my sweet. I'll help you overcome your apprehension," she begged, waving him forward.

Gingerly, he took several more steps towards her, and then stopped to one side of the window. The same window he had used as a mirror to see his reflection. Still Callum was unsure what to expect. He knew Sophie was crazy and extreme; and in a way he loved her all the more for it. But was she leading him to the gallows? Sophie jumped about gleefully and held out her hand for him to take. The moment of truth had arrived.

Dawn was here, yet he hadn't fallen down to sleep. The first day's light was drawing a square on the floor as it beamed brighter through the window. Her pale hand and her bare arm were extended out towards him across that window, through that dreaded light, and *her* arm wasn't smouldering.

With his one-hundred-and-fifty-year-old fingers trembling like that of a man half his age, Callum reached towards the light; but as the light was about to touch their tips, he paused.

"Please, Callum? You can do this. Do it for me? Reach out and touch my fingers. Trust me."

Cautiously, he let his fingertips move into the light. His pale skin dazzled, burning his eyes. His skin began to glow whiter, brighter than he could ever remember. But he could feel no burning of the skin. Sophie took a firm grasp of his shaking hand and pulled him gently into the light; his arm, his torso, his face met the new day, and still he could feel no inferno.

Callum registered the fact he was still here. Sophie's love had gone beyond her madness to reach across the universe for him. He stared at Sophie's smile of innocence, and then at the orange crescent rising above the trees. The exhilaration of seeing the sun was overwhelming that his knees weakened. The rays softly caressed his face welcoming their newborn. Silent healing tears threatened to break free. "This is amazing," he eventually stammered. "This is so incredible! I'm in the sun with no plastic for protection; - and still I'm here. I'm normal!"

Cuddled together, they watched the sun break away from the trees in its entirety. Suddenly, Sophie sensed someone behind sharing their moment. She turned and was met with the empty room; the lush furnishings, the long dining table where once she had been seated, a virgin unbroken. Who was she expecting to find? The feeling was intense though strangely peaceful. She glanced at Callum, wondering if he felt it, yet he stayed fixed to the wonders outside.

Sophie tried to focus again on the glory of the day, squeezing Callum's hand tightly for comfort.

Callum said, "I love you, Sophie; you have given me the greatest of gifts; you gave me back to myself. This is who I truly am and where I'm meant to be; in our home and by your side."

"For always and forever; I love you too, Callum."

Again Sophie felt the presence - and so close behind her this time. She turned to scan the room. Still nothing: then the softest breeze touched her face as though someone was blowing breath in the only way to gain her attention. The guttering candle blew out, smoke wisping its death. The front doors creaked open. Sophie was sure she heard them; as though someone had surely opened them with ease. She wanted to check her suspicions but the doors slammed shut confirming all. Had someone just left the house? The intensity vanished. The house seemed exorcised. The walls no longer crushed her.

The entire house seemed to wake up, yawn, and breathe a new freshness. Each room, for the first time in centuries, greeted the new sun without animosity.

Had Thomas Montford been overlooking his quest, from the other-side, all the while? From the moment Callum had arrived in Sanctuary and saw the lady that would steal his heart, had Thomas Montford been there, in spirit, overseeing things; had he been fate watching over them? If so, the two vampires he cared so much for were now standing together in the sunlight; both cured. His wishes were now complete.

Sophie was about to remark.

Callum cautioned, "Some things are better left unspoken. Though in our hearts, we must thank him. The season in our garden will always be summer. The doors shall always open graciously; they invite you in because the master of the house welcomes you here."

Callum turned towards the rising sun. He watched the light glow brighter, without protection; without it burning his retinas, without his skin blistering, bubbling, seeping, and then melting. He admired the dawn without fatigue commanding him down to lie. He celebrated it alongside the lady who had given him her heart and her remedies. Soon, there would be no need for killing. No thirst for blood.

For the first time in one and a quarter centuries, he witnessed the dawning of a new day in a new and unshielded light: normality. The quest of the vampire was finally complete.

Epilogue

EVENING FELL ON THE FORESTS. Jon opened his eyes to the lady sleeping beside him. He listened for any other sounds from within the mine and realised the others were still in the state of comatose. He relaxed, absorbing Roz's beauty; she was no longer a bitch - she was his feisty vixen. All he had ever wanted was to spend each night and day with the woman he loved, and now he was doing just that. She was good for him. So good, he had spent most of the time wondering how she would surprise and thrill him next. Death was sweet at last, and he'd never been happier. For a month now, he had existed in bliss. He and Roz were planning to leave tonight and head for Europe, travel; take in sights including Barcelona, Paris and Rome. Their adventures were just beginning. - Sometimes he wondered about Sophie and of her whereabouts, but strangely he cared little of her outcome.

Wanting a cigarette, Jon left his goddess to wake naturally and made his way to the living area. On the coffee table, his cigarettes were neatly placed alongside his lighter. But not how he had left them. Both were placed on a flat square object, gleaming brighter than water. Before he could fathom it his attention diverted to the other object placed next to his cigarettes.

Jon stared down at the items alien to the den; the small square mirror, the round gold framed glasses. Dazed, he sat down and commanded his hands to move. Careful not to break them now after all this time, he picked up the glasses and put them on. He picked up the mirror as cautiously and held it at arm's length. The mirror was facing the ceiling still hiding the secrets of its power. If he saw himself would he know himself? Would he recognise the man of his former years?

Heart thudding, palms clammy, he lowered the level of tilt until he saw a shock of black spiky hair. He grasped the mirror tighter, afraid he would drop it, and then slowly he moved it to see a forehead; his forehead.

Tilting it further, he saw the glasses and dark eyes peering back. They were glistening. Healthy, alive eyes were round with shock. They creased with his grin of amazement. Then he saw a nose and lips and chin.

He looked at the nose again: his own nose. No hair in unsightly places, no thin lips. He recognised his cheeky grin to be his own. This grin had got him into a lot of scrapes over the years – had lost him his soul. The same grin had saved his ass more than once, too. – He did recognise the man as he recounted his journey since mortality; from lost to found. Jon felt overcome; reconnected to his former identity; complete. These glasses and the mirror were a grand gift, and Jon realised the gentlemanly vampire had kept his word. - Callum had kept his promise.

Smiling in a state of inertia, Jon noticed his teeth. They were straight, white, and proportional – no fangs hungry for the bite. He studied his wild hairstyle and held the mirror steady as he ran fingers through his dark spikes. Perhaps he should steal a comb, a little gel to spike it up better? He admired the twinkle in his eyes. Shit. For the first time since the sixties, he felt almost human; normal.

Engrossed in his reflection, he watched his own fingers touch his lips like a small child understanding the concept of mirrors for the first time. He digested his features further, running his shaky fingers over his nose and cheeks whilst simultaneously feeling the tingling sensations of touch coinciding to the vision. Absorbed in the re-evaluation of his two-dimensional self, and relating it to the three-dimensional surroundings, he failed to hear footsteps approaching and rounding the curtains from the sleeping area.

"What the fuck are you doing?" Liam blurted.

Jon resigned to share the secret. "I'm admiring my reflection," he blurted a reply that seemed crazed.

"What?" Liam was confused. Gawping at the mirror, he then stared even harder at Jon's sparkling eyes.

"I'm looking at myself in the mirror." Jon chuckled, still amazed. "I'm actually fucking in here. Look. Come and see me? It's fucking great, man!"

Liam jumped over the back of the sofa, and squatted down to peer into the mirror. "Fuck me! You're in there alright!" Liam could see Jon's face in the silvery square. Thinking the mirror was magic, Liam shoved his face in the way to see himself. He should be there in the mirror too. All he could see was Jon's reflection. It was as though Liam wasn't there at all.

Jon was a little freaked out by his power; how could the light of his vampire eyes bounce off the glass and back at him with Liam's stupid head in the way?

Liam was even more put out than Jon. He fell away from the mirror, detesting the illusion. "Fucking weird crap. What's the deal?"

Jon shrugged. "The key isn't in the mirror, mate. It's in these glasses."

"That's why your eyes are twinkling like a sultry wet virgin?"

"Something like that, yeah. According to all things reflective I now have a soul. Ha! Roz will thank me because she'll be able to wear make up and check out her clothes."

"I think you can keep the weird shit. It's fucking voodoo! I don't know that I want my soul back, I quite like being without it, we've just started having fun again. I can even say the word vampire now. There's no way I'm going backwards. I'm evolving."

"You don't get your soul returned. It's an optical illusion; literally. It's a neat trick."

"Whatever, I'm not buying into it."

"I didn't have you down as the superstitious type."

"Oh right; I'm a fucking vampire; I know how Universal Law works better than anyone. I'm one step ahead of the game; I'll do things my way but I'm not fucking with mumbo-jumbo. I'm not calling my soul to be anywhere near me."

"It's not about the soul, numbskull; it's a neat trick of the light. Clever stuff; whoever invented them."

"Maybe, and that's another point. Who would go to the trouble? Who the fuck would be bothered? Where would you start? You'd have to be completely out of your box to sit there scheming this shit up."

"Yeah well, maybe? I don't expect we'll ever find out who went to the hassle. – It's all a bit complicated to explain; but you see, there was this vampire called Callum..."

The End

VAMPIRE'S REQUEST – VOLUME II

Three years later. Paulette is no longer running lost through the forest. She is on the verge of insanity due to her secret. She is nineteen and attractive; a temptation for all vampires in Sanctuary. Only her faith can keep her safe for so long as her madness reaches out to a stranger in her nightmare and beckons him forward from the shadows of her mind.

Answering her call, the master vampire returns to his town. Thomas Montford is back from the dead with a vengeance. He has his own agenda for he knows what he wants and he takes what he likes. He harbours one craving and has one persistent desire – as beneath the English Rose - virgin blood still flows...

As the vampires flit around the virgin like moths to a flame, Paulette needs all her faith to stay alive, lest they singe their wings.

———

Prequel

REQUIEM FOR THE VAMPIRE – VOLUME III

The origins of the vampire harlots: 1760 ad. – Carla Hamilton is a young genteel of noble esteem. Life is numbingly boring until she stumbles across a Highwayman under the mask of night, and engages his humour and his intrigue. This Highwayman would have a twinkle of mischief in his eyes if he were to only have a soul.

Life takes a turn for the worse when Carla meets Jake, an enemy to her father. Very soon she falls in love and falls from grace. Downwards she tumbles into her own personal hell. Amidst the heat of acrid smoke, she befriends a witch and turns to a vampire. And amongst the flames lapping at the fabric of her ruined life, she is faced with a decision. – A decision that could damn them all for eternity...

Lightning Source UK Ltd.
Milton Keynes UK
10 October 2009

144774UK00001B/48/P